MW01139637

when you're ready

J.L. Berg

Shannon —
Here's to chocolate,
jelly beans & super hot
doctors!

Published by J.L. Berg

Copyright 2013 J.L. Berg

All rights reserved.

This book or any portion thereof may not be reproduced or used in any manner whatsoever without the express written permission of the publisher except for the use of brief quotations in a book review.

Cover Designed by Sarah Hansen at OkayCreations.com

Cover Photography by Kelsey Keeton

© 2013 K Keeton Designs kkeetondesigns.com

Dedication

For Chris.

For showing me happily ever after, every single day.

Prologue

Three years earlier...

~Ethan~

I took the stationery the home health nurse brought and I placed it in front of me. The blank white pages lay there, staring up and mocking me as I struggled to begin. I didn't have much time. Clare would be gone for only a short time and I needed to get this out, to tell her how I feel. Telling her now, in person, would only cause her pain. She wouldn't understand and would only lash out in anger.

I held the pen to the page, struggling to begin.

How do you tell the woman you love to move on? To love again? The thought of her with someone else tore me up inside, but the thought of her alone forever was worse.

So this is what I had to do for her. She'd been so strong for me for far too long, and it was time I gave that back. Eventually, she would need it.

Eventually, she would find someone who would make her want to love again, and I would be there for her, telling her it's okay.

Finally, my pen met the paper and I began to write. I poured my soul out to the woman I loved.

The woman I had to leave behind.

Chapter One

~Clare~

"Miss? Do you need to see a doctor?" the emergency room attendant asked. My eyes roamed the familiar sterile walls, taking me back to the last time I'd stood in this very room. When they'd told me he...

Don't think about it. Don't even go there.

"Miss?"

I don't even know why she was asking. Why else would I be standing here? The vomit smell, the wild look in my eyes and the crying child in my arms wasn't enough of an answer for her?

"Yes, my daughter fell...she's been throwing up the whole way here. I...I think she might have a concussion," I managed to say while juggling said daughter in one arm and printing her name on the sign-in sheet on the counter with the other. I pushed back a piece of my auburn hair with my freed up hand, and exhaled in exhaustion.

Nodding, the middle-aged woman with the sandy brown hair and a nametag that said "Tammy" began to take our information, slapped those uncomfortable hospital bracelets on both our wrists and ushered us into the waiting room, assuring me it wouldn't be too long a wait. Hopefully the walls wouldn't close in on me before we got called back. I hated this place.

I sat us down in the far corner, making sure there was plenty of space between us and the other patients waiting their turn. No one needed to be sitting near this train wreck. My nerves were shot and I was still shaking like a leaf from our harrowing drive. I'm fairly sure I'd broken a number of traffic laws getting us here, but when your child was in the backseat, recreating a scene from the Exorcist, traffic tickets seemed a little less important. I knew in the back of my mind that it was most likely a normal, run of the mill concussion, and she just needed to be examined. I should have been calmer, but as soon as she began getting sick on the couch at home, I freaked out. I think it's a mom thing, we can't help it. It's our job to panic. That's what I kept telling myself at least.

I looked down at my Maddie, my four-year-old monster, currently dressed completely in pink, all of which was covered in dried vomit. She was holding onto my shirt with a tight fist, her tiny head resting against my chest. She was still sniffling from tears that had long since dried. The beautiful curly strawberry blonde hair that she'd inherited from me was a matted mess, sticking up in every direction. Her left thumb was purposely stuck in her mouth, her preferred method of calming when she was upset. I desperately tried not to think about whether or not that thumb had come in contact with anything projecting out of her mouth. *Gross.*

"I swear, child...you're gonna give me a heart attack before I turn 30," I said while absently running my hands through her disheveled hair, and gazing into the brown eyes that reminded me so much of the man I'd loved. My eyes were a deep green, but Maddie's were the color of her father's, dark chestnut brown.

The last two hours were a blur and I was still trying to recover. Parenthood was never-ending and exhausting. Being a single parent was even more so.

I hadn't planned on the single part.

"Ethan, please don't leave me!"

The memory of that night came rushing back. I remembered finding him unconscious and barely breathing, the ambulance, and the hysteria as they wheeled him in. Standing in this waiting room when the doctor came out and...*no*. I couldn't do this right now. No one needed to see an emotional breakdown in the ER waiting room. Again.

"What's a heart attack?" Maddie mumbled weakly against my chest.

"It's like throwing up, but waaaaaaaaay worse," I said jokingly in an attempt to lift her spirits. Mine too, maybe.

"Oh," she whispered back. I could see her sheepish smile peek through for a second before it disappeared. Mission accomplished. At least she still thought I was funny.

Today began as any other day. Maddie had preschool this morning, and when we got home in the afternoon, she told me about all the adventures she'd had at school. I'd listened and said "Oooh," and "Wow!" at all the right moments, making her feel like she was the most important person in the world, because she was. At least in my world.

Later, she'd gone upstairs to play dress-up in one of her many ballerina costumes. She twirled around, a vision in pink, telling me she was going to be the bestest ballerina ever.

"Baby, you *already* are the best ballerina I know!"

"Well duh, Mommy!" she replied. Such sass. I had no idea where she got that from. Absolutely none. She must have inherited that one from her father. Definitely not me. Nope.

I left her in her bedroom to be ballerina extraordinaire while I ran around the house picking up the epic mess a young child managed to create when I heard it...that heart-wrenching sound no parent wants to experience. I raced upstairs after hearing her hit the floor. As a parent, you learn quickly that the more delayed the scream, the worse it's going to be. It's like the child is working through the shock and winding their way up to the scream. It felt like a full hour before I heard that blood curdling scream. I was already at her bedroom door.

"Baby, are you okay?" I picked her up and brought her into my arms. Looking back, I realize that was probably not the most intelligent thing to do. Aren't you supposed to leave them still in case of spinal damage or something? I don't know...my parental instinct was to pick her up, so that's what I did. She cried and I consoled. This went on for a few minutes, and then she calmed down a bit so we could talk.

"What happened, Maddie? How did you fall?" I asked, looking over at her ballet barre positioned right next to her bed, putting all the pieces together in my head as she looked up at me.

"I don't know Mommy, I just fell," she said, lying through her teeth.

"Mmm, well...it wouldn't have anything to do with this ballet barre, would it?"

"Um, no?" I could see her mind going, trying to figure out something, anything that could get her out of this...but nope, her four-year-old brain wasn't fast enough, so she reverted to an old favorite, the pathetic pouty face. It works on everyone except me. I'm Mommy, therefore I'm immune.

"Okay, well I'm going to tell you what I think happened and you can tell me if I'm close or not, okay?" She nodded in agreement. "I think someone, possibly you, thought it would be fun to climb on their ballet barre and perhaps sit on it like the monkey bars at the playground."

Her eyes widened. Yep, bingo.

"Considering that isn't the safest thing for a little girl to do, I think it might be time for the ballet barre to take a vacation until we can find something safer for you to practice on." I knew I shouldn't have taken that hand-me-down plastic ballet barre from my Mom's friend, but she insisted. I don't know why, but everyone felt this overwhelming need to give toys and clothes to the widow. If I showed any of them my monthly bank statement, they'd probably have a different opinion.

Ethan was a planner, and he made sure we'd be taken care of no matter what. I could choose to never work another day in my life and we'd be fine. But being a young widow, I was still the ultimate charity case. It's been almost three years and I think there might still be enough frozen casseroles in my freezer to last through an apocalypse.

Maddie, though sad, had agreed, and we relocated the ballet barre. She was pretty bummed over losing it, I could tell. But she handled it like a champ.

"Mommy, if my Daddy were here...could he build me a ballet barre?" I nodded, unable to form words, staring at those stupid hospital walls, a reminder of everything lost. That's exactly what Ethan planned on doing when she had gotten old enough, but plans, being the bitch that they are, have a way of changing.

"Madilyn Murray?" the triage nurse called from across the room. I rose from the chair, juggling Maddie in my arms, and followed the nurse through the double doors to a small room on the left.

"We need to weigh her. Can she stand?" the petite blonde nurse asked as we entered the room.

"Oh, yes." I placed Maddie's petite body on the scale, stepping back just slightly. I didn't want to be too far away in case she fell.

"Okay, you can take her now," the nurse said, writing down the information on a notepad.

The triage nurse, whose name I learned is Nicole, goes through the many triage procedures, taking her temperature, pulse and blood pressure and asking if Maddie's allergic to anything. I always find this a strange question to ask for a young child. I mean, how many medications can a normal four-year-old possibly have taken to know a definitive answer to this question? Maddie's probably taken a grand total of maybe five medications in her short life, and I'm supposed to say no, she not allergic to anything.

"Okay, let's go over all her symptoms so I get everything into the system," Nicole said, transferring information from her little notepad into a computer.

I went over the events of the afternoon with her, the ballerina routine, the fall, flying up the stairs, and how it happened. She continued to type on the keyboard and listen. Occasionally she asked questions.

"After she settled down, we went downstairs to cuddle on the couch and start a movie. About an hour or so later, she became quiet and lethargic, which is very un-Maddie like. I was about to call the on-call pediatrician when she became violently ill. So, I packed her in the car and came here."

Nicole leaned forward, examining Maddie, completely oblivious to our stench, and it was strong. There was no way someone could miss it. People who worked in hospitals must have nostrils of steel.

"Bless your little heart. How ya doing, baby girl?" Nicole's southern accent was strong. She was not originally from here. Richmonders don't have that much twang.

"I'm okay, I guess," Maddie managed to say before burrowing her head back into my chest.

"We'll take good care of her. Let's finish up, and we'll get you settled in an exam room. I'll make sure she gets Dr. Matthews. He's the best."

"Thank you, Nicole. I really appreciate it," I said, meaning every word.

"Don't you mention it, hun. I got one at home just about the same age," she said, turning back to the computer to type again.

Nicole proceeded to ask a few more questions, briefly examined Maddie's head, made a call, and minutes later another nurse appeared in the doorway, ready to escort us down the hall.

"You take care, hun," she said, waving at Maddie and me as we walked away.

Ushered into an exam room, we were introduced to yet another nurse, this one's nametag said Theresa. She gave me a tiny hospital gown to change Maddie into before heading for the door, saying she would return shortly.

I looked at the clean, freshly laundered hospital gown with envy. At that moment, I'm pretty sure I would have given half my closet for a pair of scrubs. The last thing on my mind when we left was clothing, and I'd rushed out the door covered in vomit. The time since hadn't improved matters, and I was pretty sure I smelled awful. No, scratch that. I knew I smelled awful. Theresa seemed to be holding her breath the entire time she was in the room. Well, at least I was at a hospital. There was no one to impress here.

The door to our exam room cracked open and a familiar face peeked in.

"Clare? Oh my God! I heard one of the nurses say your name and came to investigate. Can you tell me why I had to find out my BFF and goddaughter are in the ER through some random nurse. You couldn't have called or texted?" Leah, my slightly peeved best friend said, walking into the room wearing panda bear scrubs. Only Leah could wear those ridiculous looking scrubs and still look hot. I don't know how she makes it out alive each day in the Labor and Delivery unit. If someone like her had walked in when I was in labor, all tanned and blonde with her perky breasts and model physique, while I was sweating like a pig trying to birth a child, I would have decked her. She was lucky I actually allowed her in the birthing room when Maddie was born. Although I did make her come to the hospital in her grungiest scrubs and absolutely no makeup. Petty? Yes. But it made me feel the slightest bit better.

Leah and I had been best friends since second grade, when Kara Daniels tried stealing my chocolate pudding cup in the lunchroom. Leah saw the whole thing from across the cafeteria. She got up from her chair, walked over to Kara and punched her right in the nose. That little bully fell backasswards off her seat, stunned. Leah of course went to the principal's office for it. He called her parents and she got sent home for the rest of the day. Honestly, she got off easy. When she returned to school the next day, we were inseparable and have been ever since. Kara Daniels, of course, never bothered me again. Leah and I did everything together, and even graduated from the same college, but shortly after, she decided to return to school and get her nursing license, after several failed attempts at finding a job revealed that you couldn't do jack shit with a philosophy degree.

"Leah, I'm sorry. I was going to text you as soon as we got through triage, but they just put us in here. The whole thing has been one giant blur. I thought concussions were supposed to be instantaneous. We sat on the couch watching The Wizard of Oz for over an hour. What if I made it worse by not doing anything?" I said.

"Should I have taken her here right away? What if her brain is hemorrhaging or something?" I think my blood pressure doubled with each word. I don't know why I started panicking again. Stress is a funny thing.

"Clare. Seriously, calm down." She kneeled down in front on me as I sat next to Maddie on the bed.

"You didn't do anything wrong. You know by now that you can't take her to the ER for every bump, scratch or fall," she said soothingly. "You did everything perfectly. Now shut the hell up and relax." She paused, and then scrunched her nose in disgust. "Did you know you totally smell?"

A giggle escaped out of me and I pulled her toward me for a tight hug, silently thanking her.

"No, I mean, like *really* smell. Don't hug me! Yuck!" I laughed harder. I could even hear Maddie giggling a little next to me. Leah had always been my savior when my world was flipped upside down.

"Seriously, are you doing okay? You know, being here?" she asked, knowing the last time I'd been here, having been in that waiting room holding my hand to the very end.

"Yeah, I mean. I guess." I smiled weakly. She squeezed my hand, knowing when not to push.

"Okay, well take care of my girl. I'll be back to check on you later. And seriously, find a change of clothes, cause you are just nasty," she teased.

"Thanks, Nurse Morgan. You are the bestest nurse ever," I mocked as she rolled her eyes and headed for the door.

Being here was like anywhere else that reminded me of him, the ice cream shop, our favorite restaurant, and the grocery store. It's like ripping off a Band-Aid, just have to fucking do it and get it over with. Of course, he didn't die at the ice cream shop.

I pulled myself away from going down that awful road. Leah's right, Maddie was fine. Just because there were memories here that haunted me and filled my soul with dread didn't mean that every event here would end with the same outcome. I looked over at Maddie who was now resting comfortably, and I felt calmer.

"You know Maddie? I think we'll be able to go home in no time!" I said enthusiastically. She looked over at me and smiled, right before she lifted herself up and hurled over the side of the bed, right on my shoes.

Chapter Two

~Logan~

I don't even know why I answered the phone. My best friend Colin meant well, but he sounded like a fucking broken record, and I didn't want to hear it. Mostly because everything he said was true.

"Dude, you've got to stop burning the candle at both ends. You're gonna end up leaving a bloody cloth in someone's gut or something," Colin said as I leaned back in the hard plastic chair of the hospital cafeteria, staring at my half eaten dinner. Ham and cheese sandwich that tasted like cardboard, with a side of caffeine. Again.

"Yeah, well everyone has a hobby. Some people cliff dive, others garden or practice meditation. I just happen to excel at going to bars, drinking and picking up women." I don't think he found me nearly as funny as I was trying to appear.

The fact is I was tired.

So fucking tired of everything, and...I just didn't care anymore. When I left the hospital, I didn't want to go home. I don't know why I bought that house in the first place. It was so empty. I moved to Richmond to disappear. Colin thought it was to be closer to him, and yes, it was nice having him around. When I actually bothered seeing him. God, I was an ass. But at least he had Ella. He wasn't a bachelor anymore, and as happy as I was for him, I was also envious. I hated that feeling. I hated most feelings these days. Going home to the big empty house left me wandering the halls with nothing to do but think. So instead, I went out to a bar or a club, trying to disappear in the crowds of people. Until I got recognized. Do people really not have a life? Since when did billionaires' kids become so damn interesting? It did make finding a woman to go home with easier. No one said no to a night with Mitchell Matthew's son. Too bad I didn't actually stay until morning.

"So, that's not really the reason i was calling," he said with a nervous twitch in his voice. Why was he nervous? In all the years I'd known him, Colin had never been nervous about anything. He always faced everything head on with balls of steel. I still remember the night he'd met his wife, back when I'd still be a decent guy to hang out with, before I'd turned into the bastard I was now. We were at a crowded bar around campus when he first spotted her, walking in with a date. He said he knew at first sight she was "the one" and had to talk to her before she disappeared into the crowd. Thinking he was crazy, I turned to tell him so, but he was already gone. A man on a mission. He dodged people left and right, even jumping over a table full of people to get to her. Finally reaching her table, he kneeled down in front of her, totally ignoring her date, and looked up at her with his trademark shit-eating grin and said, "You're going to be the mother of my children, and I've been sitting in this bar waiting my whole life for you. So why don't you say goodbye to this loser and go someplace with me?"

The whole bar was silent by now, having witnessed the table jumping shenanigans and heard his declaration of love. She looked around, turning red from all the attention, when suddenly her horrified face transformed into a mischievous smile. Thinking he'd won her over, he smiled back, waiting for her to say yes and follow him into the sunset or whatever.

Instead, she poured her entire margarita on his head.

The whole bar erupted in laughter and applause. Rather than walk around in defeat, he stood and strode back over to our table, red slush sliding down his face, and sat back down looking like he just scored a winning touchdown.

"Why the hell do you look so cocky? You just got turned down in front of the whole damn bar," I said, trying hard not to laugh, and not succeeding.

"Just wait," he grinned.

And so we did. We sat there and finished our drinks and ordered more. An hour or so went by, and when our third round came by, the waitress dropped Colin's drink in front of him, along with a napkin. He held it up triumphantly showing a phone number along with the name Ella. They've been driving each other crazy ever since. Unfortunately, my luck in that department had not been so good. But then, I'd been raised by a money-loving asshole, so what do I know about love?

"Why do you sound so damn nervous all of a sudden?" I asked, running my hands through my messy dark brown hair. I didn't like nervous Colin.

"Got a call from Gabe the other day. He called to tell me Melanie's pregnant. He wanted to call and tell you himself, but he wasn't sure how you'd take it. You guys haven't exactly spoken since the divorce." I was silent; I didn't know what to say. Did he expect me to react?

"Anyway, I thought you should know. It's fairly new. I think they're only a couple months along. Melanie is really excited. I know what the two of them did was shitty on an epic level, and I know they don't deserve our forgiveness, but at the end of the day, they're some of our oldest friends. And they're trying. I guess I'm trying, too. I think I still want to kick Gabe's ass again, that was fun."

"I know, Colin. I get it. Honestly, I'm happy for them. Especially Melanie. She's finally getting everything she ever wanted." Everything I couldn't give her.

"If you talk to Gabe, tell him I'm happy for them. I...I can't do it yet. I can't talk to them, not yet," I said. Of course, it's not for the reasons he thinks. I didn't deserve to talk to either of them. I'd wronged them and they didn't need me and my shit in their life anymore.

"Okay man, no problem. We're not talking on a regular basis, but I'll pass it along if he calls again. Well, I should let you get back to doctoring or something. We need to get together soon and have some man time," he said, letting out a long sigh.

"This pregnancy stuff is getting to me. Ella made me read a book about breast feeding the other day. Have you seen what a breast pump looks like? It's frightening man, I need some dude time." He really did sound frightened.

"Okay, I'll call you. Later." I said, knowing I probably wouldn't, and continued to stare at my half eaten dinner. I don't even know why he continued to call. If the roles were reversed, I would have given up by now. I'm not worth it.

I looked around the cafeteria, which had long since emptied by now. A quiet hum came from the refrigerators, and I could hear the shuffling of people's feet in the hallway. Life went on in the hospital as I thought about my ex-wife. Melanie finally got what she always wanted, a family. It just wasn't with me.

Love me Logan, just love me.

I thought I did. I tried. I gave her everything I had to give. But it wasn't enough.

Looking at my watch, I realized I was needed back in the ER. I gathered the remnants of my lack luster dinner and dumped my trash. As I walked out of the cafeteria, my mind focused back to work...at least I'm good at that.

~Clare~

I sat near the end of the bed holding Maddie's hand. She'd thrown up a couple more times and the nurse had to come in to change her hospital gown. She seemed a bit calmer now but was still pale. I was amazed by how much liquid could come out of a human being. But, looking back to my college days, I seemed to remember saying something similar as I hugged the toilet and swore I'd never drink again. And wow, it smelled in here. I was really starting to question the sanity of those who worked in a hospital or the medical field in general. Willingly throwing yourself in the middle of sick people all the time? Yuck.

A knock on the door marked the entrance of yet another person. As I turned my head, I found myself face to face with the real-life version of Dr. McSteamy entering the exam room. Is this our doctor?

Holy hell, I think I just whimpered a little.

Tall and built like a swimmer, he was sexiest thing I'd ever seen in a pair of scrubs. Like the sky right before a summer storm, his eyes bordered between gray and blue, and I couldn't help but stare into their thunderous intensity. His hair was dark brown that edged near black and had that "just fucked" look to it. The kind of hair that made you want to run your hands through it. How did guys do that? Did they spend time creating that look in a mirror, or was it really a product of being fucked? I suddenly wanted to know. Oh shit, was I drooling? Did he say something?

He was looking right at me, waiting.

"Are you the mother?" he asked. His eyebrow arched in question. A really hot question.

Seriously, Clare...get your mind out of the gutter.

"Uh, yes. I'm Clare Murray. This is my daughter Madilyn, uh, Maddie," I said, trying to cover up the fact that I had probably been standing there for an ungodly amount of time, lamely staring at him and forming my own mini puddle of drool while he tried to get my attention back on my sick daughter.

Yup, best mother ever.

"Nice to meet you Ms. Murray, I'm Dr. Matthews." Turning to Maddie, he said, "And this must be the princess."

Calling Maddie a princess earned him major brownie points and I think I even heard a faint giggle. She immediately looked up, her big brown eyes connecting with his as he began the examination.

Dr. Matthews bent down, leaned over her tiny frame and ran his hand over Maddie's head. I knew he was checking for any bumps or abnormalities, but his gesture seemed protective and my heart did a little flip flop seeing my daughter in the arms of another man.

Done with his physical exam, he settled himself at the end of the hospital bed and motioned for me to take a seat in the chair positioned next to Maddie. It was a small room, making us all very cozy. I could feel the heat radiating off his body. His really, really hot body. His eyes lingered on mine briefly and I felt the blush start to creep up my cheeks. A quick smirk flashed across his face before he began speaking.

"Well, your nurse already gave me some of the details on what led to Maddie's injury this afternoon. Sounds like you had an eventful day," he said, giving Maddie a gentle smile. She looked up at him like he was the king of the world, which surprised me. Maddie's generally not a fan of men, having not been around many in her life.

"But it looks like a classic concussion. Her skull feels normal, and I don't see any signs of swelling or bleeding. I'm going to go ahead and order a CT just to rule out anything major and make sure we've covered all of our bases. But more than likely she'll be back to her old self in a few days," he said, offering reassurance.

I nodded absently, those stark white walls started to tighten around me. It's not the fact that he wanted a test that sent me into an instant panic attack. I understood the precaution. I was glad Dr. Matthews was taking the time to do so, and I appreciated his thoroughness. It was the way in which he said it. The exact phrasing. One sentence brought the memory back to haunt me, flooding my mind and taking over my senses.

Ethan sat down next to me on the bed. He looked at me with those dark brown eyes and a concerned, loving look. He knew I always worried about everything.

"Baby, I don't need any more tests. The doctor says they're only migraines," he said. "The CT came back normal which rules out anything major. I don't want to fight with the insurance company to get an MRI. You know they aren't going to pay for it, so why bother?" He pulled me down onto our bed so that we were lying side by side.

"It's going to be fine. So please, stop worrying," he pleaded, leaning in to kiss me slowly, desperately trying to change the subject. He pulled away, looking at me with a devious grin plastered on his face. "Besides, we have more important things to think about right now," he whispered, looking down my body slowly and appreciatively.

"Oh, yeah? I can't think of anything," I said, faking a yawn and stretching my arms out wide. "I think I'm going to go to sleep. Night!"

I tried to keep my face steady, but I couldn't help the grin that escaped, and before I could cover my mouth to hide it, he attacked and I squealed with laughter. He straddled my body, pinning me to the bed with his knees and trapping my wrists above my head in his tight grasp.

"Shhh! This is the first night in weeks the baby has been asleep for more than an hour, and you're going to ruin it with your squealing horse laugh!" He leaned down to kiss me, chuckling.

"I do not laugh like a horse!" I pouted.

The annoyance in my voice melted as his trailing kisses reached my neck and meandered down to my shoulder, taking the strap of my nightgown with him. He pulled my body firmly against his and slowly made his way back to my mouth, kissing me so fiercely that every other thought melted away. Tests and headaches were left in the past.

If only I had been more persistent, more demanding...taken him to more specialists...

"Are you sure the CT will be enough? Nothing will be overlooked?" I asked, escaping from the memory that had held me captive. Fear was evident in my voice. I knew everything was fine, and what happened with Ethan had been rare, but the irrational panic was there nonetheless.

Maddie is not Ethan. Maddie is not going to die. I silently chanted, feeling the calm beginning to return.

I looked up at Dr. Matthews and he was watching me with concern and confusion painted all over his gorgeous face.

Awesome. Good job, Clare. Now the hot doctor thinks you're crazy.

~Logan~

I didn't know whether to comfort the woman in front of me or pivot and run. She seemed to be in her own world, full of pain and possibly regret, and I didn't know who or what could bring her out of it.

It'd had been a slower night in the ER, meaning we hadn't had many emergencies. So far that night, I had mended two broken arms, stitched up a knife wound for a local chef who'd had a bad day at work, and pulled a Lego out of a little boy's nose. I was about to lose my mind from the boredom. I hated days like these. I'd come to Richmond from one of the top trauma centers in the country. I had worked brutal hours, running from one patient to the next, never taking breaks, living on bad coffee and taking power naps on any empty hospital bed I could find. It had also given me a reason to not go home, cowardly choosing to stay at work rather than face a wife I couldn't love.

Moving here was a nice change of pace but on the slow nights it sometimes got to me. I don't regret my decision, but sometimes I missed the rush. Luckily, not every day was like this. It was still an ER and I had my fair share of adrenaline-inducing cases, but nothing compared to the rush of what I had left behind. The larger hospital downtown took most of the serious trauma cases, but we still had enough to keep me busy. Besides, quiet is what I wanted, and what I'd asked for.

So, when I walked into this exam room, I was expecting another mundane case, considering the evening I'd had thus far.

The smell of vomit had been the first thing that hit me when I entered, and I instantly groaned. God, I hated vomit. Give me blood and guts any day. I would rather stitch up anything then walk into a room that smelled like this. I was focused on the file, trying to re-learn how to breathe through my mouth when I looked up and saw my new patient lying in a hospital bed. She looked like an angel with a head full of long strawberry blonde curls and round cherub cheeks. She looked over at me with big brown eyes, smiled faintly and I found myself having the sudden urge to bring her into my arms, assuring her everything would be just fine. Having no idea where that came from, I turned my head away from the little girl in search of her mother, and dear God, I found her. She was breathtaking. Loose, dark red curls trailed down her back showing off a slim body full of curves in all the right places. She was wearing...hmm, well I suddenly knew where the vomit smell was coming from. She must have run out of the house in a panic. My eyes traveled back up to her eyes, shit. I don't think I'd ever seen eyes so green in my life. A man could get lost in them, never able to find his way back.

She'd been looking at me, staring actually, like she was waiting for me to say something.

Oh right, I was the doctor.

I had to tell myself to stop eye fucking her and be professional.

And I had been. She introduced herself as Clare Murray. I knew that already, having read the child's file, but it was nice to have an introduction. I'd checked out Maddie's head, feeling...I don't know what, when she curled into me as I examined her. I skipped over that quickly. I didn't like to feel...anything.

I helped Maddie lay back down, covered her with a blanket, and sat at the end of the bed focusing my attention back on the beautiful woman in front of me. She was looking over at her daughter, obvious worry in her eyes.

Her worry went from slight to panicked when I mentioned the CT I'd planned for Maddie. I'd never seen someone panic so much over a simple test before. She asked if I was sure, and then it was like she was gone. Her eyes went blank and her gaze wandered down to her joined hands resting in her lap, and she just disappeared. I don't know why, but I knew this had nothing to do with Maddie. It was too abrupt, too intense, and there was a sense of loss in her eyes. She was worried before, but below the worry I could tell she knew Maddie would be fine. She knew just as I did that it was a simple concussion that would go away on its own. Everything else we were doing was just precautionary.

I didn't know what was going on in her head, but a few seconds passed and she looked up at me, a mixture of panic and embarrassment playing across her face.

Before I knew what I was doing, I reached toward her, "Clare? Are you all right?" I asked, putting my hands on hers, trying to pull her back from the place she drifted to. Her eyes focused on where our hands had joined, and she spoke without glancing up.

"You're sure she doesn't need any other tests? The CT scan will show you everything?" Her voice quivered slightly as she asked again.

I could hear the pain in her words, see the fear in her eyes, and I wanted to erase it all. I don't know what I was doing, why this woman's pain was calling to me so loudly. It wasn't my problem to fix. I seriously needed to get the hell out of this room before I did something stupid.

I jerked my hand back, clearing my throat awkwardly. "Yes, she'll be fine, Ms. Murray. We will make 100% sure she's well enough to discharge when you leave. I'll look over the CT personally after the radiologist is done, just to be sure," I said in my most professional doctor-type voice, trying to convince myself that this was just another patient, and Clare was just another mother. Noticing the abrupt change in my tone, her head bobbed in agreement, and she returned her attention to Maddie, clearly hurt.

I took a step toward the door and silently cursed under my breath.

Instead of turning the knob and walking out the door, I rotated around, walked the three steps to the chair Clare was in, and took a knee in front of her.

Her emerald green eyes shifted from Maddie to me in surprise, widening at my abrupt change of pace.

Yeah, I know. It's new for me too.

"It will be okay," I assured her, looking over at Maddie, and then finding my way back to Clare.

"I promise."

I quickly stood, and exited the exam room.

Well, so much for not doing anything stupid.

~Clare~

What the hell was that? I thought I was crazy, but I think I may have found my date to the crazy dance. I was pretty sure that wasn't normal. Most doctors didn't kneel, vowing everything was gonna be okey-dokey. Because if so, I'm pretty sure malpractice suits would be through the roof.

We had just been wheeled back into the room after the CT and I was quietly sitting beside Maddie, watching her sleep. It had gotten late, and I swear we'd been here for three days, even though it'd only been four hours. Nothing in a hospital ever moved fast. My thoughts drifted back to Dr. Matthews and his odd exit from the exam room.

When he grabbed my hand and asked if I was all right rather than stare at me and call in the people with the straitjackets, I felt something. Something I thought I'd never feel again. I'd loved Ethan with my entire being. We'd met when I'd just started college, and he was my first love. When you have the type of love Ethan and I did, you don't expect to ever be lucky enough to find it again. It's not that I was determined to die alone, but I just figured that's how it would be. Men and women spend their entire lives looking for "the one." I'd found him and I'd been lucky enough to have eight wonderful years with him. I had my time and that was it. But when I looked up into that man's eyes as he was holding my hand, I felt something in me stir...something I'd thought was long since gone. I thought he'd felt it too.

And then he snapped his hand back and tried to brush it off like it never happened. It was like a slap in the face. I reminded myself that lightning doesn't strike the same place twice. Ethan was gone, and so was my one true love, at the age of twenty-seven. No man could ever compare to that. That's what I'd thought until he'd spun around, swearing everything would be okay. I didn't know what to make of that, but it made my heart quicken just thinking about it. It was like he was trying to erase the virtual bitch slap he'd given me and tell me he'd felt it too. Or I could be seeing a connection that wasn't there. He could just be crazy and I'd just won my very own psycho bodyguard.

A quiet knock brought me out of my thoughts, and Leah appeared in the doorway.

"Hey sweetie, how's my girl?" she whispered, sitting on the edge of the bed as she leaned over to check on a sleeping Maddie. I was a little nervous about her falling asleep, but Theresa said it was fine. They would wake her up in an hour to check on her. Honestly, I was a little envious. I wouldn't mind crawling on that bed with her and taking a nap.

"She's better, been sleeping for about fifteen minutes. Dr. Mathews said it was just a concussion, but she just came back from doing a CT just in case. And before you ask, I'm fine," I said, seeing her eyes already widening when I mentioned the CT. Sometimes, I think she knows me better than I know myself.

"Are you sure? You know it's not the same thing, right? She's not Ethan."

"Yeah, I know. I've told myself about a hundred times since he ordered the test."

"You got Dr. Matthews? Damn, you lucked out! He's fine, like I want to lick every inch of his body fine," she laughed, making an obvious change in conversation.

I rolled my eyes. "Leah! I obviously didn't notice. He's my daughter's doctor, I wasn't exactly checking him out...much," I smirked.

"I knew it. Slut."

"Whore," I countered back.

"Anyway," she laughed, "You do know who he is right, like who his father is?"

I shook my head. "Nope. Although the name sounds

familiar, I don't pay much attention to the news anymore. Four-year-olds don't get overly excited about current events or celebrity gossip."

"Right, sometimes I forget you don't live in the real world anymore. How is Dora these days?" she taunted. Leah loved heckling me about horrid cartoon characters. She knew Dora was on my top five most hated cartoon character list.

"Just as goddamn annoying as she was the last time you asked, jerk. I hate that stupid show," I snapped, which sent her into a fit of silent laughter.

She pulled herself together and said, "Anyway, Logan Matthews is the only son to Mitchell Matthews, the founder of Matthews Associates, which is like the richest hedge fund company in the world."

Of course I knew that, everyone knew that. Mitchell Matthews was known for taking his family fortune and turning it into billions on the stock market. He was a genius. Every business major in the world knew his name and studied his business's history.

"He's that Logan Matthews? What the hell is he doing in Richmond?" Shouldn't he be in New York or Paris? I might be, given the option.

"No one knows. A couple years ago, he was living in New York and married. He worked at NY Presbyterian in the Trauma Center and was gaining some serious cred in his field. He's a freaking Harvard and Yale grad. Anyway, big scandal breaks out all over the news. His wife cheated on him, and he disappeared. A few months later, he shows up here in the ER. He's been here ever since."

"Wow, she cheated on him?" I couldn't imagine the heartbreak.

"I know, right? Who would cheat on that? I mean, seriously. I've only ever seen him in scrubs and that's enough to make me want to go home and spend some quality time with my vibrator."

"Really, Leah? Maddie's like right there," I reminded her, pointing a finger at my sleeping child.

"She's asleep, and I know my goddaughter. She could sleep through an alien invasion."

She was probably not wrong about that. Maddie slept like the dead.

"So, he came here to hide?" I asked.

"Well, he hasn't exactly been hiding. No one really knows why he moved here, but according to the papers, he's quite the player and makes no effort to cover up the fact."

Well, I guess the crazy theory still stands. No player would want to touch this hot mess. A single mom, and widow to boot. Yeah, I was a huge bag full of fun.

"Hmm, interesting," I said.

"So, before you leave you should ask him out!" Leah said, out of nowhere.

"Um, I'm sorry...what?"

"Ask. Him. Out," she reiterated.

"Why? Didn't you just say he was a player?" I was confused.

"Exactly. That's just what you need. A hot doctor with no strings. It's just the right thing to get the chains re-oiled and gears working right."

"Did you just use a bike analogy for my girlie parts?" I don't know why I'm surprised anymore.

"Yep, sure did. So what's your deal? Is he not hot enough?" she asked.

Oh lord. She wasn't going to let this go.

~Logan~

I had just returned to the ER wing after going over Maddie's CT with the radiologist on call. Everything looked normal, as I had expected. I'd even had the radiologist double check, keeping my promise to Clare, and helping my nerves settle. I had to be sure before I entered that room. I had no idea why I felt the way I did. I'd never felt anything so strong for a patient or her family. Being a doctor, I always wanted to heal and protect, it was in my nature. Why else would I be working these shitty hours and surviving on so little sleep? But this went beyond normalcy. I had felt something with that woman and her little girl the instant I walked in the exam room. After spending the last three years avoiding most situations that had anything to do with emotions, it frightened me. It was exactly why I was going to make sure Maddie was safe, and then send them home. Away from me and my poisonous existence.

Having been warned at the nurse's station that Maddie was sleeping, I knocked gently at the door and quietly let myself in. Apparently my knock went unheard because as I stepped in I noticed Clare, sitting in the same seat I'd left her in, speaking with a blonde nurse from L&D. Their heads were huddled together, and slightly turned away, with their voices reduced to a low hush.

"Jesus, Leah. Just because I haven't had sex in over three years doesn't mean I'm dead. Yes, I'll admit, he's goddamn gorgeous. He's like the Ian Somerhalder of doctors...he's --- oh shit," Clare halted mid-sentence, and her eyes widened in surprise as she spotted me in the doorway. She looked like she'd just been caught with a joint in the school bathroom. Oh fuck, was she talking about me? From the shade of red her face was turning, I'd say yes.

I tried to hide my widening grin and cleared my throat...trying to remember what I was going to say.

"Ah, sorry for the um, interruption?"

Don't grin, jackass.

"I was coming in to give you the test results from Maddie's CT," I continued as professionally as I could muster.

"Right. Um, yes. Was everything okay? I mean, she's all right? You didn't find anything?" she blabbered, eyes going wild like she expected bad news.

Her hand reached out for the blonde nurse. I took a step forward because I was sorry I had scared her, but stopped myself. She's not mine to protect. She was the mother of a patient. I needed to get my shit together and let this go.

"No, the radiologist didn't find anything. I had him look it over twice to be sure. She is perfectly fine. Just a concussion. I'll have some discharge instructions typed up, the nurse will go over them and then you can get out of here. Sound good?"

Clare let out an audible breath and looked relieved. She released her friend's hand to reach out to her daughter, who'd just awoken. She took her daughter's tiny hand in her own and smiled before looking up at me.

"Yes, thank you. We would love to go home."

I locked eyes with Clare one more time, trying to memorize the emerald color that shined through them. It's true, a man could get lost in those eyes forever, but it wasn't going to be me.

Chapter Three

~Clare~

"So much for sleeping tonight," I said to no one as I set the alarm clock next to the bed for one hour in the future. Our discharge papers said I had to wake Maddie every hour the first night. She'd had the worst day ever and to top it off, she would be startled awake all night. She was going to hate me.

As I tucked her in minutes ago, she gave me her goodnight hug and kiss routine, and then said "Mommy, I'm sorry I scared you. I'm not gonna leave you alone like Daddy." Dear lord, the things kids say.

"Oh baby, I know. Daddy left us because he was sick, and it was his time to be with the angels. It wasn't his fault. I know you're staying right here with me. But maybe you could lay off the climbing a bit?" I said, hoping to lighten the mood.

A smile tugged at the corner of her mouth, "Okay, Mommy. Are you really going to build a ballet barre in my room?"

Oh, right, that. "Well, we're definitely going to try. How about on Sunday we take a trip to the home improvement store and get everything we need?" I said, praying for divine intervention. I am so defunct at home improvement, hammers and nails flee in my presence.

She bobbed her head up and down enthusiastically, and I gave her one last hug and kiss before turning off the light. My eyes wandered over to the corner where the ballet barre would go and, as I walked out of the room, I wondered how in the world I was going to make this happen for my little girl.

Ethan, if you are up there...a little help? Please?

Walking into my bedroom, I flopped down on my bed just in time to pick up my ringing cell phone which was currently blaring "Milkshake" by Kelis. God, I hated that song.

Leah.

She had an obsession with ringtones. Or maybe she just liked to mess with me. She periodically stole my phone and programmed a new default ringtone, knowing full well I had no idea how to change it. She would wait patiently, like a lioness waiting for prey, until I would call her bitching about how my phone rang in the middle of the grocery store blaring "Sexy and I Know It", or "Don't Cha Wish your Girlfriend was Hot Like Me?" by the Pussycat Dolls in the middle of a preschool play. Leah found it hilarious. Me? Not so much. When my phone started singing "Baby" by Justin Beiber in the gynecologist's office, I almost killed her. She kept that particular one programmed for weeks, slowly driving me insane. I really needed to learn how to use my cellphone.

"Hi Leah, she's doing much better," I answered.

"Oh, thank God. Thank you for taking care of my precious goddaughter tonight. I've been worried," she said. She always played up her godmother role, like she was a queen or something.

"Well, now you can calm down. She's asleep. Well, for the next hour at least."

Leah's always been like a sister to me and she loves my daughter like an aunt. I fear what she and Maddie might do together when she gets older. I may have to set ground rules. No rock concerts with Aunt Leah.

"Do you like your new ringtone?" she jeered.

"You're just lucky I answered in the first place. After tonight, I'm seriously driving all the way downtown if I need an ER. That had to be the most embarrassing moment of my life."

Dr. Matthews knew exactly who I was talking about the minute he walked into that room. The over confident grin he'd briefly flashed before examining Maddie said so.

"Why? Because he heard you say he was hot? Well, duh. He is. It's not like he doesn't know it," she said, like it was no big deal.

"Oh God and the comment about how long it'd been. Jesus, he must think I'm a nun...or a prude," I whined, finding a comfortable position on the bed. I absentmindedly twisted a dark red curl around my finger.

"Wait, aren't those the same things?"

"Shut up, not funny."

"Okay, like I was saying before we were interrupted by the very topic of our conversation. Dr. Matthews is single, and you are single...oil, gears...etc."

Wow. Subtle, Leah.

"And as I told you earlier, I have no idea why you are telling me this."

"Clare, sweetie. It's been over three years. I'm not saying go find a new husband. But at least think about the possibility of getting back out there and having a little fun," she said gently.

"Fun? I have fun," I fired back defensively.

"I mean the adult version of fun. The horizontal kind you do with the opposite sex."

Oh. Right. I'd forgotten about that kind of fun.

"I just don't know if I'm ready, Leah," I huffed into the phone.

"Sweetie, you'll never know if you don't try. What better person to test drive than a super sexy doctor?" Leah cajoled.

"Maybe you should take your own advice? When was the last time you went out on a date?" I asked, knowing full well the answer. It had been months.

Leah had been in a long term relationship with a guy

named Daniel. They were getting pretty serious and everyone expected him to propose. Then Ethan got sick and she did what any best friend would do. She dropped everything and helped me run my life for the next year. She was there for me every step of the way. When I needed a babysitter while we went to doctor's appointments, chemo treatments and counseling sessions, she was there. She picked up groceries, paid bills, and held me when I cried. She was my rock. But unfortunately, Daniel was not as understanding. He left, saying she cared more about me than him. It devastated her, and I've felt guilty ever since. She's told me over and over that it obviously wasn't meant to be, and I agree, but the guilt remains. Ever since Daniel, her dating life has been minimal.

"We're not talking about me," she answered, changing the subject.

"We're talking about you and hot doctors. I could get his number for you. You could call and say you had a question about Maddie. No, wait! You could ask for a house call!"

"Oh my God. You're insane. And no. You are not breaking into hospital records to get a phone number for me," I said. I took a deep breath, knowing full well she was not going to give up.

"I need some time. Give me a few days. Maybe we can go bar hopping or something, but I don't need to be set up with a billionaire doctor to get my mojo going again."

"All right, but I expect you to get some phone numbers when we go barhopping. No hiding in the corner booth. I still think hot doctor is the way to go. It would definitely be my pick. Yum," she said, in a dreamy voice.

I allowed myself one last fleeting memory of the moment I'd shared with the doctor today. Had I shared a moment with him, or was it just an indication that I needed to move on. Could I?

"It's time, Clare," Leah said, just as the one hour alarm went off saving me from further discussion on my love life, or lack thereof.

"I've got to go wake up our sleeping beauty."

"Better you than me. That girl is a bear when she's sleepy," she joked.

"No kidding. Just like her godmother."

After waking a very sleepy and unhappy Maddie and returning her back to bed, I readied myself for sleep. I finally eased into bed after a day that seemed like it would never end. Running my hands over the soft sheets, I tried to remember what it was like to have Ethan here beside me. It seemed like a lifetime ago that he and I were here together in this place, and yet I can still remember the exact color of his eyes, and the way he smelled after a shower when I lay in his arms. My eyes traveled over the room we'd decorated so long ago. We spent forever picking out the exact shade of gray, and the perfect furniture. The first year of our marriage was spent making this house our home. And now it was just me, raising our daughter, alone.

I can't help but think what today would have been like with him by my side. What it would have felt like to have someone there, holding my hand? Holding Maddie's hand, and assuring us everything would be fine.

My fingers reached toward the nightstand drawer next to the bed, pulling out the envelope I'd held so many times before. Still sealed, with worn edges from constantly being held, I brought it to my nose, hoping there would still be a faint whiff of his cologne, but knowing full well there wasn't.

On the front of the envelope, it simply says "*When you're ready*" in Ethan's messy handwriting. I always gave him shit for it, asking him how he could read the scribble he produced. He would laugh and admit that he couldn't. I smiled, remembering all the years of sweet memories we shared.

I found the letter weeks after he died, when I was looking through one of his drawers. Knowing him, he'd probably hid it somewhere out of the way on purpose, knowing I'd need some time. Those first weeks of grief were...well, there were no words. When someone close to you dies, it feels like they take a piece of your very soul with them. There were days when all I could do was muster up the energy to breathe. I would have done anything and everything to have a small piece of him back. When I finally found the letter, digging through his drawers, looking for something I don't even remember anymore, I looked at the words he'd scribbled down on the envelope and froze. Part of me wanted to rip the envelope open that second, but those three words kept me from doing so. For nearly three years that envelope had sat in my nightstand. On the nights when missing him would get too much to bear, I'd pull it out and run my fingers over the words Ethan had written, and feel like he was here with me. But to this day, I still couldn't break the seal.

"Ready for what, Ethan? How will I know?" I asked the silence. It didn't answer back. It never did.

~Logan~

Sitting in my usual spot at the bar, I looked around at the quiet little pub I liked to frequent on the nights I wanted to be left alone. The bar was mostly empty tonight, as it was most nights, but that's why I liked it. You could settle yourself in the corner with a drink and disappear. And that is why I came to this city, after all. If I got the itch for something more...female, I would head downtown. But in here, I was left alone, to be whatever was left of me.

"Hey Logan, you need another one?" Cindy, the bartender asked.

"Sure, why not?" I hadn't finished with the one I'd been

nursing, but I was optimistic.

"Save any lives today?" Cindy asked me that question every time I saw her. Settling into her mid-fifties, she had one of those voices that sounded like a truck driving over gravel, and her hair was hair-sprayed to the ceiling.

"Nope. Slow night. But I did pull a Lego out of a kid's nose. That was solid entertainment."

She laughed, moving across the bar to get my new drink.

Thinking about the hospital brought my thoughts circling back to the little girl with the strawberry curls and her beautiful mother, Clare. All evening, I couldn't stop thinking about them. Especially Clare. I never thought a woman covered in vomit could be so appealing. Thinking about the conversation I walked in on with her friend still makes me chuckle under my breath. I needed to Google that Somerhalder dude. Was he an actor? I had no idea who she was talking about.

"Cracking yourself up tonight, hun?" Cindy asked with a pointed gaze, dangling a freshly refilled drink before my eyes. "Maybe I need to keep this for myself, Doc?"

Feeling bold due to the memories of Clare and the whiskey currently zinging through my veins, I blurted out, "Cindy, do you think everyone's capable of love?"

Surprised, she quickly answered, "Yes, I think everyone's capable of lovin' another, why?"

"Because I'm not so sure. How do you know?"

I thought I was in love with Melanie. Hell, I'd even married her. But then I discovered the truth too late, trapping her in a loveless marriage, and driving her into the arms of another man.

Cindy looked at me like I'd grown two heads. In the years I had visited this place, we'd had conversations all the time, but they never went beyond friendly banter and her relentless flirting. It was obvious she didn't know what to do with the sudden onset of my liquid confessions.

"You okay, hun? I know a man who wants to keep to himself, and I respect that, but you're different tonight." She looked at me, her eyes full of concern.

"What's got your emotions so ripped open all the sudden?"

I completely froze. What was I doing? Bleeding my heart out to a middle aged bartender? It was ridiculous.

Whatever I felt in that exam room today was over. Clare was gone, and I needed to get on with my life. Love didn't happen in an instant. Especially for me. And that woman, shit...any decent woman, didn't deserve the train wreck of life that would come with becoming involved with me. No need to introduce someone else to a life of Logan sized failures and fuck ups. I would stick to what I was good at, what everyone expected of me.

"Sorry, Cindy. Must be the whiskey talking. Just rambling. Anyway, I'm out."

I threw a couple twenties on the bar and slid on my jacket.

"I'm headed downtown to start some trouble," I said, forcing a grin to spread, before heading out the door.

Enough thinking for tonight.

Chapter Four

~Clare~

God, I hated home improvement stores.

As I lifted Maddie into the oversized shopping cart, I looked around in fear at the enormous store and asked myself what the hell I was getting myself into. Hopefully, I could find one of those old grandfatherly type men who work here who could walk me through this. Otherwise, I was screwed. Before his stroke, my Dad could have help with this sort of thing, but he'd lost so much control in his hands that handiwork was out of the question these days.

My brother, Garrett, was pretty well trained in the art of fixing things, but was currently out of town on an extended business trip. My little brother, the executive. It still cracked me up. Just a few years ago, he was an irresponsible frat boy and now he worked for a major pharmaceutical company, traveling all over the world.

"All right Maddie, let's see what kind of trouble we can get ourselves into today!" I exclaimed, glancing down at her sweet face as I pushed the cart into the first set of aisles.

In the last few days she had completely recovered. It was like the concussion never happened, except when I delivered the bad news about ballet class. No physical activity for a week. That hadn't gone over well. She had since been counting down the days until she could return to class the following week. Her absence from class hadn't kept her from dressing in tutus and leotards every day. She's such a girl. Who says you can't watch movies in a tutu? Certainly not me.

About fifty aisles in, I was lost. How big was this store? The entire place smelled like a giant wood chipper, so they had to have wood, right?

"Maddie, we need to find the aisle that has all the wood in it. Can you help Mommy out and look for it?" I asked.

Her head bobbed up and down, eyes full of glee. She thought it was a game. This routine worked in grocery stores, as well. It saved me hours of sanity.

Seriously, am I stupid?

I should have been able to find this stuff, and where were these helpful employees they always advertised? I looked around, but all I saw were intimidating looking men who seemed to know exactly where they were going and what they needed. I, on the other hand, seemed to have made a complete circle and had arrived in the exact same spot I was five minutes ago. This was a disaster.

"Dr. Matthews!" Maddie screeched.

My head whipped around to see Maddie waving at the man who had "saved her head." Her words, not mine.

She talked about him a lot since her visit to the hospital. Apparently, he made quite an impression with her because most men intimidated her. For as long as she could remember, it had just been her and me. It broke my heart that her memories of Ethan were fading. For her, he will only ever be a picture or a bedtime story. But Dr. Matthews was different. Somehow, in a very short period of time he had been able to break down her walls and she felt safe and secure with him. To her, he'd saved her in that ER. She went to the hospital sick and miserable and he made her better. He was her new hero.

Dr. Matthews, my daughter's knight in shining armor, was reaching for something on one of the lower shelves, giving me a nice view of his perfect ass, when he heard Maddie's cry. His head rose, searching and finally found us. He appeared momentarily startled, but then gave Maddie a dazzling smile.

Damn, that man should smile all the time. Stretching his lean body to full height, he rose, and walked our way, waving back at Maddie who was bouncing up and down in the cart.

"Hey there, princess, looks like your head is back to normal," he said, gently patting the top of her head, sending her into a fit of giggles.

"Yep, but Mommy says I still can't dance for four more days!" the agony apparent in her voice, like I was torturing her. I just rolled my eyes.

"But she still lets me wear my tutu. And, she's gonna make me my very own ballet barre for my room!" she said, beaming at me. Now I was the hero again. Kids' moods could give you whiplash.

Oh God, this was going to be a disaster. Seriously, where were all the damn employees in this store? Do you think they offer installation for this type of thing?

"Wow, that's impressive. Your mother must be very handy," he said, glancing over to me for the first time. And he doesn't just glance, he roams, his eyes taking their time traveling over my body. I don't know how he did it, but that single look had me melting into a puddle. But then, I think anyone staring into those eyes would be in the same position.

His blue eyes were stunning, and so pale, almost bordering on gray. Lips curved into a small grin, with a hint of mischief, he looked like he already figured out my little secret regarding this disaster of a project.

"No, actually, Dr. Matthews, I am the exact opposite of handy. I'm actually wandering around aimlessly, hoping to find an employee who will tell me what I need to do," I confessed, confirming his suspicions.

"Call me Logan," he said. "And that would explain why you are in the plumbing section." He added, laughing. Looking around at the toilets and pipes, I blushed, "Guilty." I said, before joining him in a laugh.

"Mommy says she's good at all sorts of stuff, but building and fixing stuff isn't one of them," Maddie said.

Sobering a bit, but still very amused, he looked at me with those crystal blue eyes again, making me shiver.

"I'd really love to discover some of those hidden talents."

Oh, hot damn.

~Logan~

What did I just fucking say?

Shit, I should not be allowed in public anymore. I had just dropped the lamest pick-up line ever, in the middle of the home improvement store, right in front of Clare's daughter, no less. Thank God Colin hadn't been around to witness that little slice of failure. I would never have lived it down.

Dear God, this woman made me crazy.

I never expected to see her or Maddie again. I tried to make myself forget about that night in the hospital, telling myself she deserved better. And she did. But as hard as I tried, those searing green eyes kept making their way back into my thoughts, reminding me of a woman who had shown me another path. A path that could have been possible if I were a different man. If I were capable of giving myself over to another, but you have to have a whole heart to do that, am I'm pretty sure mine was never fully formed.

But looking up at those now familiar eyes, I felt the tension ease in my chest, and the ice loosened a bit. Seeing Clare again felt exactly the same. It gave me a deep sense of being connected and tethered. Having come from the family I did, it wasn't something I'd ever felt with anyone, and therefore I was having a difficult time trusting myself around her. I tried returning to my life, resuming my normal routine, only to be haunted by her face; a constant reminder of what I could never have.

After the quiet little pub the other night, I went downtown, finding a spot that was the exact opposite of the one I had just left. I played the part of carefree bachelor, buying rounds of drinks, doing body shots with a few overly eager women. I had every intention of following one of them home. By the end of the night, after most people had made it home, I had a young brunette pushed against the dirty brick wall of the bar, waiting for a cab to take us to her apartment. I didn't know her name, and I didn't care. I wouldn't be around by morning anyway. My hand slid down her bare thigh and pulled it around my hip. She looked at me, seductively licking her lips, her not so subtle way of giving me permission to do whatever I want, wherever I want. It was then that I looked into her eyes and saw...nothing. The brown eyes staring back at me were full of lust, but nothing else. They were the same blank eyes that I had been looking into ever since Melanie. Since her, I'd survived by seeking out women who gave nothing in return. Because it was all I could give back.

Knowing the eyes staring back at me weren't the ones I wanted, I pushed away from the brunette as the cab pulled up to the curb. Cursing under my breath, I didn't even give her an explanation, just threw her some cash and walked away.

"Well, we should let you get back to whatever you were doing. I'm sure you are busy," Clare said.

"No, actually. I was mostly done. I just needed a small part for my sink," I answered, holding up my purchase while nervously wrapping my other hand around the nape of my neck.

All right asshat, stop being creepy. Time to leave.

"I could help you," I blurted out. "I've been known to be handy on occasion. I could help you shop, and then install it for you." The words continued to free-fall out of my mouth, without any sign of stopping.

"Oh my God, are you sure?" Clare gasped in relief. I liked

creating that feeling in her.

"I don't want to take up your day off. But I would be lying if I said I didn't need the help," she confessed as she nervously bit her bottom lip. Fuck, she was gorgeous. Her hair was pulled to the side today, in a loose ponytail. She dressed casual, in tight fitting jeans and a black sweater that hugged her body. If she had any makeup on, it was subtle because all I could see were the freckles scattered across her nose and cheekbones.

"No, I don't mind at all. I'm happy to help," I assured, before turning to Maddie.

"Every ballerina needs a ballet barre. A safe one that doesn't cause any accidents." Tilting my chin down, I gave Maddie a meaningful look, followed by a wink.

My effort was rewarded when Maddie broke into a fit of giggles again, and I couldn't help but smile. She's adorable, and her enthusiasm is infectious.

Clare has done a wonderful job raising Maddie on her own. I snuck another glance toward Clare, seeing her eyes light up as she watched her young daughter. She absently ran her hand through Maddie's hair, something I saw her do in the hospital, and my eyes focused on her ring finger. I know from hospital records that the wedding ring on Clare's hand is in memoriam only. She listed Maddie's father as deceased. Call me a jerk, but after seeing her in that exam room, I checked. I don't know the specifics, but considering her age, her loss couldn't have been easy.

Helping her with this small thing was the least I could do. I knew it wasn't the real reason I was doing it, but it was the excuse I was giving myself at that moment.

"All right," Clare said, "Lead the way, foreman!"

Chapter Five

~Logan~

"I'm going to run upstairs and change quickly so I don't ruin my sweater. Just make yourself at home and I'll be right back," Clare said before walking upstairs to what I assumed was her bedroom. I was left standing alone in her family room. Maddie had already skipped off to her bedroom, intent on changing, too. Something about how Mommy didn't let her wear tutu's to the store.

Clare and Maddie lived not too far from me, in one of the smaller towns outside of Richmond. In a town like this, it was hard to believe there was a state capitol nearby. It was quaint, quiet, and full of large, aged trees and picket fences. With the warm feeling of a small town, it was still close enough to enjoy all the qualities of the city. Clare's neighborhood was full of large houses, ice cream trucks and kids on bicycles. I could see why she and her husband would have picked this neighborhood. It was an ideal place to raise a family.

I wandered around the room, checking out the large red couch, trying to imagine Clare and Maddie snuggled together, watching a movie. The walls were covered in photographs from all over the world, a castle in Ireland, the Great Wall of China, and a palace in Russia. Maybe Clare wanted to travel the world someday? A sudden fierce desire to be the man to take her consumed me and I quickly tried to dispel it.

I was not the man for her. Broken people like me didn't deserve perfection.

There was a large fireplace in the room, displaying at least a dozen photographs. With my curiosity getting the better of me, I walked over for a better look.

The first photograph was Clare with her arms wrapped around a man, who, I guessed, was her husband. At the beach, waist deep in water, they were wrapped around each other and laughing. He looked in his element, blonde hair and a deep tan. He could have passed for a surfer. Clare, with red hair and freckled skin was practically glowing next to him. Their love was obvious.

Trying to keep myself from feeling jealousy toward a dead man, I moved on.

The next picture was Maddie. Even as an infant, I recognized her. She was being held by an older woman who resembled Clare. She had the same green eyes and dark hair, now streaked with gray. There was also a photo of Clare with another younger man, dressed in a cap and gown. The two intertwined in an embrace like brother and sister. The last photo I saw was Clare on her wedding day. She was breathtaking. Standing alone in a garden, she wore a strapless gown covered in tiny crystal beads, with her hair falling loosely behind her, pulled back by a simple veil. Holding a small bouquet of flowers by her side, she turned slightly away from the camera, but you could still see her expression. It was full of absolute, consuming joy.

So much history and love was on this mantle. Clare's family was obviously tight. If someone were to look at my family's mantle, they would find one overpriced posed portrait of my father and step-mother, with nothing else, except some pricey antiques. There were no loving photos of my parents and their children, no proud moments on display for everyone to see. Hell, I'm pretty sure I don't even exist to the man I called father anymore. You only got one shot with him, and I'd blown mine the day my divorce hit the papers.

~Clare~

I stared at myself in the full length antique mirror, tucked away in the corner of my bedroom. It had been a while since I had actually done this. I still looked in the mirror when I was putting on makeup or trying on clothes, but I don't think I really *looked* at myself in years. After Ethan became sick, I was constantly on the go, taking care of him, Maddie, and everything else. After he died, I just avoided looking at myself, afraid of what I might see. I was so afraid to look in the mirror and see what grief had left me, so I just kept moving. Yes, I went through all the stages you were supposed to go through. At least I think I did. It was only recently that I felt like I had finally come to a place where I could actually say I'm a widow without choking on the words. After three years, I was confident in my skills as a mother, and now knew I could conquer being a single parent no matter what life may throw at me.

But I still hadn't mustered the courage to look at myself in the mirror. The only reason I was doing so now was the man currently standing in my family room. When he looked at me, what did he see? I don't think I had thought about it up until this moment, but when a man looked at me now, what did he see?

Did he see a tired, single mother? A widow? Or just a woman?

I leaned into the mirror, turning my cheek to the light. I can't quite explain what I was looking for, and it wasn't any attempt at vanity. I wasn't on the hunt for wrinkles or laugh lines. I think I was trying to see if, after Ethan's death and all the grief that came with it, there was any of the old me left.

Yes, I knew I was pretty. I was self-confident enough to admit it, but I spent the majority of my adult life with one man, and when you're with the right man, after a while, every other man disappeared. Yes, I noticed them, in that I knew they existed, but no one could hold a candle to what I saw in Ethan.

I knew he felt the same. I'd see his eyes melt when I entered a room. I watch them flame in heat when we shared a bed, and felt them warm when he said "I love you".

When Logan looked at me, did he see me in a similar way? Did he find me sexy?

Could I do sexy anymore? Wow, I was lame. Twenty-eight and I was asking myself if I could still be sexy. I used to be able to drive Ethan insane with a single arched brow.

"Shit, Leah is right. I do need to get out," I said to no one, again.

Whatever it was, whatever I used to have that made Ethan go crazy...I needed that back.

Even if I didn't use it. Even if it was just for me. I felt like I'd lost a part of me, the part that made me feel like a woman, and I needed it back to feel whole again.

~Logan~

"Did you grow up here?" I asked Clare, trying to keep my mind and my eyes occupied.

We had been in Maddie's room for a few minutes now, moving furniture and pulling out the supplies that she had bought. Maddie's room was exactly like the girl who lived in it - adorable. The walls were cotton candy pink with ballerina posters and family photos scattered everywhere. The quilt on her small bed was a life sized ballerina with an actual tulle tutu peeking out from the fabric. There were pointe shoes hanging next to the dresser and stuffed animals piled high in the corner next to a giant pink bean bag. It was a little girl's paradise, and somehow I knew that Clare had spent hours picking out every detail in this room, making sure it was special and unique for Maddie.

J.L. Berg

Clare set Maddie up downstairs with a movie and a snack and told her the ballet barre would be even better if it was a surprise. Maddie had happily agreed, settling into the family room with a bowl of popcorn and some entertainment. Clare had changed into a pair of tight fitting yoga pants and a long sleeved V-necked shirt. Every time she bent down to pick up another toy, I had to look the other way to keep myself from sneaking glances down her shirt, or checking out her ass. She had a really nice ass.

I said I was trying. I didn't say it was always successful. I am a guy after all.

"Yeah, my parents still live in the same house I grew up in a few miles away. I like this area of Richmond. It's far enough away that we still have that small town vibe, but close enough that I can take Maddie downtown for the circus or a Broadway show when they come to town," she said, moving about the room with a familiar grace.

"How about you?" she asked. "I know you didn't grow up here. But I don't know much beyond the last name. I mean, I know who you are. Leah told me that much, but I don't keep up much with gossip."

Ever since the divorce and the newspapers splashed my name everywhere, there were very few people who didn't know my scandalous history. My father was known for his pristine reputation, and I'd sullied it. The papers had a field day.

"No, it's a relief. It makes introductions quite awkward when the person you're meeting thinks they know more about you than you do yourself."

"Well then, why don't you tell me?" she suggested, with sincerity in her eyes.

Dear lord, what could I tell her that wouldn't scare her away?

Basics. I'd go with that.

"Well, I'm from the East Coast, New York mainly. Although I have lived in several other places while I was in boarding school. My father, well, gossip or no, I'm sure you know who my father is." Everyone knew who my father was. I hated talking about him. I hated talking about my family in general.

"I went to Yale for my undergraduate, then Harvard for medical school. I moved back to New York, where I finished my residency and began my career there. I, uh, got divorced and moved here about three years ago."

That was the edited version of the story.

Continuing to measure the walls, I marked off where I needed to drill, and noticed a silence sweeping through the room. With my back turned, I could only imagine what she was thinking. I finished my markings and turned, looking up, and wondered what I said to make her so quiet. Had I scared her off already? Should I care this much if I did?

"Wow, that was a lovely resume you just told me, but how about we just cut the shit and get to some good stuff? I want to know the real you," she said smiling, offering up the challenge.

Shit, I'm in so much trouble

~Clare~

"Well. It's not like you've given me much in return," he fired back, with a devilish grin.

He seemed astonished at first by my bold words. He wasn't the only one. I was still wondering what the hell had possessed me to demand he tell me more. He had just made me so angry. When he had been so relieved, saying that most people knew him before even meeting him, I thought maybe I would get the real Logan, something genuine. But all I got were generic resume facts about his life that anyone could find on Google. I felt a connection in that moment when he admitted something about the pressure of his life. I thought he had too, but then he had gone back to being the polished man he'd probably been raised to be. So out came my bold words and here we were.

"So, what do you have planned exactly? What do you want to know?" he asked, looking over his shoulder as he continued to work on the wall. Oh Thank God he was doing this. It didn't look too difficult, but I was pretty sure I would have already made several holes in the sheetrock.

I don't know why but I wanted to know him, what was underneath that formal exterior. Seeing him again had solidified the connection I felt in that exam room and I knew he felt it too. But, he was pushing against it, and I didn't know why. There was something in his past that kept him distant and I wanted to know what he was hiding under that well-formed exterior.

A plan emerged in my mind.

"Hold on, I'll be right back." Smiling, I walked past him and headed for the kitchen. I couldn't help but giggle when I saw his look of confusion as I walked past and exited the room.

When I returned, I held up two plastic bags in triumph.

"Jelly beans? You do know we're adults right?" he mocked.

"You may be, but I'm still deciding. Besides, one is never too old for candy. And these aren't just any jelly beans, these are Jelly Bellys. They're like candy crack."

"Okay, so you've brought in a ton of sugar, and I'm supposed to bare my soul to you now?" he asked, amusement lighting up his face.

"Did you ever play that game in college where someone would ask a question, and if you didn't want to answer it, you had to take a shot?" I asked.

He nodded, grinning.

"Well, since it's the afternoon, and I'm a Mom and responsible and stuff, we're going to do the jelly bean version. I'll ask a question, and you can choose to answer it, or not. If you decline, you have to eat a handful of jelly beans. The same goes for me with a question from you."

He still looked confused.

"And why is eating a handful of jelly beans punishment?" he asked, looking at the two bags I was pouring into a clear glass bowl.

"Ah, well see...if you pass on too many questions, you'll get sick. So see, it's just like the original game, only we're subbing sugar for the alcohol."

This earned me a laugh.

"How many handfuls do you think it takes to get sick?" he questioned.

"I think we'll just have to risk it, and find out."

"You're kind of evil," he teased, leaning across the floor to grab a bracket looking thing to screw into the wall. His shirt lifted from the movement, and caught myself biting my lip in response. The infomercial "Abs of Steel" flashed in my memory as I tried not to drool.

"You don't know the half of it." I said.

Flirting. Well, at least I could still do that.

~Logan~

"I can ask you anything?" I said, glancing toward Clare as she settled into a pink bean bag chair on the floor with the massive bowl of jelly beans wedged in her lap. She clearly had given up on helping, which I was very grateful for. Seeing her whirl around a hammer was a scary sight. I'm all for gender equality, but Maddie was right, she was definitely missing the home improvement gene.

She nodded, then smiled with confidence. "Yep, anything. Ask away."

"All right. What's your favorite color?" I quickly asked before turning back to the wall to check the progress of the brackets I'd just drilled. Total silence filled the air again.

Shit, what did I do this time?

"Seriously? You suck at this game!" I heard her say, before turning back around to get a jelly bean tossed at my head.

"Green, try again."

"Wait, green what?" I was totally confused. I'd known this woman for all of three seconds and she had told me I suck and was chucking jelly beans at my head. I didn't know whether to laugh, or worry that my ego is going to be irreversibly damaged.

"My favorite color. It's green," she clarified.

"Ah, I should have known. It matches your eyes."

Looking stunned, a beautiful blush crept up her face before she composed herself and continued.

"Okay, try again."

"Are you close to your family?" After seeing all the pictures on the mantel in her family room, I knew the answer to this question, but I wanted to see her face light up when she spoke.

"Yes, my family is wonderful. Like I said, my Mom and Dad live nearby, which is a blessing because they help with Maddie quite a bit," she explained as she fiddled with the jelly beans in the bowl. "My Dad had a stroke about 5 years ago. He recovered well, but is unable to help with these kinds of things anymore, which is why I was out braving the hardware store myself this morning."

"Brave woman."

"More like stupid woman, but at least I found you." she said before continuing. "I have a younger brother, Garrett. He recently graduated from college and started working. He's spending most of his time on the road and loving every minute of it. We catch up when he's in town, but he's young and trying to move up in the professional world. Seeing him so grown up blows my mind on a daily basis." She laughed and it was the kind of laugh that seemed to have a memory attached to it. It must have been a happy memory because the small smile she had now lit up her entire face.

I had no idea what it was like to have a family that brought that kind of smile to your face, let alone any kind of smile. My family was all about appearance and how much you could gain from each other. As soon as you made a mistake, you were shunned and an outcast. Ever since my divorce, when I finally realized I'd never make the man proud, I stopped caring what my father thought.

"So, what about you? What's your family like?" she asked as I finished drilling the last hole of the bracket securing Maddie's barre into place.

"Pass me those jelly beans."

~Clare~

"Okay, so no family questions," I said, raising my hands in defeat as he began stuffing a hand full of jelly beans in his mouth all at the same time.

"Now that is just wrong. You just committed the ultimate Jelly Belly sin."

He looked at me, his mouth full of candy, like I was crazy.

"You're supposed to eat them one at a time, unless you're creating a combo."

"A combo? What is a jelly bean combo?"

"Seriously, what rock did you grow up under? I thought every child knew a few Jelly Belly combos."

I motioned for him to come closer and he complied, putting down his tools and taking a seat next to me on the floor. Seeing all six plus feet of full grown male, wrapped in faded jeans and gray t-shirt, sitting on my daughters pink rug was quite a sight.

"Prepare to be amazed. What's your favorite dessert?" I asked him.

"Besides jelly beans?" he asked jokingly.

I nodded, giving him a pointed look.

"Okay, fine. Root Beer Float." he answered.

"And you gave me crap for liking jelly beans? Who's the kid now?"

"Well, root beer and ice cream weren't allowed in our house or boarding school. The desserts we had were so pretentious, I'm pretty sure I couldn't pronounce them until I was in my teens," he explained in an amused sort of way, but there was a shadow of something dark there. Before I could figure out what it was, it was gone and replaced by his award winning smile.

"Okay, well...root beer float coming up."

I dug through the bowl, looking for the jelly beans I needed. He watched skeptically, but leaned in closer, brushing his shoulder against mine. I could smell the aftershave on his neck, and I wanted so badly to pull him closer to me.

"You're very dedicated to jelly beans, aren't you?"

"You have no idea. Just wait until you see me with chocolate." That brought on another laugh. He had a great laugh.

I finally found the winning combination of jelly beans and handed them over for him to try. He popped the three jelly beans in his mouth and chewed, and I became mesmerized with his mouth, suddenly wondering what he tasted like.

Yum.

"That's actually pretty amazing! It really does taste like a root beer float. What's your favorite?" he asked as he finished off his jelly beans, pulling me out of my edible Logan fantasy.

"Oh. Um. Tiramisu," I answered quickly. "Chocolate and Coffee. It's heavenly."

Realizing I completely derailed out little game, I asked another question.

"So, how did a son of a stuffy billionaire learn to be so handy?"

He looked down at his hands, much too worn for his social status, and explained, "I don't know. I guess I've always liked to work with my hands. When I was in college, I lived in a shit apartment, and was always having to make repairs, so I kind of just learned on the go."

I was curious why a rich kid was living in the low rent apartments, but before I could ask, he gave me a smirk and fired back with a question for me.

"The other day, when I walked into the exam room, were you and your friend talking about me?"

Damn fair skin always gave me away. Before I could even open my mouth to respond, I was blushing, so instead I just stuffed it full of jelly beans, bypassing the entire question and committing candy treason at the same time.

"I knew it!"

"That was incredibly embarrassing," I admitted, after I swallowed my handful of jelly beans.

"I can safely say I was not embarrassed in the least. Made my night, in fact," he taunted.

"All right, it's my turn again."

In agreement, he nodded and waited for his question.

"When you're alone, away from the hospital and everything else, what do you do for yourself?" I asked. I hoped this question wouldn't be bypassed with jelly beans. I really wanted to get a glimpse of the real Logan. He was very polished on the outside, giving the image of a carefree young doctor, but it's a totally fake persona. I could see the frayed edges, and the fine lines of imperfection left by years of emotional trauma. Maybe no one else noticed because he was so adept at covering them up, or just kept everyone at a safe distance. But I saw them for what they were, scars from a damaged past. Life had left me with my own set of damage and scars, but I knew where mine came from. A life lost. What had earned him the battle wounds he so expertly hid from the world?

"I play the guitar," he answered.

I hadn't expected that one. I half expected him to pass on the question.

"How long have you played?" I asked, watching him as he stared out the window at the trees that lined the property.

"Since I was fourteen. My father believed every child should play an instrument so I was put in violin lessons when I was ten with a top notch instructor. I was terrible," he paused while I held my breath, afraid any movement might stop him from continuing.

"To avoid further embarrassment, my father ended my lessons and hired a tutor to teach me piano, which I did marginally better at. At least, enough to satisfy my father's requirement. Around the age of fourteen, thinking it would up my cool points at school, I asked if I could learn to play the guitar. You would have thought I'd asked if I could visit Satan in Hell. Obviously, his answer was no, and because I had asked, he figured I got the crazy idea from a bad influence at school. So, I was pulled out mid-year and switched to a new boarding school in a new state," he sighed, obviously still annoyed as he relived the memory.

"Your dad pulled you out of school because you asked to play the guitar?" I thought my dad was strict when he didn't let me date until I was fifteen. I had nothing on Logan.

"Yes. My father's unique." He didn't elaborate. Apparently the "Daddy file" was closed for the day.

"My new roommate Colin, who is still my best friend to this day, taught me to play that first year I was at Milton. He was probably the reason I survived." A ghost of a smile appeared across his face, and then chuckled.

"So, did it make you any cooler?" I asked.

"Colin helped with that. He sounds like a moron and can play every sport imaginable. But, he's a goddamn genius. He took me under his wing, and yeah, I did all right."

I sensed a bit of regret when he spoke of Colin and I wondered if it was a new or old regret, and if there was something currently going on between the two men.

"I don't think I've ever told anyone that," he admitted.

"Jelly beans, they're worse than booze. Okay, your turn. Ask me anything. Make it a good one," I challenged.

"Your name. I'm always curious about names, where they came from or how they were chosen. I noticed yours is spelled differently, is there a reason?" he asked, stretching to full height again to return to the wall, making the finishing touches to the ballet barre. He even picked up a mirror at the hardware store to put behind it so she could see herself as she twirled around. It was a very thoughtful touch. One I hadn't even thought of myself.

"Yes, actually. It's quite a good story. My parents honeymooned in Ireland. County Clare to be exact. They spent two weeks there and it was apparently a very successful trip because when they returned, Mom was pregnant with me. To commemorate their honeymoon, they named me Clare."

"Have you ever been there?"

"Where? To Ireland?"

He nodded.

"No, I've always wanted to. Ethan and I..."

I stopped, mid-sentence, growing still. I had not mentioned Ethan yet. I hadn't even told him I was a widow. I mean, I guess he assumed by now. But saying the words out loud to him made me suddenly conscious of what I had been doing the past hour. Flirting. In my house that I used to share with my husband. I didn't know how to feel about that. Should I feel guilty? Or relieved I had taken a step toward moving on? Was it moving on?

"Was Ethan your husband?" he asked quietly.

I nodded silently, still thinking about my sudden

realization.

"How did he, I mean...how long ago?" he stumbled over his words, before taking a few careful steps toward me.

"Almost three years. Brain cancer. Maddie was barely two," I managed to say.

"I'd say I'm sorry, but I'm sure you've heard that more times than you can count. What I can say is that from what I've seen, you've done an amazing job surviving. Maddie is a bright, kind hearted little girl. She can capture the heart of just about anyone in two seconds flat."

Letting out a tiny laugh of nervousness, I began fiddling with the hem of my t-shirt, trying to figure out what to say.

"Thank you. For everything, I mean. I know you probably had other things that needed to be done today and you –"

"WOW!!!! It's so pretty!!" Maddie exclaimed as she bounced into the room, effectively saving me from further embarrassment.

She ran to her brand new ballet barre and looked into the mirror, seeing her reflection and smiled. Jumping up and down, she abruptly turned, obviously seeing Logan in the mirror. She immediately catapulted herself into his surprised arms.

He looked stunned at first, but then melted. His arms wrapped around her, holding her as she embraced him chanting thank you, over and over again.

"You're welcome, princess. Your Mom helped too," he said, adjusting her onto his hip like a seasoned pro.

"Yeah right." Maddie commented.

She knew her Mommy well.

I stuck my tongue out at her and made a face, which sent her into a fit of giggles.

Neither Logan nor I could help but laugh right along with her. Her laugh was infectious. You couldn't help but be happy when you were around her.

Still laughing, Maddie grabbed Logan's face with both hands, looking at him square in the eyes. This was always her preferred method of getting people's attention. It was hard being small. She adapted.

"Dr. Matthew! You should stay for dinner! My Mommy can cook for you."

Well, I guess we just invited the friendly doctor to dinner.

I held my breath waiting for his answer. He looked at Maddie and then shifted his attention to me. I saw the gears in his head grinding, obviously trying to work something out. He had a look of hope when she asked, and in the brief seconds he considered her offer, his face went from hope to despair.

"I'm sorry Maddie. I shouldn't."

He didn't say he had plans, or maybe another time. He said he shouldn't. Like it wasn't a good idea. The dark shadows were floating around his eyes again, and we were all silent as we headed for the stairs. Maddie was still firmly in Logan's arms, although she wasn't laughing anymore. It was then that I realized this was the first time since Ethan died that Maddie was being held by another man, other than a family member. And now that man was leaving. The realization left me a little breathless.

Slowing as we approached the door, Logan asked Maddie "Hey princess, have you ever been to a real ballet?"

She shook her head, saying "No, Mommy tried to take me to Swam Wake, but she couldn't get tickets."

He looked at me, amused by her fumbled words, as I mouthed "Swan Lake" to correct her.

"Well, it just so happens that I have three tickets for this upcoming weekend. What do you say we all go?"

Maddie's eyes lit up in sheer manic joy, looking to me for permission.

"Logan, are you sure? That's very generous," I said, seeing Maddie was about ready to explode, waiting for my answer.

He nodded, flashing Maddie a wink. "I'm positive. Every ballerina in training needs to go to the ballet. And being a significant donor to the Performing Arts, I think it's time I cash in some of those privileges."

"Thank you. We would love to."

We would also like to know why you're so damn hot and cold all the time.

He sat Maddie down and we exchanged numbers so that arrangements for dinner and the ballet could be made and before I knew it he was gone and Maddie was jumping up and down, screaming that she was going to see the "Swammie's"!

Chapter Six

~Logan~

"When you called and asked me to hang out, I honestly thought you were dying or something," Colin said as we settled into the booth of the sports bar he had picked out.

It was late afternoon on a weekday so the bar was mostly empty. A few regulars milled about watching the screens and chatting with each other. Colin and I chose a corner booth, away from everyone else. It had been awhile since we'd seen each other and we both felt seclusion was needed.

Colin had been my best friend since grade school and yet I felt like I didn't even know the man who sat across from me. He still looked the same. Same large build from years of football and lacrosse. Same short blonde hair cut, hazel eyes and cocky attitude. But everything else felt foreign. I'd never felt so uncomfortable with him. And it was my fault.

"Yeah, I know. Look, I'm sorry," I stuttered out an apology.

There were so many apologies I didn't even know where to start. Sorry for being a shitty friend. Sorry for being an asshole, etc. The list was endless.

"Logan, I get it. You got fucked over. You put on a bit of a thick skin, okay? But dude, you gotta let someone in."

I never shared with Colin what actually happened with Melanie. That probably wasn't fair to her, or Gabe. The media made them out to be the guilty party, and yes, she was the one who cheated. But I was the one who drove her to it. I should have just let her go, had divorce papers written up early, and given her the chance to move on without the glare of the photographers. But I kept putting it off, fearing that if I did give her up, I would be admitting something to myself. Something I'd long since feared growing up, and had come to dread ever since my wedding night when I looked at my sleeping bride alone in bed, and realized I didn't love her. The consuming fear that I was incapable of loving another and there was something essentially missing in my DNA or upbringing that kept me from feeling true, deep and meaningful love.

Meeting Clare gave me spark of hope. She stirred emotions in me that had long been dormant. I still felt like I should run, leaving her to wait for someone who deserved her. But I was finding it difficult to stay away. Every time I tried to push away, I found myself waging internal civil war, completely conflicted until I ended up texting her just to get a goofy response, or calling her at night to hear her voice.

When Maddie had asked me to dinner, I wanted so badly to say yes. I wanted to be that man. But I was so scared of letting them down. Seeing that photo of Clare in the arms of her dead husband, her eyes so full of love and hope, it shredded me. I can't imagine what she must have gone through when she lost him. What if I hurt them? So I did the only thing I was good at anymore, I started to run. And it almost worked. Until I made it to the door. I couldn't walk away.

I needed advice, and the only person I trusted was the friend I had been avoiding for far too long. Thank God he was a better friend than me.

"I'm trying, Colin. I've met someone."

His eyes flared in surprise, and he nearly spit out his beer.

"Like a single someone that you plan on seeing more than once? Cause bleeding your heart to a one-night stand isn't what I was going for. Although, if you want to share other details on that front, I'm totally cool with that."

"Yes, it's one person, no to the other question." I answer.

"To which one? Seeing her more than once, or giving me the deets on your hook-ups?" he grinned.

"The second one. Not sharing secrets. Sorry man."

"You are no fun. All right, so tell me about the woman. It is a woman right?'

"Yes, asshole. Her name is Clare. I met her at the hospital, actually. She's a single mom. Widowed." There. I figured I might as well get all the shit out on the table.

Colin just stared at me blankly before running a beefy hand through his sandy blonde hair.

"What?" I asked.

"Okay, I'm going to say this in the nicest way I know how. But dude, you're kind of a dick."

I would act offended if it weren't true.

"I see from your non-reply that you agree. So, I gotta ask. What are you doing with a woman like that? You can't fuck around with her."

"I know."

"Do you? I sure hope so. Because she's not a casual fuck, Logan. You can't just bang her and leave. A woman like that is someone you stick around for. Are you ready for that?"

I remained silent, unable to answer. I honestly didn't know. But despite everything, I wanted to find out.

~Clare~

"He came over to your house?" Leah whispered from the mat next to me as I arched my body, progressing through the movements of our Wednesday morning yoga class. In the last year, I had enrolled Maddie in preschool for a few mornings each week and if Leah's schedule allowed, we always tried to make this class together. It was nice having a bit of "me time" with my best friend, even if she was currently trying to get us kicked out with her chattering.

"Yes, we ran into him at the home improvement store down the street, and he just offered to do the entire project for me. The store had me so turned around, I couldn't refuse," I whispered back, quietly moving into plank, enjoying the feel of my muscles as they flexed and lengthened. I tried to center myself; concentrating on the movements I was transitioning to when Leah interrupted me again. I really needed to find a new yoga partner.

"More like he had you so turned on, you couldn't refuse!" she exclaimed, a bit loudly, earning a scowl from the older woman next to us. Great, now I could never come back here again. We pushed back into the cricket pose and stretched back, settling into plank again.

"Leah! Shut up!" I hissed, keeping my voice lowered to a hush, hoping the grumpy old lady next to me wouldn't overhear.

"It wasn't like that. He was very nice, and a complete gentleman. I assisted and he did, well, whatever you do when you put that type of thing together, and then he left. That's it."

Mostly.

I left out certain parts, like how I playfully threw jelly beans at his head, or when I got choked up seeing him going down the stairs with Maddie in his arms.

She glared at me in disbelief, but allowed us to continue our class in peace. I think even she had been a little scared of the grumpy lady with the evil-eyed stare.

We finished up and wandered over to a coffee shop about two blocks down from the yoga studio. It was one of our favorite places to visit during the spring. The owner, Phil, was obsessed with potted plants, vintage wrought iron tables, and anything else that screamed shabby chic. And yes, if all that didn't clue you in, he was gay. It was a brutal crime against all women because the man was fine. He'd done some modeling when he was younger and it showed in his chiseled physique and turquoise green eyes. Women all over Richmond came to this coffee shop, and it wasn't just because he could make a mean cup of coffee. Gay or not, he was a fine sight to see.

After saying our hellos to Phil and getting our weekly "ogle" in, we made our way to the outdoor seating area. "You know, this probably cancels out everything we just did in class," I said, pointing to the double mochas and chocolate muffins we had ordered. Did I mention Phil baked? It really was a crime. His partner was a lucky, lucky man. I took a seat next to Leah at the table we selected. It was a beautiful spring morning with the perfect amount of sun and warmth. I leaned back in the wrought iron chair and let the heat soak into my pores, easing my tired, worn out muscles.

"Well at least our minds are clear, our bellies might as well be full," Leah said, defending our breakfast as she shoveled a piece of muffin into her mouth and washed it down with her coffee. I don't think Leah's mind has ever been clear. There are too many dirty thoughts going on in there.

"So, that was it? You totally missed your chance, Clare! It's not like you're going to keep running into Dr. Hot Ass every day. Do you want me to steal his phone number from work? I can still do it," she asked again with an exasperated sigh, clearly not done talking about Dr. Matthews.

"What? No! I mean, I have it. He gave it to me already," I said, the words stumbling out of my mouth before I could stop myself.

Crap. I'm in so much trouble.

She was giving me that look. The look that said I had broken the "girl code."

"Clare Elizabeth Murray. He gave you his number? When? Sunday?"

I nodded, unable to hide the grin that spread across my face.

"And you didn't tell me until now?"

Still not talking, I nodded, again, grinning like an idiot.

"What the hell? I hate you," she said, pouting.

"Oh stop, you do not. I didn't tell you because it's nothing. He gave it to me because he invited Maddie and me to see Swan Lake on Saturday. He obviously needed a way to contact me. It's not a big deal," I said, looking away from her penetrating gaze and taking a sip of my coffee.

I decided not to mention how we had been texting and calling each other ever since. She would probably make a big deal out of that, too. I was still trying not to overanalyze anything. He was so hot and cold, I didn't want to jump to conclusions. But every time I saw his name flash across my phone, my stomach would flutter. Our conversations started out innocent - figuring out what time he was going to pick us up on Saturday, where we should eat, but then we would somehow start talking about something entirely different. When we would start to wrap up our conversation, he'd say "I'll call you later." And *he would*.

"Um, excuse me. That's a big fucking deal. He asked you out!" Leah exclaimed.

"What? No, he didn't. Did you hear what I said? He basically asked Maddie out. I'm only there for supervision. I think he's just being nice."

God, how I hoped he was not being nice. Did he ask us because he wanted to spend more time with me, or was he really just doing it for Maddie? I had convinced myself of the latter, but I was hoping for the former.

"Men that hot don't do "nice" Clare. He's taking the two of you, but he wants to see you first and foremost. I can guarantee it. I mean, which one of you will be wearing a thong?" she asked.

"Um, neither?"

"What? Oh God, you do need work. Come on, we're going shopping."

~Logan~

"This is not a date," I chanted to myself for the hundredth time as I pulled my car into Clare's driveway. I don't know why I was so damn nervous. I was acting like a fucking woman. I changed my tie twice, cut myself shaving, and paced the floor like a pansy, just waiting for the minutes to tick down until I could leave.

I had been nervous all week. When I'd blurted out my invitation to the ballet, I was desperate. I had been standing at Clare's front door, unable to leave. I knew, standing there, I wouldn't have another random chance like the one I had that day and I couldn't leave it up to fate. Deciding to do the opposite of my status quo, I seized an opportunity and brought up the ballet. I walked out that night feeling both relieved at the thought of seeing Clare again and nervous as hell. We spent the rest of the week talking, continuing her attempt at the jelly bean game via text. We learned a lot about each other in a short amount of time. I knew where she went to college and that she majored in history. I knew she was obsessed with yoga and she knew I loved to run. When I suggested I take her out one morning for a few miles she sent back an unhappy emoticon as a response and that was how I found out Clare hated running. Every time my phone vibrated, I found myself grinning like a fucking idiot hoping it was her. Clare was witty and clever and always kept me on my toes. Best of all, she didn't give two shits who I was or where I came from.

Now, Saturday had finally arrived and I was sitting in her driveway like a fucking idiot wondering what to do. Getting out of the car would be a good place to start.

I hadn't been on a date since Melanie. Picking up women in bars and clubs didn't count as dates. With Melanie, I had never been nervous on our dates. Looking back, maybe that should have been a clue...and damn it, this wasn't a date! Now I really needed to get out of this car before she noticed me sitting out here like a stalker.

I walked up to the front door and saw the curtains flutter before hearing "He's here Mommy! Hurry up!!" followed by a little girl's laughter. Apparently, knocking wasn't necessary, but I did so anyway. I heard little feet racing toward the door as Clare shouted at Maddie to check and make sure it was me first. There was a brief pause, followed by another giggle, and the door opened. An adorable Maddie all dressed up for an evening out wiggled her finger toward me motioning for me to come closer. I leaned down to her level and she whispered, "If Mommy asks, I looked out the window, k? I already knew it was you."

Chuckling at the thought of her trying to undermine her mom, I just nodded. I scooped her up and we entered the house together.

"Maddie, you look just like a princess." And she did. She wore a teal dress with a simple bodice and of course, a tulle glittery skirt. Her curly hair was tamed and pinned behind each ear with matching barrettes and glittery silver shoes.

"Mommy took me shopping and let me pick out whatever I wanted! I look like a ballerina, huh?" she said proudly as I put her down so she could twirl around to show off her sparkly skirt. I needed to remind myself to buy everything and anything covered in tulle and glitter.

"You sure do. You'll fit right in. How about your Mom? Does she look like a ballerina?" I asked, wondering when I would get to see Clare.

"No, Mommy never lets me dress her up. She says pink tutus don't go with red hair. She's got some grown up dress on."

Just as Maddie finished her sentence Clare walked into the room and I nearly swallowed my tongue.

She was beautiful in a pair of yoga pants, but now she was downright breathtaking.

Her dress was satin, and shimmered the perfect shade of emerald green to match her eyes. The tiny straps dipped low enough to reveal just a hint of her delectable cleavage and the tight fabric hugged her every curve. She wore gold heels that made her long legs seem endless. I briefly thought about what those high heels would look like wrapped around my neck, but quickly decided, as Maddie was tugging on my arm, to shelve that fantasy for another time.

Clearing my throat, I managed to say, "You look radiant."

I wanted to say more, to tell her she looked gorgeous and downright fuckable. But this was not a date, and even if it was I'm pretty sure that statement would get me a one way ticket out the door. I may be rusty on dating, but I do remember some things. Telling a woman she looks "fuckable" in the first five minutes? That's a big don't. At least on the first date.

"Thank you. You polish up pretty well too, Doc," she declared, grinning widely. There it was again, that spark and sass from the other day when she was firing off the question and answer game, and she had it again. I felt it growing stronger each day. It was like witnessing someone's confidence returning after a huge blow to their ego. She was becoming bolder in her interactions with me, like something inside of her was slowly being rebuilt. Was she flirting? I was so out of practice with subtlety I didn't even know anymore.

The women I'd been spending time with over the last few years didn't do subtle and until very recently I liked it that way. After Melanie and all the hurt I caused her, I didn't want any feelings attached to sex. I figured it was better for all parties involved. When you have my name, there's no shortage of women, and I shamelessly used that to my advantage. It wasn't like I was a rock star. I could go to Target or the grocery store and go unrecognized. At a club or a bar where I was known to frequent, people would introduce themselves and I would do the same. Eventually they'd put the puzzle pieces together, and I would be surrounded. Leeches. They'd hang on my every word, pretending they cared. The men patted me on my back, hoping to become Logan Matthew's new best friend while the women rubbed, purred and stroked, hoping I'd take them for a spin.

"You ready to go?" Clare asked, grabbing her coat off the back of the sofa. She began slinging it around her body, but I interceded. I eased the coat over her slender body, letting my hands linger a second longer than needed, letting her subtle perfume engulf my senses. I took a quick breath to clear my head. Clare intoxicated me like no other woman I'd ever encountered. Every time I was around her, I had this overwhelming need to touch her. I wanted to hold her hand, touch her skin, and wrap her body around mine. Feeling no less distracted but knowing we needed to leave, I grabbed the small dress coat draped over the couch next to Clare's handbag, and knelt down to help Maddie.

"All set, princess?" I asked, giving her a wink.

"Yep!" Maddie sang, bouncing in the air like a jackrabbit.

"All right Ladies, let's go!"

~Clare~

He picked the perfect restaurant. It wasn't too fancy, but just enough that Maddie felt like she was given the royal treatment. He again carried Maddie into the restaurant, all of her teal colored tulle balled up in his masculine arms. It was quite the sight. And God, he looked handsome tonight.

That man filled out a suit flawlessly. The dark charcoal tailored jacket fit him perfectly and the steel blue tie he had chosen matched his eyes. After I had put on the cocktail dress Leah insisted I buy I felt overdone and out of my element. It had been years since I'd worn something so fancy. But when I came downstairs and saw those beautiful blue eyes widen in surprise, and then smolder with heat, I made a mental note to call Leah and thank her for her wisdom. I felt empowered and beautiful. It was exactly what I needed.

Maddie had insisted on sitting next to him. He laughed and said "Of course, princess!" I think he had developed his own nickname for her. I tried not to think about how that made me feel.

The waiter gave Maddie a kids menu and a small box of crayons, which sent her into her own world. Settling on a dish of light angel hair with shrimp and a glass of white wine, I placed my menu on the table and found Logan staring at me. This, of course, made me blush from the sudden attention, but he just kept staring.

"Your parents must have brought back a bit of Ireland with you when they came back from their honeymoon. Your eyes are the exact color of the Irish hillsides."

"You've been there?"

He nodded with no explanation.

"Where else have you traveled?" I questioned.

"I've been all over. My father wasn't big on holidays, so instead of putting up a tree or carving turkeys, he would send me on a trip. I would have hired chaperones and could pretty much go wherever I wanted as long as I wasn't home," he causally answered with a shrug.

"Are you an only child?"

"Uh, no. I have a sister, Evangeline, but she grew up with my Mom. My real mom, I mean, not the Stepford wife my father is married to now," he explained.

"So, you didn't spend holidays with your Mom and sister?"

I couldn't imagine not having a place to go for the holidays. Being shipped off, a big burden no one wanted to deal with.

"No, my Mom gave me up when my parents divorced. Full custody went to my father. And I don't see Eva much at all. I barely know her."

"Oh." I didn't know what else to say.

"It is the way it is. But I did get to see the world. I've been everywhere. Spain, Italy, China, and Russia." He abruptly stopped as the waiter brought us drinks and took our dinner orders.

Alone again, I asked "Not that I'm not thrilled you're talking, but why are you opening up all the sudden? You devoured half a bowl of jelly beans to avoid that family question last week."

Logan stared into his wine glass, taking a sip as he quietly pondered my question. His gaze finally drifted back up to me, and our eyes locked.

"I don't know. I feel like you see through me. The normal facade I put out there to the rest of the world? It doesn't work with you. I tried it on Sunday, and you called my bluff. When you asked about my family, I was still so stunned by how clearly you saw me. You seemed to know that was the one of the few questions that would get under my skin. I've thought about it since then, and I don't know, I guess I decided if you see through it all, what's the point?"

He shrugged, "It feels good to be honest with someone for once in my life."

I was breathless for a second, stunned by his candor. I didn't know what to say, so I took the easy way out and changed the subject.

"I've never even been out of the country," I confessed quickly. God, I was a coward.

Understanding flashed across his face, and he eased back into our first conversation.

Thank you, I silently told him.

"Really? Never?" he replied.

"No, Ethan and I were supposed to honeymoon in Italy, but I was offered a teaching position in the history department at one of the local high schools. I couldn't get the two weeks off mid-semester, so we canceled. We had always planned on going, but then well...Maddie came, and then he got sick."

Nice Clare. Excellent dinner conversation. Much better than the last one.

My eyes reached across the table until I found Maddie and smiled. I gently ran my hands over her fingers as she colored. She, of course, didn't notice, still stuck in her own little world of crayons. I don't know what I would do without her.

"She looks like you," Logan said, his eyes traveling between Maddie and me, comparing mother and daughter.

"She definitely got my hair, a lighter version, but it's still mine. But her brown eyes are all Ethan." I said, with snort, "Red hair, freckles, and pale skin. That's all me. Poor kid, she's gonna hate me as a teenager."

"She'll be a knockout, just like her Mom."

~Logan~

I've never had more fun in a restaurant. I laughed when Clare told stories about Maddie's younger years. Clare's face lit up when she explained that Maddie hated diapers as a baby and she would find her crawling all over the house buck naked. Four-year-old Maddie did not find this nearly as funny and told her Mommy saying the word "diaper" at the dinner table was "imappropriate". I had to hide my laughter behind my napkin over that one.

When our food was cleared, Maddie announced that we couldn't leave until Mommy had tiramisu. Apparently she was well aware of her mother's sweet tooth. So I ordered one for us all to share. I helped Maddie color her menu while we waited for dessert. Coloring is not a talent of mine, and Clare jokingly pointed out this fact out to me several times.

"Oh come on, it's not like you could do better," I taunted.

"Didn't you know? I'm the Picasso of menu art," she bragged, grabbing the menu to her side of the table, and began creating her own masterpiece.

A few minutes later, our dessert arrived, and Clare handed her menu back to our side of the table. I took one look and burst out laughing.

She'd drawn a plate piled high with tiramisu. It's disturbingly detailed. This woman knows her desserts. Above the drawing, she spelled out "Back away from my tiramisu and no one gets hurt!"

I looked up. Clare had confiscated the dessert and was already three or four bites in, a wide grin of mischief spread across her face.

"Ah, what? Your Mom just stole our dessert!"

"Mommy!!" Maddie scolded.

"I don't know why you are surprised. You know what I'm like around tiramisu. You should have warned him," she countered, taking another bite.

It's the most ridiculous thing I'd ever seen. It was also incredibly hot. I suddenly wanted to take a huge dollop of that espresso custard and smear it between her cleavage and lick it clean.

Adjusting in my seat, I turned to Maddie and asked, "All right, princess, what do you want for dessert? I didn't realize your mother gets hostile around Italian desserts," I teased.

"Ice cream!" Maddie cheered.

I grabbed the waiter as he walked by and ordered ice cream and more tiramisu. By the time the additional desserts arrived, Clare's tiramisu was history.

"So Maddie, your Mom told some embarrassing stuff about you. Why don't you tell me something about your Mom?" I instructed. I realized I could be digging myself a very large hole, but it was too late now.

"Oh! Okay! Um, she likes to dance, especially with me. She turns up the music real loud, and we dance all over the house. I don't think most Mommies do that, because it's really silly," she stated proudly.

I looked over at Clare, who didn't look embarrassed in the least. She just grinned before reached toward Maddie, touched her pointer finger to Maddie's nose and gave her a quick wink.

"Well, silly moms are the best. Or so I've been told," I assured her, never taking my eyes off of Clare. The more I learned about her, the more in awe I became. And the less I thought I'd be able to stay away. I was captivated now. How did she do it? Stay so strong? I had been through a lot of shit in my life, and look at me...I was pathetic. She'd been to hell and back, and she was dancing around the house with a four-year old.

As I'm staring at her, I realized her gaze is fixed on something entirely different.

"Oh, just give in already," I insisted, handing her a fork.

"Yes!" she bellowed, diving into my dessert. I ordered it for her anyway. This woman really loved sweets.

When dinner was finished and paid for, we left for the ballet. Maddie was about to burst with excitement by the time we made it to our seats.

The ballet was in a completely restored theater that dated back to 1920s. Its Art Deco elegance is something you don't see anymore, and as I watched Clare run her delicate fingers up and down the velvet seats, I knew she agreed. Her eyes danced around the room, taking it all in.

"Logan, these seats are amazing. I hope you didn't go to too much trouble."

Looking at Maddie as she bounced up and down in her teal dress, I was pretty sure I would have done just about anything to see that look on her face. Knowing this little fact should have freaked me out. Two weeks ago, I would never have done something like this, but these two women were changing me. I just hope I don't hurt them in the process.

"No, it was no trouble. It was my pleasure."

Maddie's first ballet was a total success. I held her to my side as she clapped for the dancers during the standing ovation. She loved every minute. All that excitement rushed out of her quickly though, and she fell asleep in my arms about halfway to the car. Clare and I were silent as we walked to the parking garage. I could see her occasionally glance over, looking at Maddie in my arms. There was something there, in her eyes. She was thinking, analyzing or maybe realizing something because she turned away quickly when she met my gaze.

Working in the ER, I had my fair share of encounters with children, and not all of them have been good or had happy endings. Despite the fact that I had become a complete asshole in my personal life, I still maintained a good bedside manner with my patients, especially children. I did feel for them and their families. What I felt for Maddie was something different, though. I wanted to protect her, hold her, and never let her go. It was fierce, raw and real. When she was in my arms, it felt natural to me. When I was with Clare and Maddie, I felt like I was home, or at least what I thought a home should feel like. It was selfish of me to get involved. I should run, leave them in peace to enjoy their lives without being dragged into my shit. But I couldn't stop myself. It was like the calm you felt from a drug, and I was an addict unable to turn away.

We arrived at the car and I helped Clare buckle a sleeping Maddie into the car seat. I opened the door for Clare, waiting for her to get situated before going around to the driver's side. The silence between us was deafening.

"You're quiet. Are you all right?"

"Yes. No. I don't know," she admitted.

"I know we haven't known each other very long, but remember...no bullshit? You can be honest with me," I gently reminded her.

She took a deep ragged breath, letting it release slowly from her lungs.

"Seeing her in your arms creates so many emotions in me. Warmth, pride, guilt," she began before briefly pausing to collect her thoughts.

"He's never going to be here to take her to a ballet, or pick her up from school. He won't walk her down the aisle or see her children. These are all things I know, and have known. And I'd made peace with that."

"I've upset you. I --" I began to say.

"No, you did nothing wrong. She adores you. You're the first man she's been comfortable around since Ethan. I knew from the day Ethan died that I would most likely be a single parent for the rest of my life, and I mourned all those things that Ethan would miss in her life. I guess I just realized, seeing her with you, how much she will miss in her life by not having a father. It's so stupid, but I hadn't seen it the other way around until now."

I reached across the small space in the car that separated us and grabbed her hand. Up until this moment, we hadn't touched since that moment in the ER. Her hand felt soft in mine, delicate. She turned her hand beneath mine, weaving our fingers together.

I snuck a glance down at our joined hands, before turning onto her street.

"And what about you? What are you missing?" I whispered, knowing I was stepping onto new ground.

"I don't really know. I hadn't thought about it at all. Until recently."

We reached her house and I pulled the car into the driveway. I killed the engine but didn't make a move to exit. Instead, I turned toward her and just admired the woman in front of me. The words she'd just said still clung in the air, and my body ached to lean forward and kiss her, claiming her as my own.

Her eyes locked with mine and I could see them wide with anticipation and just a hint of nervousness. The deep green seared into mine before traveling down to my lips. I nearly groaned with the need to touch her. Raising my hand, I gently traced my fingers down the side of her face, feeling her soft skin under mine. Her breath caught and her eyes fluttered closed. Wrapping my hand around the back of her neck, I pulled her closer to me so that our lips were mere inches apart.

"You are so beautiful," I murmured, closing the distance between us to finally feel her soft lips against mine.

"Mommy, are we home?" a sleepy voice from the back seat croaked.

Clare and I instantly pulled apart, acting like two horny teenagers caught making out under the bleachers. Clare jumped from the car to open the back door and retrieve Maddie, and I followed.

"Shhh, baby girl. We're home. Let's get you to bed," Clare assured.

"But I want to see more ballerinas," Maddie mumbled.

"Later princess. Promise."

I offered to carry her in so Clare wouldn't have to tackle the stairs in a cocktail dress. I settled her in bed, and Clare pulled out her pajamas. I watched in absolute awe as she performed this simple task that she'd probably done a million times now. It seemed completely foreign and fascinating to me. Maddie was all but unconscious, but Clare managed to get her changed without much effort.

She tucked her in giving her a quick kiss on the cheek.

Unable to stop myself, I leaned down, kiss her on the cheek and said, "Goodnight, princess."

Clare and I silently left Maddie's room and I followed her downstairs toward the entrance of the house. Once we reached the front door, she turned.

"Logan, thank you so much for tonight. You don't know how--"

"Go out with me," I blurted out, interrupting her.

"What?" she said, clearly amused.

"Go out with me. On a date. Just you and me."

Please, I silently begged.

"Yes," she agreed.

"Saturday. I'll call you." I grinned like a goddamn fool.

"Okay." She turned to unlock the door, looking back at me with a shy smile.

God, I wanted to kiss her. But I really, really needed to be gentlemen for once in my life.

I took a step out the door, preparing my goodbye speech and froze.

The memory of her in the car, when her breath caught, and her eyes fluttered shut flashed through me, and I couldn't move another step.

Ah, fuck it.

I quickly pivoted around, seeing Clare's brief look of surprise right before I grab her around the waist, pulling our bodies tight together, and slammed my mouth down on hers. She let out a gasp of surprise, before giving a slight moan, returning the kiss with enthusiasm. That moan was the sexiest sound I'd ever heard.

I reluctantly pulled back, both of us gasping for air.

"See you Saturday, Clare."

Being a gentleman is highly overrated.

Chapter Seven

~Clare~

I never thought Saturday would arrive.

I felt like Maddie waiting for Santa. I think that fact alone made me truly pathetic.

The week leading up to the date hadn't started out with excitement. In fact, it started with absolute dread.

After Logan kissed me, that epic earth shattering kiss, and my heart rate returned to normal, I began to panic. What was I thinking? Could I do this?

Afterward, I locked up the house and walked into my bedroom in a daze. I started to contemplate every different way I could get out of that date. I wasn't ready to date. It was too soon, right? Maybe in another five years. That sounded reasonable, I told myself as I paced the room. I eventually walked over to the floor length mirror I stared into a week earlier and took a long look at myself again.

My cheeks were flushed and my lips were swollen and for the first time in over three years. I actually looked alive. That part of me, the feminine side all women have that makes us feel sexy and wanted, was back.

I survived Ethan's death. I had come back from the ashes and lived. But until that night there was still a part of me that was missing. I could feel a sliver of it returning as I glanced in that mirror.

I hadn't lost myself to grief and I could come back whole again.

Feeling my confidence returning, I grinned in the mirror,

placed a hand over my swollen lips and finally began looking forward to my date.

The next morning I awoke in another panic when I realized I had nothing to wear. The only things I owned were what Leah dubbed "Mom clothes." Jeans, sweaters, tank tops and other random washable items. If it couldn't handle a jelly stain, I didn't own it.

I called Leah for an emergency shopping trip.

Complete silence, followed by an ear piercing scream filled the airwaves when I told her the reason. I thanked God I wasn't anywhere public because I'm pretty sure anyone standing within ten feet of me would have thought the person on the other end was being murdered while I was standing there, calmly doing nothing.

"Oh my God!" she shrieked.

"Leah, seriously calm down."

"You have a date! We must go shopping."

I was pretty sure I had already mentioned that. "I know. I'm dropping off Maddie at my parents' tomorrow afternoon."

"Good. Plan on leaving her there for dinner, cause we have some serious work to do," she instructed.

She wasn't kidding. We shopped for hours and she made me promise to go to the salon to get a mani/pedi on Friday so my nails would be freshly polished. As we were leaving the mall, she said I may want to throw in a wax. When I gave her a hard stare, she looked at me innocently saying "What? You never know! Gotta be prepared, Clare!"

I think Leah was always prepared, for everything.

And now, Saturday was finally here. Leah had just arrived. She had offered to babysit for the evening, which I thought was sweet, but I think she was doing it to be nosy.

No, scratch that. I knew she was being nosy because she

was sitting on my bed with Maddie watching me get ready.

"Mommy's going on a date. Do you know what that is?" she quizzed Maddie, absently playing with her hair. Maddie, who was seated on her lap was busy playing with her doll. She shook her head.

"Is it like a play date?" she asked Leah.

"Um, yes. But with kissing," Leah explained. I turned around from my vanity to give her a glare. She looked at me like she couldn't possibly understand what she did wrong. Leah's filter has a lot of holes. After all this time, I actually was starting to believe she didn't have one at all and just said whatever came to mind.

"Ewwww. That's gross, Aunt Leah."

"Hey, I'm not the one kissing anyone. Talk to your Mom." I hadn't talked to Maddie about this, and I had hoped to avoid it for at least another date or five.

"Who are you kissing, Mommy?" she inquired, suddenly getting very serious.

With my focus back on the mirror and the mascara I was trying to apply, I glanced at her quickly, and tried to brush off the question with a quick answer.

"Just you!" I insisted.

My exuberant response doesn't work, and she pressed on for more answers.

"On your date, who are you kissing Mommy?" she asked again, still serious.

"I don't know if I am going to kiss anyone, baby. I'm going on a date with Dr. Matthews. Are you okay with that?" I asked carefully.

"Oh. Yes!" she grinned brightly, going back to her doll play.

Leah looked at me in the mirror and we both shrugged.

Well, apparently that talk was done.

~Logan~

I pulled into Clare's driveway just as I had a week earlier, but today I felt completely different. I was still nervous, but now it felt like a different nervous, more a feeling of anticipation. Last week I was unsure of the path I should take with Clare. I wanted her. I wanted her more than anything. But I didn't know if I could trust myself. I still wasn't completely confident. After last Saturday though, when I held her in my arms and kissed her for the first time, I knew one thing. I wasn't going anywhere, and I planned on making sure she understood that today.

I took one last deep breath, got out of my car and headed for the door. As I rounded the corner of the driveway, I nearly ran headfirst into Maddie who was barreling toward me.

"Whoa there, princess. What are you doing out here?" Clare would not be pleased if she knew Maddie was out here without permission.

"It's okay. Mommy and Aunt Leah saw you from the window and said I could come get you. They've been up there forever," she huffed.

Apparently the female rituals of beauty hadn't captured her attention yet. I looked up at the window I thought must be Clare's bedroom, and saw Leah's small frame smiling down at me. She gave a small wave before disappearing behind the curtain. I chuckled wondering how long they'd been up there. Obviously long enough to drive a small child nearly insane. Poor kid.

"Forever, huh? Does your Mommy look pretty?" I asked, picking her up en route to the front door. I couldn't wait to see Clare. The week since our kiss had been long and difficult. We'd spent many hours on the phone, but I hadn't had the chance to see her in person. With my crazy schedule, I had to work double time to swing another Saturday off.

"Yeah, she's got a pretty dress on and she smells real good. Aunt Leah said Mommy should smell yummy on a date."

I choked back a laugh.

She became silent for a moment before asking, "Are you going to kiss my Mommy?"

Completely unprepared for this, I came to an abrupt stop, standing there on the front step just before we entered the house. How do I answer this? Will she hate me if I say yes? I can't lie. Not to Maddie. I looked at her for the first time, expecting a look of betrayal or hurt on her tiny face, but instead she was smiling. Amazing. It was the only word I had for this child.

"Cause it's okay if you want to," she added.

"Oh yeah?" I teased, tickling her between the ribs as we entered the house.

"Yes!" she squealed in between hysterical fits of laughter.

"Well thanks for the permission, princess." I sat Maddie down in the middle of the living room, which was just to the left of the front door. She looked at me with her big bright grin and I attacked, chasing her throughout the living room.

"No problem!" she shrieked, when I finally caught her in my arms.

"So, should I just go back upstairs? 'Cause I feel like I'm intruding."

We had been making so much noise I hadn't even heard her enter the room.

Turning, with Maddie slung over my shoulder, I saw Clare for the first time in a week, leaning against the doorframe of the living room. I suddenly felt my knees grow weak from the mere sight of her. I didn't know if I'd ever get used to seeing her without my heart rate doubling. I really hoped not.

When she asked where we were going, I simply told her to dress semi-casually, but that was all I told her. Everything else was a surprise. The dress Maddie had mentioned was simple but beautiful on her. The bright orange under an ivory lace overlay brought out the fiery tones in her hair and made her skin glow. The dress gathered at her slim waist with a belt, and it was short, giving me plenty of her long legs to stare at. She had a denim jacket tucked under her arm, and was wearing strappy sandals that wound around her ankle. She looked amazing, but I'd seen her covered in vomit and thought she'd been breathtaking. She was stunning no matter what she was wearing.

"You look...Wow," I stammered, leaning over to set Maddie down. I walked over to where Clare was standing.

"Hey Maddie, why don't you go find where Aunt Leah's run off to?" Clare suggested, briefly glancing over at Maddie and then returning back to me. Everything else disappeared for a moment. After a week away, I wanted nothing more than to take her in my arms and kiss her senseless. The look in her eyes told me she was on the same exact page.

"Oh, I'm right here. I wouldn't miss this for the world. You could cut the sexual tension in here with a knife," Leah shouted from the kitchen.

Clare reluctantly pulled her gaze from mine and circled around to Leah, who was currently sporting a messy bun piled at the top her head and a faded hooters t-shirt. She leaned casually on the granite countertop watching us, clearly amused.

"Seriously, Leah! She has ears. One of these days she's going to repeat something you say to her daycare teacher or my Mom!" Clare scolded.

"Oh please, if Maddie said something to your Mom, she would know right away who taught it to her. Laura would come after me with a bar of soap," she insisted.

"Well, at least she knows which one of us has the dirty mind," Clare said, walking to the kitchen counter to retrieve her purse. As she passed Leah, she reached over and pinched her in the ass causing her to yelp, and they both laughed.

"Ha! I'm just more vocal about mine," she argued as she rubbed her sore butt cheek.

"Not true. I'm an angel." Clare said, officially ending the conversation.

I personally would love to know more about Clare's dirty mind, but instead she went over Maddie's evening routine with Leah, who just stood in the kitchen and rolled her eyes.

"Not too much sugar. Remember to feed her dinner. And make sure she brushes her teeth," she reminded, giving Leah a pointed look.

Leah held up her hands in defense. "What? It was one time. Who says they need to brush their teeth every day?"

Clare shook her head and huffed in exasperation, leaving the kitchen to find Maddie who had arranged herself on the couch in the family room. She was reading a book with Dora the Explorer on the front. I smiled, knowing Clare hated Dora. Another late night conversation.

"Okay baby, Logan and I are gonna go. I'll see you in the morning. I love you." She knelt down in front of her daughter who was doing a good job ignoring her. Bent over, her thigh was in full view, and I desperately tried not to stare as she said goodbye to Maddie.

I was doing a terrible job of not looking at her thigh and I heard Leah snort in the background.

Busted. My covert glances were obviously not so covert.

"Love you too, Mommy." Maddie said absently, clearly engrossed in her book.

Clare laughed, "She's really going to miss me, I swear."

We headed for the door and I called out, "Bye, princess."

"Bye, Logan!" Maddie yelled from the family room.

Leah gave me a wink followed by two thumbs up as we walked out, and I chuckled.

I was starting to like her.

~Clare~

"So are you going to tell me where we are going?" I asked Logan as we continued down the scenic highway we'd been on for what seemed like forever. Spring was my favorite season in Virginia. After endless months of bare trees and cold temperatures, spring would finally arrive. The trees flowered perfuming the air, the skyline filled with color and the days were just right for trips to the park and long walks through the neighborhood. The rural highway we roamed down now was no exception. Green trees, old worn fences and the occasional farm would pass as we drove giving a sense of peace that a world like this still existed when everything else around us moved so quickly.

"Nope," he said as a wide, knowing grin spread across his flawless face.

"You're really enjoying this secrecy thing, aren't you?"

"I haven't been on a date in a long time, and yeah...surprising you? It's kind of fun," he admitted.

"You haven't dated since your divorce?" Between our long conversations on the phone and texting, he had talked about the divorce. He mentioned the cheating, and everything that happened with the press, but that was it. He didn't talk much about his life during his marriage or after his divorce. When he did, it was vague. Mostly work related or small tidbits about friends. I knew he was holding back. Whatever the reason, I hadn't pressed for information because I wanted him to come to me when he was ready. I understood heartache and pain, and we would both have to learn to trust each other with our own emotional scars. I had only skimmed the surface when he asked about losing Ethan. Sometimes, certain things were hard to admit, no matter who you were admitting them to.

"Dated, no. No, I definitely haven't done this in a while." He looked nervous, like he expected me to press for more. I didn't. Thanks again to Leah and her savvy skills for gossip, I know the reputation he earned since his divorce, but he was here with me now. I had to believe that I meant something to him, something different.

"So, are we staying in Virginia?" I asked as I looked out the window and saw another farm pass by. Exactly how far we were driving?

He visibly relaxed at the change of conversation and laughed "Yes, we don't have much longer."

After fifteen minutes and an interesting conversation that involved me admitting my obsession with Broadway musicals, we arrived at our destination. When I asked him if he liked musical theater, he looked over at me, shocked, like I'd gone mad, and said, "Clare, you have noticed I'm a guy, right? Because if not, I can pull this car over right now and make that abundantly clear."

I stared at him stunned, face turning an awful shade of red, imagining all the things we could do in that car alone. As my mind raced with a hundred different fantasies, he just smirked and said, "Breathe Clare." I took a big gulp of air into my lungs as he started his tirade against musicals. "I loathe musicals. Randomly breaking out into song? What's that about? It's just plain wrong."

I burst into laughter and we proceeded to argue the pros and cons of musical theater. Somehow I didn't think I'd be convincing him to see "Cats" anytime soon.

We turned onto a gravel road with a worn sign that had "The Thompson Plantation Bed and Breakfast. Est. 1809" printed in wispy elegant script. I turned in my seat, a bit confused and said, "A Bed and Breakfast? A bit presumptuous, aren't we?" I joked as we traveled down the tree lined single lane road.

"One can only hope," he grinned. "But no. We will be enjoying dinner. Only."

"Oh."

"Who's the presumptuous one now?" he laughed.

"Hey, you're the one taking me to a -- holy shit!" I yelled, stopping myself mid-sentence when the house came into view.

The word house was an understatement. It was huge. The colossal white mansion sat along the glistening waters of the James River. We had been driving so long and talking so much, I hadn't realized we were even following the river. Massive, dense gardens surround the house from every side, holding every flower imaginable. It looked like a postcard come to life.

The house was everything you would expect of a southern plantation, with black plantation shutters, huge white columns, and a wraparound porch. I could just close my eyes and envision what it must have looked like during the Civil War with elegantly dressed women wandering around the gardens worrying about their men as the slaves performed their duties, wondering if things would ever be different. So much history stood in this structure.

"Oh my God, Logan. This is amazing." I grabbed the door handle, dying to jump out of the car and explore. As a history major, or "history nerd" as Ethan used to call me, I had a love for everything old. It was one of the reasons I loved living in Virginia. Once I became a single mother, I had little time left for myself. My inner nerd had been seriously deprived over the last few years. Right now, she was bouncing up and down in excitement.

"So, good surprise?" he asked, still seated in the car.

"Yes! Perfect. Now let's go! I want to see everything!"

Laughing at my enthusiasm, he opened his door, quickly running around to open mine. He was too late. I was already out of the car, practically foaming at the mouth. I was like a kid in a candy store. My eyes were darting everywhere. There were gardens, an old barn, the house...I wanted to see it all!

"I figured a history lover would have visited all the local

plantations by now, but I took a chance on this one because of its location and the fact that it was a Bed and Breakfast."

"It's magnificent," I sighed. It was. Whoever owned the property took precious care of it. The pristine gardens had winding paths, budding roses, and ivy covered arches that all lead to a view of the James River that went on for miles.

"Come on. The Innkeeper, Ms. Thompson is expecting us," Logan said, taking my hand and pulling me toward the grand entrance of the estate.

His hand felt warm and solid in mine and it began stirring something inside of me I hadn't felt in a long time. I had the same feeling last week when he pulled me in his arms and kissed me senseless. Desire.

Walking along the path, I allowed myself a few moments to shamelessly look Logan up and down. God, he's sexy. He wore dark jeans that rested low on his hips and hugged his ass and a tight fitted button down shirt that matched the dark color of his hair. He looked edible. The bottom button of his shirt was left undone, and I could see his belt buckle and a bit of skin peeking out whenever he moved just right. I wondered if that button was purposely undone because it was currently driving me insane. All I wanted to do was run my hands under that shirt and pet him until he purred.

He was still sporting his "just fucked" hairstyle, the norm for him I realized, and it was just as hot as it was the first time I saw him, all messy and tossed to perfection. We reached the front of the estate and just as I was contemplating what it would look like with my hands buried in it, he glanced back, basically catching me in the act of eye fucking him.

Oops.

One side of his mouth pulled into a mischievous, lopsided grin. His eyes alight with humor, he took a step closer to me so that we are inches apart.

"See something you like, Clare?"

"That's got to be the cheesiest thing you've ever said to me," I teased, even though, yes there were quite a number of things I saw at the moment I liked. But I just couldn't let that cheeseball line go. It was horrible.

He shook his head, clearly amused, saying, "You must be the hardest woman in the world to flirt with."

"Ohhhh that was flirting? I'm sorry, I didn't know," I mocked.

"Maybe I need to try harder," he whispered in my ear, pulling my body flush against his, sending shivers racing down my spine.

Gently brushing the hair off my bare shoulder, his fingers trailed down my back to rest at my waist. All joking between us was gone, and I looked into his eyes with raw need.

"You are so beautiful, sweet Clare."

Just as he started to lean in, his soft lips mere inches from mine, the Innkeeper came barreling through the door.

"Welcome to Thompson - oh! Sorry! Didn't mean to interrupt!" she said, suddenly noticing our intimate embrace.

Taking everything in stride, Logan gave me a quick wink, "No apologies necessary, Ms. Thompson." Logan politely responded, turning to face our host, but keeping his hand firmly secured around my waist. I was so glad he was the one speaking at that moment because he was obviously the more mature one. I wanted to scream "Go away!" so we could go back to the kiss she interrupted.

"It's so nice to finally meet you in person. I'm Logan and this lovely woman is Clare. We very much appreciate your hospitality this evening."

Ms. Thompson, an older woman who reminded me of my grandmother fell instantly under Logan's spell the moment he spoke and was practically swooning. Her eyes were roaming all over my date. I held back the laugh that was currently lodged in my throat. I had to give the old woman credit though, she had good taste. "Well, why don't you two come on in, and we'll get you all set for your garden tour?" Ms. Thompson suggested brightly, leading the way into the expansive house.

The interior of the house was just as stunning as I knew it would be. I couldn't help but run my hands over the hand-carved banister, or brush my fingers along the antique furnishings. The family had done an amazing job of keeping everything maintained and the history preserved. There wasn't a single modern looking item in view. It was as if you had stepped back in time. Ms. Thompson assured us that the house was equipped with all the modern conveniences, but they had made sure with each upgrade that the integrity of the house was maintained.

Ms. Thompson wasn't giving us an official tour of the house until later, but I still found myself stopping at least a dozen times as we made our way through the halls to admire one thing or another. Being the ever gracious host, Ms. Thompson entertained my curiosity with interesting tidbits and facts from her family's history. Logan must have enjoyed history himself because he stood with me, listening intently to every word and even asking questions of his own.

We finally made our way to the main parlor, a large room with antique sofas and family portraits hung on the walls. There was a large picnic basket set on a coffee table with a neatly folded blanket set to the side. A single red rose sat on top of the blanket.

"Wow! What is this?" I exclaimed.

"Well, I wanted you to have something special on your tour of the gardens, so I packed you a little something." This was a "little something"? What did the woman consider a meal? Logan might have to use a wheelbarrow to get me out of here.

She grabbed the large wicker basket and blanket and

handed it to Logan. She offered Logan the rose and a wink and pushed us toward the front of the house.

"Now off you go! I've got a meal to prepare! Enjoy!" she commanded sweetly as she walked in the opposite direction, humming softly to herself.

Logan took the perfect red rose and handed it to me, never breaking eye contact until he reached over to kiss me softly on the cheek. I bit my lip in a vain attempt to keep the blush from creeping up my face. With a quick wink, he adjusted the basket to his right hand and grabbed mine with his left and we head for the door. Since that moment on the porch when we almost kissed, he hadn't stopped touching me. As we walked through the house with our host earlier, his hand sought out mine, or he'd wind his hand around my waist. It was like he was making sure I was still there and I didn't want him to stop.

Walking back outside, we took a left, intent on the larger of the two gardens. Ms. Thompson said this was the better of the two and perfect for a late day picnic. I personally didn't know how you could choose a favorite, but I wasn't a gardener. Anyone who could keep a flower alive was a genius in my book.

The late day sun felt warm against my skin as we began our stroll down the garden path, meandering through arched trellises and flowering trees. Looking over at Logan as he carried the large basket and had the blanket tucked under his arm, I chuckled.

"You sure you can handle that heavy basket all by yourself, Logan?" He insisted on carrying everything, and I carried only the red single rose. Sometime male chivalry is dumb.

"You wound me, Clare." He moaned in mock pain, gesturing to his heart with our joined hands.

I giggled, "Ahh, poor Logan. Did I hurt your feelings? Do you need a lollipop? Maddie always likes suckers when she's upset." I preferred chocolate. Lollipops did nothing for me.

Looking mischievous, he said, "No sucker, thanks. But I can think of something else to lick that would make me a great deal happier."

"Perv!" I yelled, playfully hitting him on the shoulder with my free hand.

"You walked right into that one, and I wasn't lying," he laughed.

"You would think with a best friend like Leah I would have learned not to say things like that by now!" I huffed, trying to sound indignant but failing miserably due to the grin I couldn't seem to shake.

"No, please don't. I am a huge fan of your oblivious dirty talk."

"I do not talk dirty!" I cried.

"We'll see," he said, no longer joking. Those two little words held promise and possibility and I took an audible gulp as my mind started racing with indecent thoughts. Okay, yes. I did have a dirty mind. Sue me.

"Is here a good spot for our picnic?" Logan asked, pointing to a bright open space located underneath a flowering dogwood tree.

"What? Oh! Yes!" I babbled, realizing I'd been so completely engrossed in my Logan fantasy world I had barely noticed we had already been through half the garden by now. Weren't women supposed to be able to multi-task? Apparently only ones who were getting regularly laid.

Logan spread out the blanket and we both began unpacking the overflowing basket, settling ourselves Indian style across from each other on the large blanket. When Ms. Thompson said she packed "a few things" she was being a bit modest. Inside the basket there was a large array of fruit, cheeses, breads and crackers. The sugar addict in me also noticed the cookies, brownies and....jelly beans? I looked up at Logan and he just smiled. She also gave us a bottle of chilled white wine, a corkscrew and wine glasses. It was a feast, and this was only our appetizer.

"This is, wow. Amazing. How did you set this up? And don't think I haven't noticed we are the only ones here," I said. I was very curious how he managed to empty out a six bedroom inn on a Saturday.

"I wanted our first date to be about us. No busy restaurant or crowded streets. We can do all of that later, but today I just wanted to be about you and me. It's amazing what a bit of money and a lot of charm can do. And I have that," he grinned. "Plus Ms. Thompson's a bit of a romantic, so it didn't take much to twist her arm," he added.

"It's lovely Logan. Every part of it. Thank you."

"Well it isn't over, so don't give me a perfect score yet. There's still time. I could still completely fuck it up!" he joked.

"Even so, I think it'd still go down as the best first date ever," I confessed.

His eyes flashed up to mine quickly in surprise, and then I realized what I just said. This wasn't a simple first date for him, I realized. He must constantly be wondering what or who I'm thinking about. I wondered if he feared he'd never measure up. If he thought he would constantly come in second place to a ghost. I wanted to ask him and then soothe his fears because it wasn't what I was thinking at all. But not here. Not on our first date, in this beautiful garden, when everything is so perfect. So, instead of using words, I did the only other thing I could, I showed him. Leaning forward on my hands, I gently placed my lips on his. He groaned at the contact, and all of a sudden his control snapped. He snaked his arm around my waist and hauled me onto his lap. Tilting my head to the side, he deepened the kiss and plunged his tongue inside, consuming me. With my legs wrapped around his torso, I felt him hard and ready between our bodies and I instinctively ground against him. I was completely lost in him, and the world disappeared.

"Stop, ah fuck. We've got to stop," he gasped, desperately trying to catch his breath as he leaned his forehead against mine.

"Why?" I breathed, still stuck in my lust haze.

"Cause if we don't, I'm going to take you here right in the middle of this garden. And that's not the way I want our first time to go."

"You've thought about our first time?"

"Jesus, Clare. I think it's been the number one thing on my mind since the moment I walked into that exam room. It's a wonder I can even function at work," he admitted.

I giggled, my body shaking slightly which caused him to wince.

"Okay, you on top of me? Not helping my resolve. I'm starting to reconsider," he groaned as his eyes roamed up and down my body.

"Fuck," he cursed and promptly picked me up at the waist, sitting me down next to him.

I giggled again. I really shouldn't have, but I did find it kind of humorous.

Call me crazy.

"So, our first time, what's it like in your head?" I questioned him.

"You want me to describe it, Clare? I'm not sure how that's going to help my current situation."

Distracting himself, Logan picked up a bunch of grapes and began popping them into his mouth, one at a time. I mimicked him, taking my own bunch of grapes from the giant basket in front of us. Apparently we both need a bit of a distraction.

"Well, yeah, if I play a starring role, I'd like to know about it. And what makes you think there will be a first time?" I teased.

"Woman, you're trying to kill me, and really? After that? I'm quite positive we'd be in the middle of our first time right now if I hadn't put the brakes on," he boasted, giving me a cocky stare which caused me to blush. Saving me any further embarrassment, he continued, "I don't have an entire scene planned out or anything, but I am a guy. I can't help but imagine you spread out, like a feast before me, allowing me to take you in every way imaginable."

Oh God. Can't breathe.

"Look. I haven't had the best track record since my divorce. I've been labeled a lot of things, and for the most part I've earned them all," he admitted, his voice full of regret.

"I want a clean slate with you, Clare. You're special to me. I don't know what we're doing or where it's going but I've never felt anything like this, and I can't mess that up by doing the same shit I've always done."

I was speechless. I don't think I had ever been so turned on from a man telling me why he didn't want to have sex with me before. Forgetting myself, I leaned over again and kissed him, pulling his body to mine. He came willingly, and we ended up right where we were minutes ago, devouring each other with fiery frenzy. In our fervor, he pushed me down to the blanket, and I felt his hard body on top of mine. His hands slid up my leg and slipped under my dress to grab my ass. He groaned in surprise when his hands touch nothing but fleshy backside thanks to the thong Leah talked me into. God, his groan was sexy.

"Dammit Clare, you really are trying to kill me, aren't you?" he whispered, scattering kisses down my neck and shoulder.

He sighed, his eyes taking one last lingering glance at my body before saying, "We need to get back to the house before I say fuck it and just fuck you."

Damn.

~Logan~

Somehow we made it back to the house. I couldn't remember the actual trip and I think I may have cried or at least whimpered a little along the way.

I might not survive Clare. She was truly my ultimate temptation. I never wanted anything more and yet fought so hard against it. But I knew I needed this. I knew she needed this. I had to start this off right. She deserved it, she deserved everything.

I had planned this quiet date so we could get to know each other more. Our phone calls and texting had done a fairly good job so far, but I was selfish and wanted her to myself for the entire day.

This, however, was not how I envisioned the day going. Not that I was complaining.

No, definitely not complaining.

But Christ, she was a widow. She hadn't touched a man in over three years. I had planned on being careful, conservative and sensitive. What I had not planned on was her kissing me, followed by us nearly ripping each other's clothes off in the middle of an old woman's garden.

Clare was quick with words and comebacks and we had a great time joking with each other. But while she was bold with words, she was timid with physical contact, blushing at the mere mention of something dirty. I understood that considering her circumstances. Her husband had died and in the last three years she had been a mother only. I think some part of her had forgotten how to touch a man, and in a way, made her innocent again. As happy as I was to be the man to show her again, I understood I had to go slow. What I hadn't counted on was her gaining the courage to make a move so bold, so soon. When she leaned over on her hands and knees and kissed me under that giant dogwood in the garden, I lost myself.

"What are you smiling about?" Clare asked as we approached the front door to the house.

"Mmm...Not telling," I teased.

"Well, that's not fair," she pouted, folding her hands over her chest in mock indifference.

I stopped just inside the beautiful white house and turned, looking into those piercing green eyes of hers.

"You. I'm smiling because of you. You've taught me to smile again." I didn't think I would ever have anything to smile about again. Now, I just had to make sure I didn't fuck it up and lose her.

She looked at me, stunned. Shit, did I go too far? Say too much, too soon?

"Thank you," she whispered, gently rising on her toes to kiss me.

"No, thank you."

The house tour Ms. Thompson gave us was outstanding and I loved seeing Clare so animated and full of life as she asked questions and made discoveries in each new room. Built before the Civil War, the house had quite an extensive history, and Ms. Thompson, a direct descendant of the original owners, knew it all. With each new room she had a new story to share including stories about her own family which included four children and twelve grandchildren.

I glanced over at Clare, who was currently looking out the window in the ornately decorated dining room, which showcased much of the gardens we'd been in earlier. I wondered if she was remembering our picnic because I know I certainly was. She looked over her shoulder at me and blushed, quickly looking away. I guess that answered my question.

Our host came in carrying yet another covered silver dish and set it down on the large table.

"Ms. Thompson, do you know if we are supposed to get a storm?" Clare asked, still looking out the window, but her gaze had shifted upwards toward the sky.

I joined her at the window, looking up and noticed the sky was turning black.

"I believe the weatherman said there was a slight possibility of a thunderstorm, but its only late April, so I wouldn't worry," she replied as she set up the table for our meal.

Clare nodded her head in agreement but took one last look up at the clouds again. They did look ominous. And if there was one thing I had learned in the short years I'd lived here, Virginia weather was unpredictable.

I rested my hand on her waist, pulling her to my chest, loving the feel of her there against my body.

"Let's eat. If a storm comes we can always drive home after it passes," I reassured her.

Letting out a breath, she nodded. Her smile and the light mood from earlier returned.

"You're right, I'm sure I'm worrying for nothing."

Ms. Thompson finished up and made herself scarce. We seated ourselves at the table, looking at all the prepared food. The table was covered, with barely an inch of wood showing due to the massive amounts dishes and platters covering the surface.

"Did she know it would be just the two of us?" Clare asked, her eyes surveying the table.

I laughed, "Yes, but I don't think she remembers how to cook for two people anymore. Plus I think she might have a crush on me."

"Oh, she definitely does. I caught her giving you a once over on the porch when we arrived, and I saw her checking out your ass when we went upstairs a bit ago," Clare quipped, completely amused.

"That's one randy old lady, I'll give her that," I added, not exactly sure how I feel about a Grandma checking out my ass.

"Well, at least she has good taste...but if she gets handsy, I may have to bitch slap her."

"Defending my honor, huh? That's kinda hot. Well, minus the Granny part," I added.

She gave me one last amused look before we began our meal. Ms. Thompson might be one of the best cooks I'd ever encountered. She had taken southern cooking to a whole new level, creating modern dishes with a down home feel. No wonder her Bed and Breakfast is one of the best in the country.

I heard Clare moan as she took her first bite of the pork loin smothered in a cranberry and peach chutney.

"Oh my God, we're taking this woman back with us. Go find a bat. I'll get the duct tape," Clare declared, taking another bite.

I laughed. It really was good.

We dined on pork loin and ratatouille, roasted sweet potatoes and asparagus, and baskets of bread. It was divine.

Around our second glass of wine, the rain started. One thing I loved about Virginia was the rain. It could be sunny one minute, and pouring the next.

Right now the rain was coming down in sheets, beating against the roof and rattling the windows. The sun had long since passed and the deafening sound combined with the darkness outside made it feel like we are the only two people in the world.

"Tell me about your wife," Clare requested, completely catching me off guard.

"Of all the things we can discuss on our first date, you want to talk about my ex-wife?"

"She was a part of your life and a part of you. I want to know everything about you." She paused and gently reached her hand across the table for mine. Our fingers touched and became entwined together.

"I'm sorry. You don't have to if you're not ready."

"No, Clare. It's not that. It's painful, yes. But not in the way you're thinking. I'm worried that after I tell you about her, you'll look at me differently."

Like the cold-hearted bastard I am.

"Whatever it is, you can tell me. No bullshit, remember?" she reminded me, giving me an encouraging smile.

"What do you want to know?" I sighed, not wanting to have this conversation but knowing she needed to know me, even the ugly sides of me, if we were going to continue.

"Everything. Anything? Whatever you want to tell me."

I want to tell her nothing, because I'm a coward, but I knew I couldn't do that. So I decided to start at the beginning.

"I met Melanie when I was in med school. She was attending Harvard for her undergraduate work in economics and psychology. She was beautiful and cultured. She came from a wealthy family, but she wasn't the least bit pretentious, and she had all these lofty notions that she was going to change the world. She wanted to visit third-world countries and would spend hours telling me about her dreams and aspirations. For a young man who had been told what to do for his entire life, she was fascinating. I asked her to marry me as soon as she graduated."

I paused, not wanting to continue, afraid she would hate me for what I was about to say.

"My life was crazy during med school but it became insane during my residency. Being newly married *and* a newly practicing doctor was like mixing oil and vinegar. I was never home, and I quickly realized I didn't want to be. When I was home for long periods of time I just mentally checked out. And she knew it. I didn't love her, and I never had. I confused fascination for love, not knowing the difference. I think I was so enthralled by the idea of being loved that I took something I shouldn't have, without thought for the consequences. Melanie had loved me from day one, and I couldn't give her a damn thing in return. What's worse is I kept her, hoping I'd someday start to feel something, anything. But all I ever felt was guilt."

Unable to look at Clare, I stared out the window while I made my confession. I watched the rain slam against the window, unable to look her in the eyes because I was so afraid her face would be filled with disgust. Would she leave now that she knew I was incapable of loving someone? I finally looked at her and found her looking at me with something entirely unexpected.

Compassion.

"Is it so horrible to want to be loved, Logan?" she asked.

"No. But chaining someone into a marriage just to have it? That's unforgivable," I insisted.

"When you married Melanie and said your vows, did you believe you were in love with her?"

"Yes," I said without hesitation.

"You can't blame yourself for this, Logan. Wanting to be loved so desperately is not a crime," she assured me, holding my hand firmly in hers. Her hand felt so soft and delicate in my own.

"Is that why she cheated?"

I nodded, adding "I don't blame her. I kept her in a loveless marriage, and I was never there."

"Did you know him?" she inquired.

Clearly, she still hadn't looked me up because this particular part was a media favorite.

"Yes. He was one of my best friends, Gabe. He'd been at Harvard the same time as Melanie and me, studying law. He moved to New York to pursue his dream of working in the projects. We always used to give him shit for going to Harvard on his Daddy's dime to earn a law degree he planned on using for pro bono work. But, he was exactly like Melanie. He wanted to change the world. She volunteered to help in his office doing light administrative work a few hours a week. I hardly paid attention when she told me," I admitted.

I shifted in my seat, uncomfortably.

"How long before you found out?" she asked.

"Six months. My wife had been sleeping with one of my best friends for six months and I didn't even notice," I confessed. I had been so involved in my own thoughts, and my own world, I had actually stopped paying attention to her. So much so that she carried on a six month affair and I had no clue.

"I'm sorry Logan, it must have been painful."

It was, but not for the reasons she was thinking.

"Looking back now, I can see it. Melanie and Gabe are perfect for each other. They're running that law firm together now. She provides counseling and he gives legal support. Colin told me they're expecting their first child this fall. And honestly, I'm happy for them, for her. She deserves it, all of it."

"You deserve it too," she said softly, tracing my palm with her fingers.

"Thank you."

"So...I saw Ms. Thompson set up a ton of desserts in the other room. If we don't go over there soon I'm going to get cranky, and I'm not nearly as cute when I'm cranky," Clare announced, lightening the mood with her addiction to sweets.

I couldn't help but laugh, thankful we were done with the heavy conversation for the moment. I was also relieved she was still looking at me the same way. I didn't deserve it, but I'd still take her anyway.

"Okay, let's go!" I exclaimed, rising to follow a quickly moving Clare to the parlor. She was already eyeing the massive display of desserts and squealing with delight.

"This woman is insane! There's enough dessert here to feed an army!" she cried, zeroing in on the chocolate covered strawberries and profiteroles before noticing the best part.

"Oh my God, she made Tiramisu! Did you tell her to do this?" she asked before turning to look at me.

I just grinned in answer.

"Of course you did." She sauntered over to me, swaying her hips, before reaching out a hand to grab mine.

"Thank you. This has been the perfect date. You're amazing"

Just then, a huge clap of thunder shook the house, followed by a flash. Clare screamed, closing the distance between us to rush into my arms, just as the power went out.

Well, so much for perfection.

Chapter Eight

~Clare~

"What the hell was that?" I screeched as I burrowed my body further into Logan's firm chest.

"Uh, thunder?" he uttered.

"Well, duh. But holy shit, that was close. It couldn't have been more than a mile away."

One thing I noticed right away...okay, two things. The first thing, Logan smelled really good.

Like really, really good. I don't know if it was cologne or a scent that was just uniquely Logan but I wanted to bury my face in his shirt and take a deep breath so I could have a memory of it permanently stored in my olfactory senses.

The second thing. It was dark. Like pits of hell dark. Having lived in the South my entire life, I had learned to endure strong storms. But they still freak me out, which is why I was currently curled up like a five-year old child in a grown man's arms. Well, it probably wasn't the only reason. My only saving grace was the fact that when the power went out in a suburban neighborhood, it was never completely dark. You still had neighbors that ran backup generators and headlights from cars passing by.

But the Thompson Plantation Bed and Breakfast?

It was pitch-black, make-you-wanna-scream-for-your-Mama dark.

"Are you all right, Clare? You're shaking," Logan asked, his voice full of concern.

"Sorry. That scared the bejesus out of me. I don't like when the power goes out," I confessed.

"I'm actually really enjoying the lack of power," he said, squeezing me tighter.

"Oh man!" I suddenly wailed.

"What?" his voice alarmed and full of sudden concern.

"The desserts! I can't see the desserts! I want my desserts!" I whined.

He chuckled. "That took all of thirty seconds!"

"Don't make fun of me, I'm in agony here. There's sugar over there, and I can't see it. If Ms. Thompson doesn't come with a candle soon, I'm just gonna wing it and dive in with my hands."

He thought I was kidding, but I was totally serious. I never mess around when it comes to dessert.

Just as I was contemplating exactly how to get into the dessert without ruining my dress, Ms. Thompson nosily bumped into the room with a candle in hand.

"Well, that was exciting, wasn't it? You two okay? Didn't scare you too bad, did it?" she asked as she began lighting candles scattered about the room.

"No, we're fine. Just a little startled. We were just admiring the dessert table when the power went out. You did an amazing job," Logan commended her, causing our host to become embarrassed under his praise. As she lit the candles, everything started to come back into view, including the desserts.

"Well then, continue on. Don't mind me. I'm going to look for a radio and see if I can get any updates on the weather," Ms. Thompson said before marching out the room with determination.

I scurried up to the table, grabbed a plate and started taking a bit of everything and a lot of the tiramisu. It was such a thoughtful gesture to have her include my favorite dessert. And the jelly beans during our picnic…

And now I was thinking about the picnic again. Every time I looked at him, I remembered the way his hands felt moving over my body and how his mouth moved against mine. I had no idea what came over me, but if he hadn't yelled stop, I'm not sure I would have. The heat and chemistry between us had awoken a part of me I thought was gone. Something raw and real. I didn't know where our path together would lead, but tonight I felt like anything was possible.

Logan fixed his much smaller dessert plate and we both took a seat on the comfortable sofa in the parlor. He poured two cups of coffee from the carafe Ms. Thompson left on the coffee table, and I snuggled into the feather pillows, angling my body toward Logan as I dove into my plate piled high with desserts. I moaned in delight as the sugar and chocolate melted in my mouth. I felt contented and happy.

"So, what do you think she's going to do with all those leftover desserts?" I feigned innocence.

He laughed, "Don't worry, she's sending all of it home with us. I made sure of it."

"Yes!" I shouted but then said, "Geez, how much did you pay this woman?"

He just rolled his eyes so I continued to eat.

"You have chocolate, right there," Logan said, leaning forward and motioning to my mouth. His eyes zeroed in on my lips, full of heated intensity.

"Oh."

I opened my mouth, reaching out with my tongue to catch it, but he beat me to it, licking the chocolate from my lip, before kissing me long and slow.

He eased back; his eyes alight with fire and grinned, looking very smug.

"I think I got it."

"You know, I think I could have taken care of that myself," I snickered.

"But my way was much more fun. And besides, Maddie told me I could kiss you, so I plan on doing so. A lot," he assured me.

"She did?" I asked, surprised.

"Yes. When I got to the house today, she gave me her permission to kiss you. I politely said thank you, and then chased her around the room while she squealed. Good times," he grinned.

"I really have no idea why she's feels so safe around you."

"Hey!" he cried, dejected.

"No," I giggled, understanding how that could have been misunderstood.

"I didn't mean it like that. I just mean I don't understand why it was so instantaneous. You walked into that exam room and she trusted you immediately. She's never treated another person that way," I explained.

"I felt it, too. With her. With you, too," he paused before saying, "I always feel that need to care for my patients, but when I leaned down in that hospital bed and she curled up in my arms as I examined her, I don't know...something inside of me clicked. I've never felt so fiercely protective over a patient before. If that's even one tenth of what you feel as a parent, I don't know how you do it. I suddenly couldn't imagine the thought of her in pain. And then I saw you. Even in those vomit soaked clothes, you had me on my knees. When I mentioned the CT and you panicked? I saw that fear in your eyes and all I wanted to do was make it go away."

I've never told him why I panicked in that hospital room.

"Ethan," I explained, "He kept getting these horrible headaches. His doctor ordered a CT first. It came back normal. Months went by and we thought everything was fine. But he kept getting headaches and I got more and more nervous. But Ethan swore it was fine because of that CT. Finally, I convinced him to go see someone else. His new doctor ordered an MRI, and that's when they found the tumor which hadn't shown on the CT," I said in a low voice, still hating myself for not pushing harder. If I had been more adamant, sent him to a doctor sooner, would he still be here?

But then I would have never met Logan.

Sometimes life didn't make any sense and you just had to stop thinking.

"It's very rare for a CT to be wrong. You know that by now I'm sure?"

I nodded.

Silence filled the air as we finished our coffee. It wasn't an awkward silence that was so typical on a first date, but the silence of two people who were comfortable enough to know that sometimes words didn't need to be said.

I finally took a glance up at him from my coffee cup, noticing his eyes looked more gray than blue in the low light. The room smelled of burning candles and shadows flickered along the walls as the flames danced. Logan's hair had fallen into his eyes a bit, and I absently brushed it back, letting the inky black strand slip through my fingers.

"We seriously suck at dinner conversation, don't we?" I said, still enjoying the feel of my hands in his hair.

"Yes, awful," he agreed. "We should definitely make out instead," he added playfully.

"Horndog," I teased.

Ms. Thompson strolled back into the parlor, candle in hand, muttering an apology for her interruption. She looked like she has bad news.

"Again, I'm sorry to interrupt, but I just heard on the radio that the main road out to the interstate is blocked by a downed tree. It may be morning before they can get it off the road. I think you two are stuck here for the time being."

Oh my God, I was stuck in a Bed and Breakfast with Logan. I didn't know whether I should jump for joy or pass out in fear.

Logan turned to me, worry clearly showing on his face.

"I'm so sorry, Clare. Is Maddie going to be all right? Should I figure out a way to get us home?"

It was a sweet gesture and I was really wondering how he planned on getting us home, but I declined.

"No, it's fine. She's fine with Leah. I just have to make a phone call."

Oh God, that was going to be interesting. No doubt Leah would have some advice on what I should do.

"Okay, have you ever gone a night without her? Will you be all right?" he asked, still concerned. He was always checking on both of us.

"Yes, she's spent the night at my parents quite a few times. She'll be fine," I assured him. He looked visibly relieved.

Ms. Thompson had been politely quiet during our exchange and now placed herself back into the conversation saying, "Okay, good. Now, should I make up one room or two?"

Well shit.

~Logan~

Clare looked to me as if I was supposed to answer the question. Oh right, because I was the organizer of this grand date? Well, this was definitely not in the plans and I had no fucking clue what to do.

"Ah, um...well."

I'm stuttering. I'm fucking stuttering!

I stood, unable to sit there anymore. Pacing the floor, I turned back. They were both looking at me now. Two sets of eyes waiting for an answer. Why should sharing a night with a beautiful woman be such a difficult decision to make?

Body said good idea.

Mind said bad.

Fuck.

"Two, please," I answered quickly.

A brief look of disappointment flashed across Clare's features and then was quickly replaced by something else. Rejection?

She felt rejected? Oh, hell no. That shit was not happening.

Ms. Thompson said her goodbyes and went off to prepare our rooms for the evening. I swiftly grabbed Clare's hand, pulling her from the couch and rotating her around in my arms, as our bodies collided together against the nearest wall. She needed to understand how badly I wanted her.

I pressed my body against hers, letting her feel every hard inch of me. She gasped and her eyes went round in surprise.

"Do you remember what I said to you in the garden?" I asked.

She nodded breathlessly.

"This isn't a casual fuck for me, Clare. I refuse to screw this up like everything else in my life."

Her eyes softened at my words and she opened her mouth, no doubt to rebuff my words, and soothe me. But I was in no mood to be soothed. She thought I rejected her in refusing to spend the night with her, and that seriously pissed me off. Lifting her at the waist, I grabbed her legs, wrapping them around my body, and rocked myself deeper against her core. She gasped, her eyelids lowering as she let out a small moan.

"But don't think that me making the decision, the very hard decision, to refrain from taking you up those stairs to make love to you all night long, has anything to do with me not wanting you," I reiterated before I released her legs, letting them drop gently to the floor. I still kept her pressed against the wall, our bodies tight together.

"Am I clear, Clare?"

She simply nodded, eyes wide, as a sheepish grin spread across her face.

"Good, now go stand way over there, across the room, while I think about old men running naked on a beach," I begged

She busted out laughing as I pulled away from her and dropped my hands to my knees, panting. I glanced up as she walked over to the over side of the room, clutching her sides in hysteria.

She was cracking up while I could possibly be dying of blue balls, all because I wanted to prove a point.

~Clare~

I never felt so bad for a man, but I couldn't stop laughing. He actually looked like he was in real pain, with his hands on his thighs, and his breathing heavy and staggered.

Could men die of blue balls? Should I Google this? Hmmm...

He looked up at me, straightening, looking much better. Okay, good. At least I wouldn't have to explain to Ms. Thompson why he looked so...ill.

"I'm good. Thinking about naked old men. Works every time," he admitted.

Ewww.... "I so didn't need to know that."

He gave me that lopsided grin I loved so much and joined me on the other side of the room, his attention focused behind me.

I followed his eyes, and saw a large painting in the corner of the room. It was hard to see in the dim light, but once you did, you couldn't look away. It was of a young woman dressed in period clothing from the late 19th century. She was beautiful, with dark brown ringlets and a fully adorned Victorian gown. Her skin was the color of porcelain, which was in stark contrast to the deep red of her cheeks and lips. Her vivid green eyes reflected a deep emotion and I took a step closer trying to discover it.

"Ah, I see you've found Catherine," Ms. Thompson announced as she re-entered the room. Logan and I had been so mesmerized by the painting we hadn't heard her.

"Pardon?" I said, still staring at the painting. It had an almost haunting quality to it that made it difficult to look away.

"That is Catherine Ann Thompson. She was the eldest daughter of my great-great grandfather William Conrad Thompson," Ms. Thompson said proudly.

"She's beautiful," I told her.

"Yes, she was. I found that painting in the attic after my father died and I couldn't let it sit in the darkness anymore. It's too beautiful to hide."

"Why would anyone want to hide it?" Logan asked.

"My family was ashamed. She broke a betrothal, secretly marrying a man outside her social class. It was quite the scandal," she remarked as she quietly fixed herself a cup of coffee and settled herself on the sofa adjacent from us.

"Catherine, as you mentioned, was beautiful. She had many suitors and her pending betrothal was the talk of the Commonwealth. Our family was very wealthy, owning the majority of the tobacco fields in the area, and my Grandfather knew an alignment with the right family could create a powerful business merger," she sighed, taking a sip of her coffee and continued, "Love wasn't a factor in marriage for wealthy families back then. It was all about power and wealth, and William knew his daughter's beauty and his good name could get him more of both. She was soon engaged to Edward Norton, the son of a cotton gin tycoon."

I couldn't imagine having my fate set without my consent. How times had changed. I looked over at Logan, suddenly grateful that I was able to choose my life. I couldn't imagine the terror of standing in a bedroom on my wedding night with a stranger, expected to give myself to someone just because I was a good match on paper. The wedding night I shared with Ethan, though sometimes painful to remember now that he was gone, was magical, full of love and commitment. It was as every wedding night should be.

"What my great-great grandfather hadn't realized," Ms. Thompson continued, "is when he was out creating business deals and mergers, Catherine was falling in love with someone her father had never heard of. No one knows for sure how they met, some say she lost her chaperone while in town, others say it was while she was out in the fields picking wildflowers while he was painting. The point is, they met. His name was Jakob, a son of an immigrant from Germany. No one knows how long they secretly saw each other, but we do know he was the one who painted her."

Yes, I could see it now. That emotion I saw shining in eyes, and tugging at her full red lips. Love. She loved the man who had captured her image on the canvas.

"What happened to them?" I asked, knowing it couldn't possibly have ended well if she ended up being the shame of the family.

"When her father came home and announced she was to be married, she panicked. Unwilling to marry a man she didn't love, she and Jakob ran away. When she returned, she was married and carrying Jakob's child. Her father disowned her, kicking her and her new husband to the curb. By this time, the civil war was in full swing, and Jakob did his duty and enlisted. He didn't want to leave his new wife, pregnant and alone, so he left her in the care of his parents. As he left, he swore he would return to her before the baby was born."

"He never made it back?" I whispered, grabbing Logan's hand in fear my guess was correct.

"No, he did. He was injured near the beginning of his service, but quickly recovered. But during his recuperation, the Confederate military discovered his talent for painting and found another use for him. He was sent all over the South painting war scenes to boost morale and enlistment. Because of his new freedom, he was able to come back to Virginia for the birth of his child. Catherine's labor was difficult, as many were back then. Jakob lost them both that night. He carried her lifeless body back to the plantation that night, and banged on the door until someone answered. William came to the door, furious to be woken at such a late hour, until he saw Jakob holding his daughter's body. 'What have you done?' he said, 'What have you done?' he screamed. Jakob, a broken man, was barely unable to speak, tears running down his face. He placed her on the front porch, kissed her one last time and asked her father to please take care of her...and he disappeared. He never returned to the Army. A deserter. But many years later, this portrait appeared on the front porch. We assume it came to us after his death but no one ever took the time to find out for sure."

"So tragic. What did her father do?" Logan asked her quietly.

"Despite her father's shame, he did bury her in the family plot. Her grave is marked with a simple stone that reads 'Catherine'. Ever since I put that painting up, sometimes I swear I can hear her walking through the halls, calling for Jakob, wondering where her long lost love is. The floor boards will creak, or the curtains will flutter. Maybe I'm just a superstitious old woman," she smiled, taking another sip of her coffee. "But I always wonder if she remained here waiting for him."

I took one last look at the painting, hoping she and Jakob were somewhere else, together and at peace.

Ms. Thompson led us up to our rooms. Logan and I had said a quick goodnight in the hall and went our separate ways, both deciding a quick goodbye was best. Our impromptu host for the evening had loaned me something to sleep in. I couldn't think of anything better than a long, hot shower, aside from sliding into bed with the man who currently resided in the room next to me.

As my dress slide to the floor, I let my thoughts drift back to those brief moments this evening when Logan had my body pressed against the parlor wall. That could have been one of the singular hottest moments of my life. He had been so enraged, turned on and out of control. It was a titillating combination.

I stepped into the shower, letting the hot water cascade down my body, remembering the feel of Logan's hands as they touched my sensitive skin. It had been so long since I felt anything so intimate. Unlike Leah, who had an entire drawer of toys that she individually named, I wasn't nearly as adventurous. It had been years since I felt the release of an orgasm. When Ethan died, that desire died, too. It took a defunct ballet barre, a trip to the ER and a very special man to stir it awake again. I knew it wouldn't be the same with just anyone, and having Logan touch me today left me aching.

My hand wandered down my body, becoming bolder with every touch and caress of my skin. Moving down my hips and slowing working back up, I grasped my aching breasts, pinching the sensitive nipples and rubbing the tips. Need blossomed in my belly, making my movements bolder. Would it feel this way if Logan touched me here? Needing more, my hand descended to the juncture of my thighs, spreading the tender folds with my fingers. My heart was racing, and my breath became ragged in anticipation. Knowing Logan was in the next room, mere inches away, drove me further, my fingers slipping into my tight, wet core. My knees suddenly weakened from the contact, and I braced myself against the shower wall with my other hand. My fingers brushed my clit, oh God, it felt glorious.

For a split second, I worried that Logan might hear me, but

the new, bolder Clare took over, and she didn't care. I sunk my fingers in further, moving them in and out, rubbing my clit at the same time. My stomach muscles tightened, and I felt a familiar flutter begin to bloom deep in my pelvis. My fingers moved more quickly in and out as my mind replaced my fingers with Logan's hard lean body.

"Oh God," I moaned out loud.

Just when I thought I might pass out, I came, seeing stars as I called out my release. My knees finally gave way, and I sunk to the bottom of the shower in a mindless puddle.

Somehow, maybe years later, I managed to eventually stand and finish my shower. I couldn't imagine what I just cost Ms. Thompson in water.

Completely sated, I finished my nightly routine, or what I could considering the lack of toiletries. I slipped into the borrowed night shirt and climbed into bed, utterly relaxed.

I was dreaming when I abruptly awoke, startled by a noise in my room. I kept still, listening intently. Suddenly, the floor creaked as if someone was walking toward me and I screamed. I flipped on the light next to me and found myself in an empty room.

"What the hell?" I swore.

I jumped again when there was a loud knock on my door.

"Clare, are you okay?" Logan asked, before barging in completely, concern clearly showing on his face.

He obviously left his room quickly when he heard me scream because he was wearing a pair of boxers. Only. And holy shit, the view was nice. My eyes roamed over his broad shoulders and chiseled chest. He had those sexy hip bones I loved on a guy that created a perfect "V" framing his tightly packed abs.

"Clare, are you all right?" he asked again.

Mmmm...Right. He said something.

"Oh, yes. Sorry, I heard a noise. It sounded like someone was in here. It freaked me out. Guess the ghost story got to me a little more than I thought," I answered quickly.

"Oh, good. You worried me, I– what the hell are you wearing?" he questioned, noticing my night shirt for the first time.

"Oh!" Completely embarrassed now, I answer, "Ms. Thompson lent it to me so I wouldn't have to sleep in my dress. Do you like it?"

The night shirt in question reached down to my knees and nearly swallowed my size four frame. It was periwinkle purple and had the words "#1 Grandma!" written in bright yellow script.

"It's hideous," he laughed.

"Yes, I know. What you have on is much, much better," I added, continuing my leisurely journey up and down his body.

Taking a cocky step forward, he faltered before stopping himself altogether.

"I should go," he said, keeping his feet glued to the floor, not taking a single step toward the door.

"Stay with me," I pleaded.

I could see an internal war brewing in his brain.

"Just hold me. I don't want to sleep in this room alone. If I hear another creak, I'm heading for the car," I stated. And it was the truth. I loved old houses but I think Ms. Thompson might have ruined this one for me. Who knew I was scared of ghosts?

"Okay," he agreed as he joined me under the blankets. His skin brushed mine, so warm and comforting. He wrapped his arms around me and I curled up onto his chest, throwing my leg over his, feeling cherished and secure. He smelled like the soap from the bathroom, clean and safe.

His hand absently ran up and down my back, causing me to shiver.

"What's your father like?" I asked.

He hadn't mentioned his father much. I knew they didn't get along.

"The exact opposite of yours I suppose," he mumbled, still stroking my back.

"Was there ever a time you got along? Did something happen?"

"My father isn't like most fathers. He's cold and calculating. When I was young, he set expectations and goals for me. I had a track and a plan. Private school, Ivy League and then some pre-approved career. Lucky for me, I loved medicine, which was a relief. I knew I'd rather do anything in the world than work for my father. As long as I followed the plan, I received his approval. Not praise. Just approval," he explained, his words as emotionless as the man he was describing.

"When I married Melanie, she met his approval. She was from an approved family, had wealth of her own. When the divorce became public, my father basically disowned me. I haven't spoken to him since. My father is all about image. And I tarnished that."

He paused, as he often does in the middle of a memory, as if he was trying to find the words to express it properly.

"I moved down here to disappear. I realized I'd been living my entire life according to his predetermined plans, and I was done. With all of it. I wanted to find my own path, separate from my father's expectations."

"And have you?" I asked.

"What?"

"Found your own path?" I whispered.

"I'm starting to."

Chapter Nine

~Clare~

The next three weeks passed in a blur. When Logan and I returned from the Bed and Breakfast, we returned as a couple. Waking up together, wrapped in each other's arms, we couldn't go back any other way. There was no nervous pacing around the phone wondering if he was going to call and ask for a second date because everything between us fell naturally in place. Logan spent every free moment away from the hospital with Maddie and me. He would join us for a movie during the day when he had to work a night shift. He'd take me out for dinner when he had a night off. He fit into our lives seamlessly, like he was supposed to be there. A missing piece.

There were still nights when I wandered through the halls staring at memories scattered all over the walls reminding me of the life I had once shared with Ethan. The man I thought I had an eternity with. My heart still ached for him and I missed him every day, but Logan helped me heal and I felt my wounds closing tighter the longer he was around.

I was falling for him, and falling fast, and I wasn't the only one. Maddie thought Logan hung the moon and loved spending every waking moment with him. There were times when I would question myself for allowing Maddie to give her heart to another so easily, knowing she could get hurt, but I was learning to let my instincts guide me and everything inside me was screaming that this was right. So I let her fall right along with me and took a leap of faith that we wouldn't get hurt in the process.

"Logan, are you and Mommy having a play date tonight?" Maddie asked as the three of us sat around the fifties inspired diner sharing an ice cream sundae on a sunny May afternoon. This was one of Maddie's favorite spots to come during warm afternoons. The waiters wore white uniforms and knew her by name. She loved to fiddle with the miniature juke boxes, making me read every song title and artist.

"Nope. Your Mommy is spending the evening with Leah doing super-secret girl stuff. I'm not allowed," he teased as he scooted his spoon around the ice cream pushing the nuts to my side of the bowl. He hated nuts.

I stuck my tongue out at him, and he returned the favor, laughing. Maddie giggled at our childish behavior before digging out an enormous bit of strawberry ice cream and shoveling it into her mouth. She looked like a chipmunk storing food for the winter.

"Well, it's not like you are going to be lonely. When does Declan's flight arrive?" I asked.

Declan was a one of Logan's friends since boarding school and was an up and coming actor in Hollywood. I'm sure Leah knew all about him, including his shoe size, his favorite type of food and who he was currently banging, but I had chosen not to mention his visit because he wanted to keep a low profile. As much as I loved her, Leah was anything but low profile. A Civil War film he was starring in and executive producing was scouting the area. Declan was here to follow up on a few possible locations the location manager had found.

Apparently production was his true love and acting was just something he fell into. Having looked him up online out of sheer curiosity, I could understand why. With a rock hard body and a bad boy image, Declan was seriously hot.

Since I was spending the evening with my best friend, Logan was spending some time with one of his. Although Logan didn't look too happy about it. Something told me their relationship was strained and Logan would rather not being spending a night with his longtime friend. But he agreed anyway, and after picking him up from the airport, they were going to meet Colin for dinner and go do whatever else boys did for entertainment.

"He arrives in an hour, which means I need to head out," he announced in answer to my question.

"Okay, have fun. But not too much fun," I said with a quick wink before leaning across the table to give him a brief kiss goodbye.

"Promise," He grinned, sliding out of the booth. Before leaving, he bent down to Maddie, ruffled her hair and gave her a quick tickle in the side, which caused her to laugh.

"See you later, princess."

"Bye, Logan!" Maddie said before returning to the sundae.

I watched him as he disappeared out the door and walked to his car. He tossed on a pair of sunglasses and ran his hand through his disheveled hair before gracefully sliding into his car. Yum.

My attention returned to Maddie, who was currently shoveling ice cream in her mouth like it was her last day on earth.

"Hey! Leave some for me!" I said, pushing her spoon out of the way with my own.

She giggled again and we continued to eat the ice cream, talking about preschool and enjoying our time together for the rest of the afternoon.

"Okay, I think that's everything Mom," I noted, managing to haul the last of Maddie's things into my parent's house. Who knew a four-year-old required so much stuff for a sleepover? I swear I used to pack less when she was an infant. It took us forever to get here because we sat in her room arguing over how many stuffed animals she had to bring with her. We compromised on three, which was two more than I had wanted, but four less than she had originally requested.

"Okay, sweetie. I'll take care of the rest. Just put it all in her room and I'll make sure she's washed and fed." God, I loved my Mom. She was a saint. As soon as Maddie was born, my Mom turned one of the spare bedrooms of the house into "Maddie's room" with pink and purple wall paper, gingham curtains, and a beautiful handmade quilt for the twin bed. Until she was old enough, there was a portable crib in there, but that was long since gone. Even before Ethan got sick, my Mom and Dad were always willing to take Maddie if we needed a night off. Both of them were retired, so I think having the chaos of a young one in the house gave them something to look forward to.

"Thanks Mom. I really appreciate this. Leah and I are looking forward to a night out," I confessed.

"It's no problem. You know I don't mind taking her. For whatever reason," she lingered, making clear she knew more than she was letting on.

"You know, don't you?" I asked bluntly.

"Yes, Leah mentioned you were seeing someone."

Annoyed at my mother and BFF for talking behind my back, I asked, "I swear, did you adopt Leah somewhere down the road, and I just didn't know about it?"

"You know she's always been like a daughter to us. But you are my actual daughter. You could have told me. Are you ashamed?"

"What? No! I'm not ashamed. I just thought...I was afraid you would be angry, or...feel betrayed," I admitted.

I made the difficult decision to move on, but had my parents? It was still something I struggled over, and something I battled with constantly. But I didn't give them the choice when I made my decision, and I didn't know how they would react.

"Oh sweetheart, no. You loved Ethan more in the few years you had together than most people do in a lifetime. You gave that man everything and he gave you everything in return. But don't think you are done because of it. Ethan died, yes, but you didn't. When you married him, he became our son and I loved him more than I can say. His death hurt us all, but that doesn't mean you should carry that sorrow forever. I want nothing more than to see you happy again," she assured me.

My Mom always seems to know the right words to say and the exact moment to say them.

I nodded, letting the tears fall freely down my cheek. And just like she used to do when I bruised a knee or came home from school with another broken heart, my mom pulled me into her arms and held me. Her warm, familiar embrace gave me the comfort only a mother could.

"Does this man make you happy, Clare?" she asked softly.

"Yes Mama," I answered, pulling back to look into her beautiful green eyes that mirrored my own.

"Do you love him?"

"I think so. I don't know yet," I answered honestly.

"Take your time, sweetie. Know your heart before you give it away."

Later, as I was readying myself for a night out with Leah, my thoughts drifted to the conversation I had with my mom, and I found myself looking over at my nightstand, the keeper of my husband's last words. I hadn't forgotten the letter. I still pulled it out late at night when I needed to feel him close to me. When the memory of him felt too far away and I couldn't quite remember the exact sound of his laughter or the way he looked in the morning when he'd just woken up, I'd touch those frayed edges and remember.

The familiar sound of the drawer sliding open calmed me as I once again pulled out the worn envelope and held it in my hands. I ran my hands over the cryptic message written on the outside, remembering the years I had with him and how suddenly it all had changed. We were supposed to have forever. I would have gladly spent every day of my life with him, never regretting a single second. But he was gone and all that remained was me and Maddie....and an unopened letter. Taking one last look, I placed the letter back in the drawer, hoping one day I'd be ready for whatever lay sealed in that envelope. But it was not today.

"So, let me get this straight? It's been three weeks since your super-hot and heavy date?" Leah practically shouted in my ear, trying to be heard over the crowds of people in the popular downtown bar we had chosen for the evening. Downtown was a madhouse on the weekends and I usually tried to avoid it, but Leah loved the crowds and the excitement. She said sitting back watching people make fools of themselves all night was the best free entertainment in the entire city. I personally would rather be home in my fuzzy slippers reading. But whatever. At least I looked hot.

I nodded, taking a sip of my drink. White Russian, yum.

"And you still haven't had sex?" she asked, swirling her cranberry and vodka around with a straw.

I shook my head in confirmation.

"Wow, that guy must have balls of steel!" she laughed.

"Oh my God, you're horrible. He said on our first date I wasn't a casual fling for him and he wanted this to work. I'm letting him work through that, however long it may take."

And good God, I was starting to think I might spontaneously combust if he waited any longer. For a guy known as a walking man whore, he had the patience of a saint when it came to me. Or so it seemed. For the last three weeks, he'd been the perfect gentleman. I would have thought he was losing interest if I hadn't caught the heat in his eyes when he thought I wasn't looking.

We had barely spent a minute alone in the last three weeks and I think it was part of his master plan. Having Maddie around meant he couldn't jump me, so he kept her around like a sobriety sponsor. When Maddie wasn't around we went someplace public. It was exasperating. The other day he came over to give Maddie a guitar lesson. It was the first time I'd heard him play. He was amazing, and also failed to mention he could sing. After fifteen minutes I was barely able to sit still, I was so turned on by his long, talented fingers strumming that guitar. I abruptly asked Maddie to take a few minutes and go play in her room and then I pounced, straddling him on the couch and kissing him with fierce passion. I thought I finally was making headway when his hands went under my shirt and cupped my breasts, but then he shot off the couch, panting, muttering something about a plan.

"See, you should have just taken my advice when you called home that night of your date. You would be sitting here a much, much happier woman," Leah scolded.

I rolled my eyes recalling the conversation I had with Leah that night in the Bed and Breakfast. It took a full five minutes to convince her that there really was a downed tree in the road that was preventing us from getting home. She thought I was making some lame excuse for not coming home in order to stay the night with Logan. Finally, after she believed I was telling the truth, it took another five minutes for her to stop trying to convince me to sneak into his bedroom late that night, completely nude, telling him I was cold, and needed help getting warm. I had no idea where Leah thought this shit up. She must sit around, daydreaming pornographic scenes all day.

"No, I definitely shouldn't have. I think it's sweet. And I fully support him," I said defensively.

"Uh huh, and how many times have you masturbated in the last two weeks?" she asked.

"Leah! I can't believe you would ask such a question!" I snapped, feigning innocence.

She just looked at me, waiting for my answer.

"Fine. Every day, happy?"

"Not as happy as you, apparently." We both laughed and raised our glasses, toasting to the countless times we'd spent together laughing and sharing our lives.

Our waitress continued to bring us rounds as we emptied our glasses. I think we were about three drinks in, and my head was starting to feel fuzzy, when she saw him.

"Oh my God. I think I just saw Declan James walk in. What the fuck would he be doing here, in Richmond?" she shrieked in excitement, hitting me on the arm to get my attention.

Oh shit.

Not good. So not good. She was gonna be pissed when she saw who he was with.

"And, what the hell? He just walked in with your boyfriend! Something you forgot to tell me, Clare?"

Crap.

~Logan~

So far, so good. We made it through dinner and no one seemed to notice Declan. Or me. Not that I was usually recognized outside of bars and clubs. It did help that he had a baseball cap pulled tightly around his head and dark glasses. The bar we just walked into, after dropping Colin off at home, was one he picked and I wasn't too confident in his choice. It was packed, bodies pressed together, filling every square inch. But it's what the guy wanted and I was letting him run the show.

Even though he hadn't reached true fame yet, Declan was on his way. He played a supporting role in a movie last year that had created a lot of Oscar buzz, and now he was suddenly on the radar of every major director in Hollywood. But Declan was choosy. He refused to do a movie based on how much money or fame he could gain, and instead chose roles based on the script, producers and director. I don't know much about Hollywood, but I don't think there were many actors left like Declan, which made him a nightmare for agents and a godsend for the screen.

I had known Declan since we were kids. His father and mine were friends, which meant Declan and I spent a lot of time together when we were still too young to be shipped off to boarding school. We were not the best of friends until later on in life. Even as toddlers, our Nannies would find us wrestling over toys. I was stuck up and snobby, constantly worrying over what my father might think. Declan was the opposite; constantly getting into trouble and causing fights every chance he had. By the time we reached high school; he had been kicked out of every boarding school his Dad could find, until he finally resorted to private tutors. He had always been a bit of a wild horse, not easily tamed. Acting has calmed him down a bit, but I still wondered if he would ever be fully domesticated. It was one of the reasons I didn't want to be around him. He reminded me of my past. A past I wanted to forget. A past I was desperately trying not to remind Clare of, and I wanted him gone before he had the chance to show her.

As we made our way through the bar, I could see his eyes scan the room, looking for exits or surveying the crowd, I couldn't be sure. It was one the things I had noticed that changed about him, he was constantly alert. A bit of his carefree attitude was gone and I feared what real fame might do to him if he was already this intense.

As his eyes continued to analyze the crown, he narrowed in on a leggy blonde seated at a table in a corner. Her eyes were filled with laughter as she held her drink in one hand and made excessive hand gestures with the other. Declan looked mesmerized and hungry. It appeared he'd found what he was looking for. Maybe I could go home.

Wait a second! I knew that blonde.

Leah's eyes locked with Declan's and widened. She leaned across the table and whispered something to Clare, who was seated with her back to us, and she visibly stiffened. Was she upset that I was here? I wasn't exactly happy about Clare and Declan being in the same room, but I wasn't leaving now. Not now that I was so close to her.

Oh God, she thought I was a stalker.

Leah looked back up at the two of us, eyes still full of excitement. It wasn't until she saw me standing next to him that her expression suddenly went from confused to pissed. Putting the puzzle pieces together, I finally relaxed. Guessing from the obvious scolding Clare was getting, I wagered that she left out the part about Declan being a close friend of mine and his visit to Richmond. It didn't appear to be going over well.

Leah composed herself rather quickly and whispered something in Clare's ear. Clare nodded before turning in herself toward us to wave. She plastered a smile on her face that I knew was fake, and I couldn't help but laugh. Poor Clare. I knew she was probably just raked over the coals and was in need of some serious saving.

I looked over at Declan who hadn't broken eye contact with Leah until he saw Clare's wave.

He finally glanced in my direction, confusion and a bit of humor showing on his face, and said, "Friends of yours?"

"Uh, yeah. That's my girlfriend and her best friend Leah," I stammered.

"Girlfriend? You?" he arched his brow in surprise.

I nodded. We hadn't discussed Clare. I wasn't ashamed of her, but for Declan, monogamy is a four letter word that wasn't uttered in his presence, so I figured he wouldn't understand.

Based on the last few times we hung out, I really didn't want to talk about women with him. At all.

He shrugged, "Well, why don't we go say hello then?"

We made our way over to the girls' table and Clare slid over to make room for me next to her. As I leaned down to kiss her hello, my lips lingered, savoring the sweet taste. The last three weeks had been the best of my life. They had also been the most torturous. Even since that first date, I'd been trying to give her time. It may be time she doesn't think she needs, but she does. She had lost someone and I didn't want to be just a replacement for him. I wanted to be the one she wanted. I also needed time to prove to her I was worth it. I think I needed to prove that to myself as well.

But the waiting was pure hell. Every smile, every brush of her skin set me on fire. I had spent three weeks in a perpetual state of need. I don't think I'd jacked off so much since high school. But, as each day went by, my will started to falter and my walls crumbled a bit more. Time or not, I didn't think either of us could hold out much longer.

"Hey, funny meeting you here," I whispered against her ear.

Smiling, she answered, "Great minds think alike, I guess."

I gave myself a moment to look her over from head to toe. She was wearing a tight fitting halter top that tied at the nape of her neck and showed off her shoulders and back. Rimmed in kohl, her eyes smoldered, the brilliant green still shining through. She was wearing a sexy jean skirt which showed off her toned legs and I could feel the high heel of her pump as it slid up my calf.

Momentarily distracted by her foot game, I realized Declan and Leah were sitting across from us, staring.

"Oh, I'm sorry!" I shouted, which caused Clare to laugh.

"You haven't been introduced. Leah, this is Declan James. Declan, this is Leah Morgan. And this," I wrapped my arm around her shoulder, "is my Clare."

Everyone said their "nice to meet you's" and "how do you do's" and we ordered a round of drinks.

The conversation was nice and everyone seemed to be having a good time when Clare mischievously looked over at me and then Declan and said, "Tell me something about Logan that I don't know."

I groaned, shifting uncomfortably in the booth, which caused a wave of laughter across the table.

Declan smirked at Clare's request and I swear I heard Leah swoon. Seriously, the dude isn't that good looking, is he? I looked over at Clare, and she was staring at me. Okay. Good. My friend could keep his balls tonight.

Remaining quiet, he didn't say anything right away. He seemed to be pondering or plotting...I couldn't tell. Unfortunately, there's a lot of shit he could tell her. He was obviously enjoying this moment.

"Logan was always the good boy growing up," he said, looking at me, his smirk turning into a full grin.

Well that's not too bad.

"Until I took over. Do you remember those few weeks between our junior and senior year, Logan?"

Shit.

"Declan," I warned.

The girls' eyes went wide with curiosity, egging him on. I gave him the evil death stare, but he just shrugged and continued.

"I hated Logan with a passion. He was the most uptight, boring kid I ever met. And that's saying something when you hang out with rich people all day long. Luckily, since both of us were in boarding school, we didn't see much of each other past grade school. That summer though, our paths crossed at this uppity social function held at one of our parent's friend's estates. It was the same old shit. Everyone was dressed in formal wear, parading around, talking about how they were taking over the world. I opted out of the party and went to go find my own entertainment."

"You mean you fucked one of the waitresses in a closet?" I interrupted

"Yup, far more entertaining," he grinned, his hazel eyes full of dark mischief.

"Anyway, as I'm leaving, I see Logan; all dressed up in his monkey wear, talking to his parents' friends, trying to impress a father who didn't even know he existed."

Clare's hand found mine under the table at the mention of my father and I appreciated the support. But what I really wanted to do was throw her over my shoulder and get the hell out of there. I didn't want to talk about my past. I fucked up, couldn't we just move on?

"We hadn't seen each other in years and the differences between us were as clear as day. He'd taken the path most righteous, and I'd taken, let's just say, an entirely different fucking path. I headed out the door and was about to start my bike, when I heard someone running up to me from behind. I turned around, expecting my father and another speech about responsibility, but it was Logan. Why did you follow me, Logan?"

I just shook my head and sighed before answering.

"Because I wanted to know how it felt to break the rules for once."

"You wanted to live, Logan. And I showed you, right?" he asked.

"No, Declan, you showed me what it was like to drink, fuck, and party. You gave me exactly what I wanted - a summer of debauchery. But it wasn't living."

This conversation had really taken a nosedive.

"Well, you can only give a man the tools," he shrugged, before adding "but the rest is up to him. He kept coming back, though. Every time his life went to shit he'd come back to his buddy Declan and I'd show him how to live again. When was the last time, Logan?" he asked, clearly knowing exactly when the last time was.

"I think we've had enough of this conversation," I said, the threatening tone clear in my voice.

"Okay. Oh! One more thing!" Declan shouted, that cocky smile still plastered all over his face. I almost stood up and decked him right there.

"He snores in his sleep," he added, obviously trying to lighten the mood, and I felt myself relax for the first time since we sat down. I knew the conversation wasn't over and Clare would ask about my time with Declan. But I didn't want to talk about it in a bar, with our friends present.

The conversation lightened from there but I only half listened to Leah explain her job and Declan talk about his upcoming project. I was unable to move on from the previous conversation.

I spent those few weeks with Declan in high school doing everything and anything I wanted to, and I had gotten away with all of it. My father didn't notice a damn thing. I'd been working my ass off to please him for years, doing everything he wanted, and then I went on a three week bender and he didn't even notice. I should have thrown in the towel right then, told him to fuck off, and gone off and found my own life. But, I couldn't. I was too damn scared to go up against my father. Turns out it wasn't as bad as I thought it would be. It was painless, because he didn't care.

"Clare, how about a round of pool?" I suddenly asked, needing to pull myself out of the funk I was currently swimming in.

"Pool?" she asked as she finishing off the drink she'd been nursing.

"Oh, it's okay. I'll teach you if you can't play. Come on, it will be fun." I stood and grabbed her hand. She threw Leah a mischievous grin over her shoulder, and we headed for the pool tables.

"Do you play a lot?" she asked me, suddenly looking very nervous.

I grinned. This was going to be fun. I'd never taught a woman how to play pool before.

"Not a ton anymore, but I use to be fairly good in college," I admitted.

"And you'll go easy on me?"

"Of course," I promised, grabbing a pool cue and heading toward an empty table.

"I'll go first and break so you can see how it's done. Okay?"

She nodded, a wry smile tugging at the corner of her mouth. I gathered up all the balls, took my first hit, and scattered balls everywhere. Two stripes landed in the pockets. Not bad for my first turn.

"Okay, so now I'm stripes and you're solids. It's your turn. Grab a pool cue behind you," I instructed. She turned, grabbed a pool cue from the rack and joined me at the table.

"Like this?" she asked, her mouth now so close to mine I could feel her breath.

"Yep. Take a shot." I whispered.

"Huh?"

"Your turn Clare. It's your turn." I chuckled.

"Oh! Right."

She took a slow walk around the pool table, looking at every ball, almost like she was surveying every option and angle, like a seasoned pro might do. She finally took her shot, sending two solid balls into the corner pocket.

She looked up at me, smiling sweetly, "Beginners luck, I guess."

What the fuck?

She moved to the other side of the table, took another shot and sank two more.

Walking up to me, she smiled again, then bent over, giving me a nice view of her ass, sinking one more ball. As she turned around, I pounced, pinning her to the table between my arms.

"I think I've been hustled," I purred in her ear.

She giggled, wrapped her arms around my neck and kissed me, which made me wish we were anywhere but a crowded bar. She pulled back and I saw the mischief in her eyes. She giggled again and that's when I realized.

Clare was kind of drunk.

"I'm sorry, I couldn't resist. You looked so eager to teach me," she laughed, swaying in my arms.

"How in the world are you so good at pool?" I asked.

"Ethan. It was how we met," she explained, her mood light and happy.

"Leah and I were at this dive bar near campus and we were attempting to play a game of pool. We were already half drunk on beer we'd bought with our fake IDs. Some guys came over asking if they could join us and we said sure. One guy became particularly interested in me, asking if I needed help with my game. He was drunk and smelled God awful. He tried doing that thing guys do where they lean you over the pool table showing you how to aim."

I was so glad I didn't try that.

"Anyway, Leah had found a guy she was really into and they were busy making out in the back. I could not get Mr. Grabby Hands to take a hint. Our game was over and it was just me and him standing there alone. Just when I thought I'd have to go hide in the bathroom for the rest of the night, someone spun me around and kissed me. I mean, seriously kissed me. I pulled back, stunned, wondering who I'd just kissed...and there was Ethan. I'd seen him around campus, but never talked to him. He wrapped his arm around me, and looked over at the guy and said 'Hey, thanks for looking after my girl, man!' He walked me home, and that was the beginning."

I tried not to flinch hearing her talk about Ethan kissing her, but it wasn't easy.

She shrugged, continuing, "Turns out he was there playing pool with his roommates and saw me across the room and just had to help. We went back to that bar all the time and he taught me to play."

"He was a good teacher, because you're kicking my ass," I confessed. I was glad she was able to tell me something about Ethan without sadness, even if my male pride was slightly wounded. It meant that she was healing, and that gave me hope.

"Well, I haven't given you much of a chance," she admitted.

We agreed to start over. This time at least I knew what I was up against. We played a few games and she still kicked my ass, but I did manage to win one. Just as we were finishing up, I saw Declan and Leah headed for our table.

"Hey guys, I think we're gonna head out."

"We?" I asked. That was a surprise. Well, not on Declan's part I guess. He had eyes for Leah all night.

"Yeah. Leah said there's this old cemetery around here that dates back to the Civil War. I want to sneak in and see it. It might be a great location for us to do a night shoot."

"That's the weirdest and creepiest thing I've ever heard," I told him.

I really didn't know what to say. Should I say no, and try and defend Leah's honor for Clare? Would she get mad if she found out they slept together? I knew Declan. If she left with him, they'd end up in bed together.

I looked over at Clare, and she was just shaking her head, grinning, looking completely unsurprised. Apparently, I had nothing to worry about.

"Hey Logan, I'm assuming you can get Clare home?" Leah asked, her face full of humor and mischief.

"I can absolutely do that," I answered quickly, glancing over at Clare as she smiled and bit into her lip.

She looked sexy as hell.

Shit, she still looked drunk.

A smiling Leah gave Clare a little wave and walked off with Declan, who gave me the male equivalent – the head nod. Pulling his baseball cap tight, he lowered his head, wrapped an arm around Leah's waist, and disappeared into the crowd.

As my eyes returned to Clare, I saw her walk over to the back wall and put away our pool cues. She circled back around to me, slowly and seductively, her eyes filled with desire.

Oh God, hadn't I been tempted enough in the last month? Now I had to fend off my drunken girlfriend, all in the name of honor. Being a gentleman sucked ass.

"Maddie's at my Mom's," she said, pausing to run a finger down my chest, as her eyes bored into mine.

"All. Night," she punctuated each word, making her wicked intentions clear.

Yes.

All gentlemanly thoughts rushed out of my head and were replaced by two words.

Fuck yes.

My entire body screamed yes as it came to full attention. I pulled her by the arm, dragging us out of the bar as fast as humanly possible. Once outside, I quickly walked us to my car in the parking lot, grateful I had a space toward the back in a low lit area. Bad for thievery. Good for what I have planned.

"Get in the back," I demanded.

"We're not going to your place?" she asked, opening the back door and slipping inside.

Joining her, I closed the door, "If I take you home with me

Clare, I'm going to fuck you. Repeatedly," I said, taking a deep breath, "But you're drunk."

Clare's confusion quickly turned to shock, letting out a small gasp hearing my bold words, but it was quickly replaced with something else entirely. Desire. "You wouldn't be taking advantage of me. I know what I'm doing," she assured me with a shy smile.

"Oh, I'm not worried about that. I know you want it," I replied with a wolfish grin, as I ran my hand up her lush thigh.

"I just want you to remember it. All of it. In vivid, technicolor clarity. And that can only be achieved if you're sober. When you and I come together for the first time, I want you to remember every touch," I ran my hand up her arm and down her back, causing her to shiver. "Every moan."

She did just that as I leaned into her body, slowly kissing her neck and tugging on her earlobe with my teeth.

"Every wave of pleasure," I ran my thumb over her nipple through her shirt, and gently tugged, causing her to gasp.

"So what are we doing in the back of the car?" she whispered breathlessly.

"Making the best of the situation."

~Clare~

And with those words, he pulled me to his body, capturing my mouth in a soul-searing kiss.

"Straddle me," he demanded.

I didn't hesitate, placing my knees on either side of his firm body. Raking my hand through his hair, I pulled and weaved my fingers through the thick strands, eliciting a low growl to rumble from his throat.

His hands were everywhere, roaming up my thighs, on my ass, and under my shirt. Finding my breasts, he gently rubbed my nipples through the fabric of my lace bra, causing a friction that put my body on edge. With one hand, he undid the tie at my neck holding my shirt, letting it slide down to my waist. Logan's eyes were on fire as they looked me over.

"You're so beautiful," he murmured.

Without warning, Logan pulled the lace cups of my strapless bra down, and his mouth was on me, sucking on my nipple, causing me to scream out.

"Oh God!" I cried, as he rolled my nipple with his tongue, letting it graze across his teeth, gently biting down, which caused me to nearly explode. With his other hand, he kept my body still and pinned to him, so he could start the torture all over again.

Snaking around to the front of my body, and under my skirt, his hand left my breast to cup my core.

"Do you want me to make you come, Clare?" he growled.

"Yes, God, yes," I begged.

Answering my plea, he slid my thong aside, spreading me wide with his long fingers.

"Shit, you're dripping wet," he said as he ran a finger lazily over my drenched clit before finally sinking it deep inside me.

A deep sensual moan erupted from me as he added one more, slowly moving them in and out of my body, making me ache.

"God, you're so fucking tight. Ride me, Clare."

Following his orders, I placed my hands on his shoulders, rising up and sliding back down again on his stationary hand.

"That's it," he said, "fuck my fingers."

He added one more, thumbing my clit at the same time.

"Faster," he commanded, his voice growing rougher by the second.

That tightness deep in my belly began to build and I could feel my body soaring higher. With his thumb, he flicked my clit, and that was all it took. I come unglued, crying out in pleasure.

"Oh God!" I screamed, the orgasm claiming me until I was unable to hold myself up and I collapsed into Logan's arms.

"Holy fuck. That was the sexiest damn thing I've ever seen," Logan said.

"I think I almost passed out." I giggled against his chest, feeling my buzz from the many drinks I had consumed returning.

I felt a smile tug at his lips against my forehead, and he kissed me, running his hands through my hair.

"We better get going. It's almost Last Call. This parking lot is going to be flooded in a few minutes, and I don't want anyone seeing that look on your face but me."

I giggled again. How much did I have to drink? Hadn't I read something in Cosmo once about orgasms actually making you feel more drunk because of the adrenaline or something? Or maybe I made that up.

"Don't we, um, need to take care of you?" I asked sheepishly, lifting my head so I could look into his eyes. His beautiful blue eyes.

"Clare, I'm holding on by a string here. Offer me something like that, and I'm going to have you naked in this back seat in five seconds," I nodded, still giggling and he rolled his eyes.

We adjusted ourselves and got in the front just as the crowd from the bar descended. Wow, he wasn't kidding.

And oh my God, I had just got freaky in a parking lot!

He drove me home, holding my hand as we talked about Leah and Declan leaving the bar together.

"Do you think they hooked up?" I asked.

"Well, Declan isn't known for being subtle, and he had his eye on Leah from the minute we walked in that bar. What about her?"

"Leah hasn't really been with anyone since her breakup, so I wonder if she'll take her own advice," I said, looking out the window as we merged on to the interstate.

"What advice?" he asked.

"Oh. Well, when I first met you, and ah, noticed you…"

I looked at him, his eyes glittered with unheard laughter. Smug bastard.

"She said it was time I go out and have some fun, of the male variety. She said I didn't have to date, just have some fun."

His eyebrows drew together, and he frowned before shaking his head. "That's terrible advice."

"Well, she did suggest you as a starter," I teased.

"Well, not too terrible of advice then. One night with me and you'll be mine forever," he promised as he brought my hand to his lips and kissed my knuckles, which sent chills up my spine and heat down to my core.

"But I don't think I have it in me. The random one night stands. I don't think I'm built that way," I admitted.

He shook his head in agreement, "No, you're not. Jumping into bed with a stranger involves a lack of feeling and emotion for the people you get involved with," he said. "You are too good a person. Too loving and caring. You could never sleep with someone with the intent of never speaking to them again."

"You make me sound boring," I mumbled.

Giving me a sideways glance, he said with assurance, "The woman I just saw come unhinged in the backseat of my car was anything but boring."

I smiled at the compliment, but his words were still echoing in my head.

"Is that why you did it? So you wouldn't have to feel?" I questioned. We hadn't talked much about his checkered past since his divorce two years ago. The gory details had been skimmed over a bit, but he knew I was familiar with it.

"Yes," he admitted. "When Melanie left, I felt relief. Pure and utter relief. She'd done the one thing I was too much of a coward to do. Then the guilt came and I felt sick. Shouldn't you be torn up when your wife leaves you for another man? I should have felt rage, but I didn't. I'd lived every day of our marriage with this overwhelming sense of guilt. Seeing the way she looked at me, her eyes filled with such love and devotion, and I couldn't return those feelings. I'd always been so fearful I couldn't love someone and there was my proof," I tried to interrupt him and tell him he was wrong, but he just continued.

"After a few months with all those emotions running rampant, I just became numb. The only thing I held together was my career. It's always been a type of solace for me. Like I said, following a random stranger home from a bar requires a lack of feeling, and that was me."

He laughed for a brief second, and I could hear the pain echoing in the sound.

We pulled into the driveway and he shut off the engine. Grasshoppers chirped in the nearby bushes, and the dozen air conditioners that lined the street hummed in unison. Summer was coming to Virginia and the air was growing more humid with each passing day.

"What Declan said," he started to say before I cut him off.

"Logan, it doesn't matter," I tried to assure him.

"It does matter. I need you to know. I haven't been a saint. I can't even count the number of women I've slept with and used to avoid my own pain since my divorce. Declan was my only friend who supported that type of behavior. He was my enabler, and he has been for the majority of my life."

He looked defeated, dejected.

I didn't know what I had to say to make him understand. I didn't care what he had done or who he'd done it with. As hard as it was for me to picture, I didn't even care if he and Declan were out picking up bar trash the night before we met. He was mine now.

I didn't judge him for anything. We both had pasts. Yes,

they were vastly different from each other, but they were still baggage with both carried into this relationship.

Just like in the garden, words failed to show the depth of my feeling at that moment. So I leaned across the seat, looked in those gorgeous blue eyes, and kissed him. It was a kiss completely opposite of the frenzied passion we had just shared. This kiss was slow, meaningful, and was meant to be savored.

When he walked me to the door that night, his mood was lighter and happier as if a heavy weight had been lifted. I seriously think he had been waiting for me to run for the hills and every time I didn't, he became a bit more secure. Logan could hold his own and walk circles around anyone when it came to anything remotely sexual, but a two-sided relationship was new territory for him.

As we reached my front door, I turned, my lips curving into a smile.

"Sure you don't want to come in?" I teased.

"Temptress."

"Ok, don't say I didn't off–" Before I could finish my sentence, his mouth was on mine, our tongues twirling together in a punishing rhythm. His arms wrapped around my waist pulling me closer, as I coiled mine around his neck.

His lips left mine, trailing kisses over my chin, down my neck and then up to my ear. His voice low and seductive, he whispered, "Find another night for Maddie to spend with Leah or your parents. Because the next time we're alone, you're mine."

Chapter Ten

~Clare~

"Clare Elizabeth Murray! You little slut!" Leah nearly screamed as we made our way through the aisles of one of our favorite clothing stores.

It was a Monday morning, and I was enjoying a few hours to myself while Maddie was at preschool. Leah had the night shift today, so she and I decided a little retail therapy would be nice. Leah searched the clearance rack, her long blonde hair pulled to the side in an artfully designed braid that would have taken me hours to create. Today she wore a short summery dress that made her look like she'd just stepped off a runway in Paris. God, I hated that woman.

"Leah, would you freaking shut up! I think China heard you!" I scolded.

"News flash! They probably heard you moaning in the back of that car Friday night!"

I groaned, completely embarrassed. The store clerk was seriously trying to ignore our conversation but I could hear her muffled giggle behind the rack of clothes she was pretending to sort.

"Okay, we are done talking about me. Let's talk about you and how you totally bailed Friday night. And don't tell me it was to go to some lame cemetery," I said, changing the subject and calling her out on her one-nighter.

She opened her mouth and shut it again, speechless. What the hell? Leah was never speechless. Like never. She always had something to say about everything. Sometimes I wish she came with a muzzle.

"We went to the cemetery. He's working production on this film, apparently that's his true love. Acting is just something he fell into 'cause he's got a pretty face. But that's it. He took me home."

"You are a goddamn liar, Leah."

"Am not," she said. I could tell she was lying by her sudden interest in a ridiculously ugly dress. There was a reason it was on the clearance rack. There was no way Leah wanted to buy it. She was avoiding me.

"Are too."

"Am not!" she repeated.

"Are too," Annoyed now, I said, "Oh my God. Are we children again? Have we reduced ourselves down to Maddie's age now?"

She looked at me, trying to give her best poker face. Problem was, Leah didn't have a poker face. She was usually an open book, willing to tell anyone virtually anything. Sometimes I wondered if her thick skin came from being raised by an alcoholic dad, but she always brushed it off and said this was the way God made her.

"You mean to tell me you left a bar with a Hollywood celebrity who is hotter than fuck, which by the way, if you tell Logan I said that, I will kill you, and you didn't sleep with him? That's like your ultimate fantasy!" I confronted her.

"Okay, fine! Yes, I slept with him!" she snapped, before pulling us to into a dressing room and closing the door with a huff.

"And it was amazing. Like five times amazing, okay? I've been having sex with vibrators for so long I'd forgotten what an actual man felt like...and this one? Holy shit! He was like an Olympic gold medalist for orgasms."

"So why didn't you want to tell me?" I asked, still wondering why we were hanging out in a dressing room. And if we were, I was at least going to start trying on the dresses I picked out.

I start stripping down for my first dress as she took a seat in the corner and explained.

"Because I knew you'd make a big deal out of it. You're in that 'I just fell in love!' stage, and it's radiating off your damn body in waves. You're naturally going to want everyone around you to feel that same exact thing. And this is the exact opposite of what you have. It was purely physical and a one-time thing. Okay?"

"I'm in love?" I asked, completely forgetting everything else she just said and focusing on the one thing I still hadn't come to grips with.

"Well duh," she snorted.

"Isn't it too soon?"

"Does love have a time restriction?" she asked.

"Then why haven't I opened the letter, Leah?"

"I don't know, sweetheart. I don't know," she said, standing to pull me into a tight hug. We stood there in the small dressing room, holding and supporting each other, like we'd done for the last twenty years. With her head resting on my shoulder, Leah whispered, "Your rack looks fabulous in this dress. You should wear this one. He'll lose his shit when he sees you in it."

"You always know the right things to say," I joked.

"I know. I'm like a super-hot version of Yoda."

I snorted, giving myself a long pause before saying, "You'll be there Wednesday morning?"

"There's nowhere else I'd be, Clare."

I tiptoed into Maddie's room, hoping to catch a few moments alone with her before she woke. The clothes I had carefully laid out the night before were laying across her rocking chair, and the CD I put on repeat was still chattering on about sheep and numbers. I gently sat on the edge of her bed, looking down on her tiny face, trying to remember how it looked three years ago today. She was barely into her toddler years, just starting to leave infancy. When I held her in my arms sobbing, I thought she looked so big compared her to the tiny baby we'd brought home. Looking down at her now, I felt that overwhelming lack of control every parent has watching their child grow before their eyes, unable to stop it, or slow it down. How had she gotten so big? She would start kindergarten next year, and he wasn't here to see it.

He was gone.

It had been three years, today.

Maddie shifted in her sleep and made an incoherent noise before her eyes fluttered open and focused on me.

"Hi Mommy," she mumbled, her voice still sleepy.

"Hey, baby."

"Whatcha doin'?"

"Just looking at how pretty you are," I smiled, reaching down to smooth out her tiny red curls.

"Are we going to go visit Daddy today?" she asked.

"Yes."

"Do I get to wear my pretty dress?"

"Of course, baby," I choked out.

"Do you think Daddy would like my pretty dress?" her voice filled with curiosity over a man she would never know again.

"Oh definitely. Green was Daddy's favorite color." It was the color of my eyes.

Just breathe, just breathe.

She remained silent for a second, pondering something before saying, "Mommy?"

"Yeah, baby?" I said, my voice coming out in a whisper.

"I miss Daddy."

Holding back tears, I nodded. It was all I could do. I pulled her in my arms and nodded again, because I did too. I missed him. So damn much.

We met in the late afternoon, which is the same time we met every year since we lost him. I don't know who came up with the idea, but it was a tradition we had kept. That first year is a bit of a haze, but every year, on the anniversary of Ethan's death, we gathered at the cemetery and grieved. My parents, my brother, Leah, and a few of his friends. Everyone who was still living and mattered in his life.

We huddled together, hands linked, and our heads bowed, letting the silence be our opening hymn. My father was the first to speak.

"Thank you all for coming again. Ethan wasn't just a son-in-law to me, he was my son. He came to us without a family, and we gave him one. In return, he loved our daughter and gave us Maddie. He loved them with everything he had until his very last breath."

His voice quivered as he struggled to continue, "So, with that...I think I'll start."

Every time we gathered, we each told a memory of Ethan, and then placed a seashell on his headstone, a small symbol of the surfer boy who left us all too soon.

"The first time I met Ethan was when Clare brought him home during Thanksgiving break. When she called us to say she was bringing home a boy from school, the warning flags went up, but she assured me he was just a boy from out of state who didn't have any family. So, when I caught him in the kitchen with his hand up her shirt, I turned to Clare, asked her to exit the room to give the men a few minutes to chat."

I shook my head. I couldn't believe he was telling this story. I thought he was going to kill Ethan that day. It was just a good thing it was that moment he chose to catch us that weekend. There were several other worse occasions he could have walked in on.

"So, I walked up to the boy, expecting him to look scared shitless."

I gave him a stern look, and he just looked back confused before understanding blossomed across his face.

"Oops, sorry Maddie. Papa has a potty mouth," he snickered.

She let out a little giggle as she gripped my hand, looking beautiful in her lightly smocked green dress.

"But he just stood tall and said, 'I know what you're thinking, sir, but I want you to know I love your daughter and I plan on making her happy for the rest of my life.' I looked him over, shrugged and said 'Okay, but keep it clean in the house, will ya kid?'"

Everyone laughed the pained laugh people do when they were wavering between laughing and crying. Many tears would be shed today, but we tried to make sure the good memories were kept alive as well.

We went around the circle, sharing stories. Some were funny, some were a bit sad. Leah was next to last and told the story of Ethan becoming a father.

"He was scared to death. I thought he was going to pass out," she laughed, shaking her head and wiping the tears from her eyes. "Then he saw Maddie and it was love at first sight."

Tears dripped down my cheeks, remembering that moment when we became parents. It was the scariest and happiest moment of our lives.

When everyone had finished their stories and placed their shells, only two remained. Mine and Maddie's.

Everyone's eyes focused on me. I was always last.

"When you plan to share a life with someone, you never for a second stop to wonder how long that life may be. Even if I had known I would only get a handful of years with him, I still would have said yes and never looked back."

Looking down at Maddie, I squeezed her hand and took a deep breath, centering myself before I continued.

"Before the cancer and the chemo. Before the headaches and the tests, there was Ethan, me, and our little surprise Maddie. Ethan was the most laid back and carefree person I've known, except when it came to finances. He was meticulous." A couple knowing chuckles filled the air in agreement.

"When we got married, we had a plan. A financial plan. We both would work for five years, save, buy a house and then start talking about kids. His entire plan was reduced to a pile of rubble when I took that pregnancy test one morning. We went from having everything planned to nothing, and I'd never seen him happier. We bought a house and watched my belly grow. It was the best time in our life."

Looking down at the simple headstone, I took another breath and finished.

"I look back and think about how different his last couple years would have been if we had actually been able to follow through with that God awful plan. We would have wasted them working ourselves to death, saving money for dream we would never see. Instead, our lives became a blissful combination of chaos and joy when Madilyn Grace entered our lives. She was the gift we never knew we needed, and she gave Ethan the one thing he needed before he left this world, to become a father."

Looking over at Maddie, I held up my shell, and asked, "You ready?"

She nodded and we took a final step forward, placing our shells on Ethan's headstone together.

"I love you, Ethan," I said at the same time Maddie said "I love you, Daddy."

The crowd began to dispense, hugging each other as they went. Everyone asked if they could do something, take us out, or bring us food. It was like this every year. I politely declined.

No, Maddie and I would be fine alone. We always were.

When everyone had gone, the only people that remained were Maddie, Leah and me. And the shells. Ten in total, all lined up.

We said one last goodbye, linked arms and headed for the car.

I saw him a split second before Maddie yelled, "Logan!" and took off in a run, catapulting herself in his arms, and burying her face deep into his chest.

Stunned, I temporarily forgot how to breathe. What was he doing here? And why did I have the sudden urge to do the exact same thing as Maddie, and bury my head into his chest willing him to make the hurt go away. Tears blurred my vision again as he made his way to us. Leah motioned for Maddie and she reluctantly pulled away from Logan to join her, "Come on, short stack. Let's go home. We'll meet you there?" she asked, looking to Logan. He nodded briefly, turning his attention back to me.

A few moments of silence passed, the only sound coming from the sway of the trees and birds flying above. He looked at me intently, waiting for me to speak first.

"What are you doing here? How did you know?" I asked, the words stumbling out of my mouth in a rush.

"Leah told me. Why didn't you?" he questioned, pain clearly echoing in his words.

"I don't know," I answered, "I figured this was too much, too soon. I didn't think you'd want to be here for this...for a woman you'd just started seeing. I mean, we haven't even slept together," I threw out the last part in a rush, hating myself for even saying it.

"Jesus, Clare. Do you think I'm only here for sex?" he hissed, clearly hurt.

"No, I'm sorry. I don't. I just, I don't know...I thought you wouldn't want to be here," I admitted.

Breathing deeply, he took a step forward, angling my chin so he could look me in the eyes. "Clare, this...what we're doing. It has to be all or nothing. And I want all of you. When you cry, I want to be the one holding you. No matter the reason. So please, let me hold you," he whispered.

I went willingly into his arms, doing exactly what I wanted to do since the moment I saw him. I buried my face in his chest and let out a sob I had been holding back all day. It felt cathartic and supremely overdue, like a dam spilling over after years of neglect.

"I still love him, Logan," I confessed.

"I know, baby. I know. It's okay," he soothed.

His arms wrapped around my small frame, his large hand cradling my head as tears flowed. I don't know how long he held me like this. It could have been minutes, hours, I don't know, but he didn't waver. He just held me, letting me have this day to grieve, to remember.

~Logan~

Holding Clare while she grieved for another man was probably the hardest thing I had ever done. While logically, I understood it, and could convince myself it was normal and healthy, and exactly the way it should be. The man, the Neanderthal male inside of me was screaming. He was banging his chest, growling, and yelling because I had just spent the last hour holding my woman, yes mine, as she grieved another man that she still loved. Insecurity threatened to take over as we drove back to the house in silence and I wondered if she could ever love me as much as she loved him. Would I ever measure up? As if sensing my unease, Clare's hand covered mine, calming me. She had become my constant when everything else was a chaotic mess.

I took her home and Leah left shortly after, leaving the

three of us alone. I helped Clare throw something together for dinner and we put Maddie to bed early. She was asleep within minutes, the exhaustion from the day claiming her almost instantly. Swaying on her feet, Clare was minutes away from collapsing herself. I lifted her in my arms, savoring the feel of her body close to mine, and walked the short distance to her bedroom. It was the first time I'd been in there, carefully avoiding the room she'd shared with her husband.

I gently laid her on the bed and pulled the covers over her tired body. Her eyes had already drifted shut, sleep finally taking hold of her. She looked beautiful like this, and I could lie here for hours watching her sleep. But I was not staying here, in this sacred place, without permission, especially today. I quietly made my way to the door when I heard her shift.

"Logan, don't leave me," she murmured.

I froze. "Are you sure?" I asked, turning to meet her eyes as she looked at me from across the room.

"Yes. Please, just hold me."

"Always," I vowed.

I came to the opposite side of the bed, quietly undoing the buttons of my shirt as she watched through sleepy eyes. I kicked off my shoes, unbuckled my belt and dropped my jeans. Pulling the covers down, I slid in next to her, never breaking eye contact. Realizing she was still completely clothed, she lifted her hips to slide her jeans off and cuddled in next to me, wearing only a tight t-shirt and panties. God, she was gorgeous. Laying on my side, I wrapped my arms around, fitting her to my body. Her back to my front.

Hating myself for it, but knowing I had no choice, I asked, "What was he like?" I had to know her, all of her, including this man who would forever own a piece of her heart.

"He was the perfect balance of crazy and responsible," she began. "He'd be the first one to suggest something stupid at a frat party, but he'd beat everyone out the door for early morning classes on Monday. He was the only person I knew who carried perfect grades and never studied," she said, giving a quiet laugh.

"He was an orphan. His parents were killed in a car accident when he was a teenager and he was lost without them. When I brought him home for the first time and my family took him in with open arms, he said he finally felt grounded again."

She paused and I kissed her shoulder encouraging her to continue. I think she needed this as much as I did.

"He loved to surf. I used to call him my surfer boy. We always looked ridiculous standing next to each other. He was blonde, tan and muscular, and I was a skinny redhead who hated the beach because it made my skin burn. But we made it work, and I did eventually grow to love the beach."

We lay still for a long time and I listened to her breathe. Just when I started to wonder if she had fallen asleep, she rolled over in my arms, staring into me with those emerald green eyes.

"I don't compare you to him, Logan. I don't keep a checklist trying to figure out which one of you will win 'Clare's Great Love' contest. Ethan, as much as I will always love him," her voice faltered, "is gone. And I can't live my life married to a ghost. You are here with me now. And I want all of you."

Squeezing my eyes tight with emotions I wasn't used to having, I kissed her forehead and thanked God I was the one who walked in that ER room.

I awoke to the feeling of something, or someone rather, poking me in the head. My eyes fluttered open to find Maddie staring at me, a doll in hand and a smile plastered on her face as she said, "Can I sleep with you?"

I was surprised she wasn't screaming, "Why are you in bed with my Mommy!?" I shrugged, letting her climb in next to me, but instead, she climbed up and over me, causing me to grunt, as she kicked me in the side and kneed me in the ribs. How the hell was Clare sleeping through this? I looked over and she was peacefully sleeping, the epitome of calm, while I was getting punched. Maddie settled herself between the two of us, pulling my hand so it rested over her tiny body, like a miniature version of spooning. She snuggled deeply and sighed, obviously contented with her new sleeping arrangement as she reached over to drape a hand over her Mom's side. We now created a three person spoon, well four, if you counted the doll. I drifted back to sleep with a grin on my face, and a dull ache in my ribs.

I awoke again, this time with the sun shining through the windows, the smell of bacon and the sound of laughter drifting up from the stairs. I could listen to that sound for the rest of my life and never grow tired of it. Quickly rising to change back into my clothes from the day before, I rushed downstairs and found a pajama clad Maddie, wooden spoon in hand, bouncing up and down to...is that Usher? Clare was at the stove flipping pancakes and shaking her hips, which made Maddie burst into fits of laughter.

I leaned my long frame against the side of the fridge waiting, wondering when they would notice the intruder, hoping I could catch Clare off guard.

Clare danced over to one of the kitchen cabinet and retrieved a plate. Still dancing, she turned, gliding over to me, completely unsurprised by my presence.

"Good morning," she said smugly before placing a chaste kiss on my lips.

"How?" I tried asking.

"Mom." She shrugged as if it was enough of an explanation. She laughed, realizing I still looked confused and elaborated. "I have eyes in the back of my head. I see everything," she said, making it sound like it was one of the

Seven Wonders of the World.

"It's true," Maddie confirmed.

I chuckled and began helping Clare dish up breakfast. I had never done this before. Had a family meal. It was the most normal thing I'd ever done.

Taking a moment from her cooking duties, Clare pulled me away from the prying ears of Maddie "Thank you. For last night. For yesterday, for everything," she stumbled out the words, obviously trying to find the right ones.

"You don't need to thank me, Clare. There is nowhere else I would rather have been."

I meant it. These two had managed to bring more joy to my life in the last month than I had in the entire thirty-two years of my life. Seeing both of them yesterday lost, grieving and hurt...it will never happen again. They had a new protector, and it was me. I would keep them safe. No matter what.

Chapter Eleven

~Clare~

"Just breathe," I told myself for the hundredth time as I stood on Logan's front porch staring at the brass knocker that adorned his door. While his words regarding the next time we were alone may have totally turned me on at the time, I was now a complete and total disaster. It had been a week since he slept in my bed and held me while I told him teary-eyed memories of Ethan. I don't know how he knew, but I needed that. I needed him to know Ethan, at least through my eyes. I didn't think I would ever find someone to care for after Ethan died, and now that I had, I didn't want Ethan's memory to fade. I knew I couldn't be in a relationship with two men, but I also couldn't forget the man who taught me to love in the first place. After all, he gave me Maddie, the ultimate gift.

When he met me at the cemetery, held me in his arms as I sobbed and let me grieve the man I had loved and lost, I knew. I may have already been there, or on my way, but seeing him so selflessly giving himself to me in my grief. That made it real. When I awoke the next morning, and found Maddie cuddled between us, his arm wrapped around her, in a protective embrace, I knew I wanted this man to be my future.

The front door I had been staring at opened, startling me.

"You gonna stand out here all day?" Logan asked, leaning against the door frame as he casually threw a kitchen towel over his shoulder.

"Ah, no. Sorry. Scatterbrained."

"You mean nervous?" he said, motioning to the overnight

bag that was slung over my shoulder.

Blushing, I nodded. The overnight bag had been a huge cause of contention between Leah and me. She told me to pack it. I told her it was being presumptuous.

"Presumptuous, Clare?" she said "He invited you over for dinner. After telling you the next time you were alone, he was going to ravage you senseless. I think you're being a little dense. Pack a bag so you don't have to brush your teeth with your index finger."

I gave in and did as I was told. But having never packed an overnight bag, I had no idea what to bring. When I dated Ethan, we were in college and in the same dorm. If I spent the night in his room, I just ran back to my own in the morning for a quick shower, and vice versa. I didn't know what went in a "spending the night at my boyfriend's house" bag. Did I pack pajamas? Or was that prudish? Did I bring shampoo, or should I just use his? I settled for the minimum. A change of clothes, a sexy nightie, a bit of makeup and a toothbrush.

"No need for nervousness, Clare. You hold all the cards tonight," Logan winked as his eyes traveled the length of my body, making me instantly flush.

"Did I mention you look amazing? Downright fucking beautiful," he declared.

And every bit of nervousness I had evaporated as his pale blue eyes meet mine.

He could have me. Here. Now. Any way he wanted.

"Dinner, Clare. We have to eat first," he breathed in my ear.

"Right. Food," I said, blushing.

Chuckling, he led me in through the front door and I took a look around. I had only been here briefly to drop things off or to pick him up, so I had never actually been able to take a leisurely stroll through his house. You would expect a young bachelor like Logan to be somewhere downtown in a loft apartment, full of steel and high end furniture. Instead, Logan's home was from the turn of the century and tucked away in an older neighborhood outside of Richmond, not too far from my house. I ran my hand over the hand carved banister that probably dated back to the nineteenth century as we made our way to the fully remodeled kitchen.

"Logan, your house is stunning. It's definitely not what I would have expected when I first met you," I admitted.

"And now?" he questioned, opening the fridge to grab a bottle of wine. He was dressed casually tonight, jeans, a black t-shirt that showed off his tight stomach and arms, no shoes. It was sexy.

"I can see it. It suits you." And it did. I could see his trademark style everywhere. From the acoustic guitars that lined the living room to the global artwork and photography of places he'd visited that decorated the walls. He had created a home, and he probably didn't even realize it. He didn't spend much time here, but somehow he had created a space for a family. It's like he was waiting for it to be filled, hoping the empty space in his heart will one day be filled as well.

"You're cooking for me?" I asked as he moved to the stove and began stirring something in a pot.

"I did ask you over for dinner. Did you think we were ordering pizza?"

When my answer came in the form of a wry smile, he laughed, tossing a kitchen towel in my direction.

"You did think I was going to order a pizza! I'll have you know that I can cook, woman!" Grabbing the kitchen towel he tossed on the floor, I walked to the stove to take a peek in the pot.

"Marinara? You're making spaghetti?" I guessed.

"Ah, no. I'm making pizza," he answered quietly

"You're *making* pizza?" I said, doing everything I could to keep from laughing.

"I said I could cook. I didn't say what!"

"All right," I relented, heading over to the sink to wash my hands, "what can I do to help, Emeril?"

Shaking his head, he pointed to the cutting board filled with mushrooms and various other toppings, "Start slicing the toppings. God, you're a pain in my ass!" he laughed.

We settled into a comfortable rhythm, while I sliced and he rolled out the dough. He spoke about his last shift at the hospital and the busy evening he had. I discussed how Maddie decided she needed to go to the beach. I had been looking up favorite destinations all week.

"We should go together," he suggested.

"Yeah?"

"Yeah," he affirmed, "but not just any beach. We should take her someplace great. Pick someplace and we'll go. Anywhere."

"Okay," I answered, a little out of breath. Had we just planned our first trip? Butterflies fluttered in my belly, and I tried and tame them by changing the subject, even though all I wanted to do was jump up and down screaming "He's Mine! All Mine!" To absolutely no one. Maybe I'd save that one for a more public place. On second thought. Maybe I should keep that little cheer to myself.

"What are you smiling about?" he asked as I realized he was staring at me.

"Huh? Oh. Um. You."

His sly grin shifted into a high beam smile, and wow. He was stunning when he smiled like that. I mean, he was always gorgeous, but when he smiled like he did right now, he was downright panty melting hot.

"Good," he stated.

Once the pizzas were out of the oven we skipped the dining room table and instead opted for the floor in front of the fireplace in the living room. Logan gathered pillows, a few blankets and a tray, and we took our plates and wine and settled comfortably into our makeshift picnic.

"You really like picnics, don't you?" I asked him.

"I really like picnics with you," he corrected, before adding playfully, "They always go really well for me." He took a bite of his pizza, and I did the same. I nearly moaned as the flavors hit my palette.

"Oh yum. This is good, Logan."

"See, I told you I could cook," he defended himself.

"I'm never ordering pizza again. I'm just calling you from now on," I said, diving into my second piece.

"So that's all I'm good for now? Pizza?" he mocked.

"Oh no, you have many, many uses." Wow, look at me. Seductress extraordinaire.

After I finished off everything on my plate, I had the need for something sweet. "So, you made pizza for dinner. What are you making me for dessert?"

"Dessert? Oh crap. I forgot!" he exclaimed.

"You damn well better be joking, Logan Matthews," I warned, folding my arms across my chest and pouting.

"Do you really think I would risk certain loss of limb and not have dessert for you? I'm many things, but stupid is not one of them. I'll be right back," he announced, jumping up, tray in hand, headed for the kitchen.

Moments later, he returned, with the tray again, but this time it was filled with ice cream, candy, fudge and whipped cream. I clapped my hands together like a five year old child.

"Ice cream sundaes!"

"It's the best I could do. You don't want anything I baked," he confessed, as he rested the tray back down on the floor.

"It's great! Absolutely perfect!"

I started to build my masterpiece, loading it up with goodies. He even bought coffee ice cream. He never missed a thing. Logan dug into the vanilla and we made our sundaes in a comfortable silence.

"Why didn't you ever go back to teaching?" Logan asked as he added the finishing touches to his sundae.

"I honestly don't know," I admitted "I guess I had always planned on going back, but just never got around to it. When Ethan first got sick, the school was very supportive. If I needed a day off to be with him during chemo, they gave it to me without question. But then he got worse, and the days turned into weeks until I eventually had to take a leave of absence. I told them I'd return when he got better, but he never did."

I remembered looking in on Maddie as she slept, days after becoming a single mother, knowing my life would never be the same. Knowing I couldn't possibly leave her alone, and feeling like I needed her more than anything in the world.

"After his death, I could have gone back. They hadn't filled my position, and I had the entire summer to grieve, but the thought of leaving Maddie killed me. I never thought I'd be a stay at home Mom, but I just kind of fell into it. Thanks to Ethan's meticulous planning, we have more than enough to live on for quite a long time, and I knew I'd never get these years back. I have considered looking for a position next year though, after she starts kindergarten. I do miss teaching. Teenagers are an interesting breed."

"Oh, I bet," he laughed. "I feel sorry for the boys in your classes,"

"What? Why?" I asked, confused.

"Having you as a teacher? They probably had to hide their mammoth size boners the entire class period. I know I would have."

"Oh my God! That's so not true!" I gasped, grabbing a chocolate chip from the nearby bowl and chucking it at his head.

He ducked and the chocolate sailed past him and landed near the fireplace. All laughing aside, his voice grew serious,

"You have no idea how devastatingly beautiful you are, do you?"

"No," I whispered as he angled his body toward mine.

His fingers brushed the burgundy colored curls off my bare shoulder as his mouth found my collar bone.

"You're breathtaking," he murmured, kissing the curve of my neck and nipping my ear lobe causing me to shudder.

"Absolutely stunning," his lips traveled up my chin as his hands wrapped around my back to haul me closer.

"And so goddamn fucking sexy," he growled before he claimed my lips as his own, branding me with his mouth, and taking my very soul with his kiss. Our tongues moved together as he leaned forward, pressing me into the nest of blankets and pillows laid out before the fire.

He pulled back and his eyes quietly searched mine, "We don't have to do this tonight. I'll wait. For however long it takes, Clare. I'm yours," he whispered like a prayer.

Being sure to never break eye contact, I carefully brought my hands to the buttons of the sexy green dress I'd worn, slowly unbuttoning each one. His eyes flared with heat, but they never left mine. Finishing the last button, I pulled the two pieces of fabric apart, hearing his hissed response.

"Touch me, Logan."

He didn't hesitate. He pulled me up around the waist, my legs instantly wrapped around his torso as his mouth devoured mine. Sliding the rest of my dress off my shoulders, his eyes seemed to memorize every curve of my body. I should have felt exposed and intimated in just my black lace bra and thong, but I didn't. I felt seductive, confident and sexy as hell. Deciding Logan was a little overdressed for our party, I moved my hands under his t-shirt and felt the hard ridges in his stomach and his killer upper body as I pushed the shirt up. He took over, doing that hot thing guys do with their shirts, grabbing the back of it and yanking it off, leaving nothing but Logan.

Every muscled sexy, edible inch.

He saw the flash of desire in my eyes as he reached a hand behind my back for the clasp of my bra. Oh so slowly, he slid the straps down my shoulders, letting the bra fall to the floor. Gently, he laid me back down on the blankets, and sat back on his heels to admire the view.

"God Clare, you're perfect," he said, looking at me like I was a feast and he couldn't decide where to start first. Leaning down with his eyes still locked on mine, he took a nipple in his warm mouth, causing my body to bow off the ground. His hand cupped my other breast as he worked my nipple with his mouth, rolling it, flicking it and pinching it with his teeth. I moaned as his mouth shifted, working my other breast with the same lovely torture. Just when I thought I might actually come from this alone, his mouth traveled down my belly, stopping at my panty line. Glancing back up at me, he grabbed the two strips of fabric at my sides that made up my thong and slowly slid it down my body.

"Jesus," he cursed, "Spread your legs for me, Clare," he demanded, his voice low and rough.

I did as he said, spreading my legs wide, exposing myself to him completely.

"So fucking beautiful."

I felt his hands caress my ankles before they moved to my knees and finally my inner thighs, pushing my legs wider. His head lowered and he slowly kissed is way up my thigh, working his way closer to my core. I was shaking with need and wet with desire.

"Do you want my mouth on you, Clare?" he asked as he fingers grazed my slick folds, causing a wave of pleasure to zing through my body.

"Yes!" I pleaded.

"Remember how I said you hold all the cards tonight? You have to tell me what you want."

"Oh God, do it Logan, please!" I begged. I had lost all control and had no problem with begging him to get what I so desperately needed.

"You need to be a bit more specific, sweet Clare. What do you want me to do?" He was taunting me, driving me wild with his sexy voice as much as with his fingers as they continued their lazy journey.

"Lick me, Logan," I demanded.

Before the words were barely out, his head descended and I was in heaven, my body ignited in flames as his tongue and mouth began their dark dance. Licking and teasing me, he pierced my body deeper, driving me closer to the edge. I moaned and cried out as the pleasure grew, building, climbing higher until I screamed out my release.

Still reeling from my orgasm, I almost didn't notice we were moving. With my arms and legs wrapped around his body, he carried me upstairs to his bedroom, carefully laying me on the bed. Done in dark grays, with splashes of red, Logan's bedroom was very masculine and neat. But it could have been purple and covered in unicorns, and I probably wouldn't have noticed as soon as he started to undo his belt buckle. I noticed the slight shake in his hands, and wondered how much he was restraining himself. The jeans and boxers came next and he let them slide the floor, leaving him bare before my eyes for the first time. Clothed Logan was sexy. Naked Logan was every woman's fantasy come to life. His body was flawless. Muscular and lean in all the right places, thanks to years of running and weight training, and lord, he was huge. Fully erect and begging to be touched. My tongue darted out to wet my lips as I thought about wrapping my mouth around his hard length. As if he could read my mind, or maybe my facial expressions were really that obvious, Logan groaned as he walked forward.

"I still have the taste of you on my tongue and if you keep

looking at me like that, this is going to be over really quick."

Stopping at his nightstand, he opened it to pull out a condom, and then hesitated before settling his eyes on me.

"Clare. All the other women before you," he breathed out.

Uh, why are we talking about this? Now?

"I never brought them here. I've never brought a woman to my bed. Ever," he confessed, looking at me with those stormy blue eyes. Trying to comprehend what he just said, it dawned on me.

"Wait, never? But you were married." I said.

"We had separate rooms. I set it up that way in the beginning because I thought it would allow her more sleep with my crazy schedule. Looking back now, I realize it was my attempt to keep distance," he recalled.

"But what about earlier, when you weren't married? Surely, you had her over?" I seriously couldn't believe we were sitting here naked talking about his ex-wife. I seriously couldn't believe I could form a sentence right now, with him looking like that, other than "Seexxxxx."

"Ah, no. We always lived apart, and when we were together, we were at her place. Never mine. I'm sure she noticed, but she never said anything."

"Oh." I didn't know what to say.

"I wanted you to know, because you are the only woman I've ever wanted to share my bed with, or bring home. Clare, you are my home."

And with that, I melted. Ex-wives and pasts are forgotten as I gave myself to him completely. Our bodies tangled together, as his hands and mouth mapped my body, taking over and fueling my desire.

Feeling his hard body on top of mine, I wrapped my legs around him, pulling him closer, feeling him hard against me. Pausing briefly, he reached for the condom on his nightstand, but I grabbed his hand instead.

"I'm on the pill," I assured him. Having had horrible cramps since the day I turned thirteen, I'd been a lifer.

"Are you sure? I was tested right after I met you, but I would still understand," he said, doubt clouding his features due to a past filled with regret.

"I trust you, Logan."

He closed his eyes, savoring each word, before kissing me slowly until we were breathless.

Breaking apart only to look me in the eyes as he vowed, "From this moment on Clare, you're mine." He sealed his words as he entered my body with his own, filling me completely. He paused briefly, allowing my body to adjust to his, running his hands up and down my thighs.

"So beautiful," he whispered, pulling out and thrusting back into me, making me gasp and moan at the same time. Every move, every caress was slow and sensual and his eyes stayed constantly locked with mine. He gently stroked my hair and kissed me slowly as we made love. In and out, his body moved against mine, as I felt the pressure begin to build inside of me. As if sensing my climb, Logan's thumb reached down between us to find my clit, flicking it once, twice and I'm done, pleasure spiraling out of control.

With my legs still wrapped around his hips, he lifted me up in his lap, keeping us joined.

"Ride me. Like you did in the car, Clare," he instructed.

Placing my hands on his broad shoulders for leverage, I moved, sliding up and down his hard shaft, riding him as his arms wrapped around my body and our eyes locked.

"That's it, Clare. You feel so fucking good," he moaned before devouring my mouth again, palming his hand on the nape of my neck. With a growl, I was instantly on my back again, Logan moving us around the bed as if I was weightless. Like a guitar string that snapped, the last shred of Logan's control disappeared as he pushed my knees forward with his palms and drove into to me, sending me into a second orgasm as he came apart, letting out his own release with a roar. Both still breathless and unable to form words, he gathered me in his arms, pulling the blankets over us, as he began stroking my hair. Soon, the exhaustion of our lovemaking took its toll and sleep claimed me.

~Logan~

I awoke the next day, finding the room filled with sunlight as it streamed through the old windows, illuminating Clare's beautiful red curls who slept against my chest. She's was so beautiful. I kept telling her that, but I don't think she would ever understand the world through my eyes. Her beauty radiated from every pore. It wasn't just one feature, or characteristic. It was her, entirely. Her body, the way she carried herself and the kind of person she was made her beautiful.

Unable to stop myself, I ran my hand down her cheek, loving the feel of her skin, reminding me of how it felt to have her body moving with mine. Last night had been life altering for me. I had joked with Clare that once she was with me, all other men would be ruined in her eyes, but it was the opposite. I would never want another woman the way I wanted Clare. After experiencing something so cataclysmic and monumental, I could never go back to my old life of bar hopping and one night stands. Clare and Maddie were my future, and I would give anything to become the man they deserve and needed.

"Hey," Clare said with a faint smile, her voice groggy and full of sleep.

"Good morning, beautiful." I answered, bending down to kiss her full lips.

"Last night was..." she began.

"...amazing," I finished.

"Well I was going to say 'absolutely fucking amazing', but yours works too."

Grinning, I shook my head. "Such language, Clare."

She rolled her eyes and started laughing. I began laughing with her.

"So, are you going to cook breakfast for me, too?" she asked sweetly.

"Of course. But first I thought we should shower. You know, because being dirty is bad," I suggested as I slowly pulled the sheet down exposing her perfectly rounded breasts, causing her nipples to harden instantly.

"Yes, wouldn't want to be dirty, would we?" she agreed, obviously playing along with my ridiculous game, as her eyes darkened with desire.

Ripping the sheet off her body entirely, I rose and threw her over my shoulder. She squeaked as I headed to the bathroom.

"Logan! Put me down!" she squealed.

"Nope, sorry. Gotta make sure you get to the shower properly. I'll have to join you, too. To make sure you do a good job."

She giggled, smacking me on my bare ass, before I sat her down in front of the massive shower.

"Holy shit, this place is huge!" she exclaimed.

"Yeah, I wasn't a fan of the granny style the previous owner had, so I had it completely gutted and redone. Doesn't exactly fit with the age of the home, but I figured they didn't have bathrooms back then, so who cares?"

I loved this bathroom. I had always secretly envisioned sharing it with someone, which is why it had double sinks and an extra-large shower, both of which would come in handy today. I ducked my head in and turn on the shower, and waited for it to warm up before we entered. I didn't waste a second, pulling Clare flush against my body, letting her know how much I wanted her. Last night our lovemaking was slow, a buildup of two people getting to know each other's bodies, but today was about passion. As soon as our bodies collided, I had her pinned against the shower wall, spreading her legs wide.

"Wait," she said. I stopped completely, not knowing if I had hurt her or taking things too quickly.

"Turn around, with your back against the wall," she commanded, her voice full of purpose.

So fucking hot.

Letting her legs slide back to the floor, I turned around, and followed her orders, keeping my eyes on her, wondering what she had planned. I found out seconds later, when she immediately dropped to her knees, taking my hard cock into her warm wet mouth.

"Fuck!" I cursed, as she slid her mouth down my entire length, and pulled back, sucking me root to tip. The delicious torture continued as she rolled her tongue over the sensitive head of my cock, then slid back down, taking all of me. Her cheeks hollowed as she sucked in and out, over and over, my hips involuntarily thrusting to meet her welcoming mouth.

"Clare, I'm gonna come," I called out, giving her a warning if she wanted to pull away. But she just wrapped her hands around my ass, pulling me tighter against her mouth and continued. My balls tightened, and my cock grew ever harder until I came. Hard. Panting, I stared down as Clare took every last drop I gave her, and then looked up as she licked me clean.

Holy fucking shit.

Without thinking, I knelt down, grabbed her around the waist and wheeled us around to our previous position against the shower wall. After watching her lick me clean, I was already hard again, and I wasted no time, surging into her as I wrapped her legs around my waist. I relentlessly slammed my body into hers, driving us both to ecstasy.

"Oh God, yes!" she screamed as I thrusted into her over

and over again.

I felt my balls start to tighten again, and I knew I couldn't hold on for much longer. Clare's inner wall started to squeeze my cock and I knew she was about to come.

"Logan!" she yelled, and I felt her release, as her body tightened even more, gripping my cock like a vice, sending me into another endless orgasm.

After I caught my breath, I carefully slid us both down to shower floor, afraid my knees might buckle.

"This is by far the best shower I've ever had," Clare said, breathless.

"I agree. We should do this every day."

She laughed, shaking her head, and smiled. And there it was, the new reason for my existence.

To make her happy. No matter what.

We finished our shower, letting the water slide down our slick skin as we washed each other's hair and bodies. I left her in my bedroom to dress as went to the kitchen to make breakfast. Seeing her in my house and in my bedroom brought something out in me. It was foreign, and unlike any other feeling I'd known, but I recognized it for what it is. Pure male possession. She was mine now, in every way, and each minute she was here in my bed and my arms, made that feeling grow. I had never felt possessive of Melanie. When I discovered she was cheating on me, I lashed out, finding Gabe and taking my fist to his face, but only because I thought that was how I was supposed to react. In reality, I understood why she strayed. I was never there to anchor her in the first place.

As I began heating up the griddle, I heard her walk into the kitchen and felt her arms wrap around my waist from behind.

"You're making me pancakes?" she asked, resting her head against my back.

"And bacon," I added, pointing to the package of bacon

sitting next to the stove.

"Mmm..you're my hero."

Turning so I could face her and see those vivid green eyes I'd become enchanted with, I laughed before asking, "I could really get you to do just about anything if I used food as the incentive, couldn't I?"

"Well, it really depends on the type of food you're offering. Veggies? Probably not. But if you offered me a chocolate cake with peanut butter frosting? Well then, yes. I'd probably become your sex slave for life. Wait, where are you going?"

Walking over to my cell phone, I picked it up and start punching buttons.

"Finding a bakery obviously," I answered.

She thought I was kidding.

"You are not!" she squealed.

"Oh, I so am. And then I'm going to lick every bit of frosting off your delectable body." I promised darkly.

"Um."

She was speechless. I don't think I had ever reduced her to speechless before. Score one for Logan.

Just as I was about to punch in the number for the bakery I found, a call came in on my phone causing me to groan.

"Shit," I muttered.

"Who is it?" Clare asked, her voice was full of concern and she stopped pouring the pancakes to check on me.

"My mother," I told her before I hit receive, bringing the phone to my ear.

"Hello Mother," I answered.

"Oh Logan darling! How are you? It's been so long since I've heard your voice."

Well, I did have a phone. She could call me. But I didn't say that. I had learned that even when I did speak to her, my mother only heard what she wanted to.

"I'm well, thank you," I said politely, as I started pacing the kitchen. Whatever reason she was calling for, I hope she got to the point soon. Her voice was ruining my mood, and Clare didn't need to get caught up in the fucked up mess that was my family.

"Good, good," she replied, before continuing. "Listen, I have wonderful news! You'll never guess!" Oh I was sure I already knew. Before I could even respond, she blurted out, "I'm getting married! Again!"

Yep. I knew it.

"To whom?" I asked, mustering up as much excitement as physically possible. I had no idea why I even bothered.

"Robert Erikson. He's a banker. We've been seeing each other for a while now. Surely, I've told you about him?" She hadn't, but it didn't matter.

"Well, that's wonderful mother. When's the big day?"

"In four weeks! You have to come! It's going to be lovely." She continued on, telling me about wedding colors and the venue, and a million other things I didn't care about. I heard about half of it as my focus centered back on the beautiful redhead currently making pancakes in my kitchen.

"Well, that's really soon. I'll have to check my schedule at the hospital," I said, fully planning on doing the exact opposite, with a follow up call a week later apologizing for my absence.

"I know we would both love for you to be there," she emphasized.

We said our goodbyes, and I walked back to where Clare stood in the kitchen. I wrapped my arms around her waist, feeling myself settle, and center.

"So, your Mom? You've never talked about her," Clare asked cautiously.

"That's because she's a gold-digging, self-centered woman who cares more about her next purse or pair of shoes than she does about her children," I answered bluntly.

"She's getting married?"

I nodded my head, saying "Don't get too excited. I think this is number four, maybe five. Weddings are her thing. Marriage...not so much."

Scrunching her brow, she asked, "What do you mean?"

"I don't know all the particulars because no one in my family talks to each other, but from what I've gathered over the years from various household staff and family friends is, at some point, my parents actually loved each other. I'm guessing that's how Eva and I came about."

I couldn't imagine my father feeling warmth toward anyone, but apparently for a short time, my mother was his world.

Sitting down with our breakfast, Clare looked at me with those bewitching green eyes that begged me to continue, and so I took a breath and carried on.

"A short time after Eva was born, my father caught wind from some family friends that Mom's flamboyant behavior was not going unnoticed in their social circles."

"Flamboyant?" she questioned.

Pushing the food around on my plate, I answered, "See, the type of social circle my father belonged to, and still does is refined, full of old money. Traditional. My mother showing up with pink high heels would have been considered scandalous."

"He left her for being different?"

I nodded. "He quietly had divorce papers drawn up, and less than a year later married my robo-stepmother. There is nothing more important to my father than image." The words rang so true in my head. I hadn't spoken with the man since I moved. Since he told me I'd fucked up, and was an embarrassment to him. It wasn't like I was arrested for DUI. My wife cheated on me, and yes it made the papers. Shouldn't a father be supportive and be there for a son in a situation like that? Not mine. Nope. Out of sight, out of mind.

"Is that what he did with you?" she asked.

"What? Cut me off? Yeah, but I wasn't living on his money anyway. Every dime he's ever given me, I've put away and invested. I worked throughout college to pay for all my expenses, and have been living off my own income ever since. I knew my father wasn't reliable, and didn't want to ever be financially dependent on him," I explained.

Apparently I had inherited one thing from him, a good financial sense. Planning for my eventual banishment was the best thing I could have ever done, but it meant that I always knew he would eventually do so. Well I had news for him, if he ever wanted to take a look at my stock portfolio he would find out that I'd learned quite a lot from him over the years. The small amounts of money he'd given me for graduations, living expenses and other accomplishments had grown exponentially. I was worth millions.

Thanks Daddy.

"So are you going to your mom's wedding?" Clare asked cautiously, leaning back in her chair as she sipped her cup of coffee.

"No," I answered immediately.

"Logan. She's your mother."

"Only on paper. She gave up all rights to me and left me with that man. Alone." I snapped.

Her elegant fingers wrapped around my arm tenderly, making me regret my bitter words.

"Just think about it, okay? We could go with you. I'd like to meet her, to know someone in your family."

That was the last thing I wanted. Bringing her and Maddie into the batshit crazy world of the Matthew's family? Hell no. But more than that, I wanted to make her happy. So I just nodded.

"Okay, we'll go."

Chapter Twelve

~Logan~

"God, Logan, would you stop fidgeting? It's going to be fine," Clare said as I pulled into the packed driveway of the upscale neighborhood.

Fine. Sure, whatever.

"Dad was very kind to Ethan when they first met. His black eye healed quite quickly," she assured me, completely serious, as my eyes widened in horror. She was silent for what seemed like forever before she broke out into explosive laughter, actually grabbing her side and doubling over.

"Not funny, Clare," I muttered.

"Oh my God. Not true. That was hilarious! Maddie, that was funny right?"

I heard Maddie giggle from the backseat.

Evil women.

"You seriously have no idea what I'm going through, do you?" I wailed, shaking my head in disbelief.

"Logan, they're going to love you. You need to calm down. It's not like my Dad is going to take one look at you and know every single sordid detail of our relationship," she said with a wink.

Thank God for that. I don't think I would be living if he knew the things I had done with Clare. To Clare. In Clare.

Okay. New train of thought. Definitely didn't want to be walking in there with a hard-on.

Bad, bad idea.

"Okay, let's do this," I said, grabbing the bottle of wine

Clare had picked out as a hostess gift.

We got Maddie out of her bright pink car seat that had now taken residence in my SUV for the past two weeks. After installing it one afternoon when we were headed for the movies, it just stayed. I think Clare actually went out and bought another one so we wouldn't have to switch. Seeing that permanent fixture in my car did something to me, and made me feel important to Maddie's life in a small way. It felt like we were taking a stepping stone to something bigger.

As we made our way to the front door, Maddie grabbed both of our hands, yelled "One, Two, Three!!" as we lifted her up, one arm each and swung her, laughing as she squealed with delight. Three months ago I would never have known how to play this little game, and now it had become second nature.

Clare didn't bother knocking, just opened her parents front door yelling "Mom! We're here!" She got a response back from the backyard telling her everyone was outside. We sat the bottle of wine down in the updated kitchen decorated in muted tans, cherry wood and stainless steel.

"Nice kitchen," I commented.

"My parents' present to each other now that they are finally tuition free for the first time in years."

"Speaking of which, is your brother going to be here?" I asked, wanting to meet the elusive brother with the very demanding job.

"I think so. Mom said he should be, assuming he doesn't have any last minute assignments. I haven't seen him in ages."

Clare opened the slider to the backyard. Maddie immediately took off, headed for the swing set that I'm assumed was placed in the corner of the lot especially for her. I don't know how my parents would react to me having a child, but I know they wouldn't build a swing set or take her overnight if needed. That was what Nannies were for.

The large yard was filled with quite a few people for the afternoon cookout, including Leah who joined Maddie at the swings.

When I asked Clare what the occasion was, she just looked at me confused and said, "No occasion, just a cookout."

Apparently they had them all the time. My family needed a reason to gather, otherwise why bother?

Clare pulled us towards an older couple standing near the center of the yard, chatting with several guests.

Clare fell naturally into the woman's arms, and they embraced lovingly. "Hi Mom."

"Hey, sweetheart," Clare's mom said in reply.

She exchanged similar greetings with her father, the man's eyes never leaving mine. Clare was kidding about her dad roughing me up, right? Because right now, he looked like he was holding back a right hook.

"Mom, Dad. This is Logan Matthews. Logan, these are my parents. Thomas and Laura Finnegan."

I offered my hand, but Clare's mother surprised me and gathered me up in a hug.

"It's so nice to meet you, Logan," she said.

She pulled back, and her eyes, the same green eyes I'd become addicted to, were brimming with unshed tears. Panicked for a moment, thinking I had upset her, I searched her face and found her smiling.

Happy tears. She's happy.

I was speechless.

"Mom, you okay?" Clare asked, wrapping an arm around her mother.

"Oh yes, honey. I'm wonderful."

Dad, on the other hand, didn't look quite so approving of me as he turned to Laura and Clare.

"Ladies, do you mind giving Logan and me a minute to get to know each other?"

Clare gave me an encouraging smile before nodding to her father and exiting with her mom.

Fuck. I'm screwed.

"Logan, why don't you join me for a beer?"

Uh, okay. Not how I expected this to go, but I'd go with it.

"I'd be happy to, Mr. Finnegan," I said cheerfully.

"Call me Tom, Mr. Finnegan always makes me think my father's around," he joked. He was relaxed, but there was still that look in his eye. That appraising, calculating, judging look.

We grabbed two beers and planted ourselves in some nearby chairs, silently watching everyone mill about in the backyard. I watched as Clare greeted several of the guests, hugging various friends of the family. Tom wasn't what I expected, although my perceived notions of a father figure were slightly skewed. In every single memory of my own father, he wore a suit. I'd never seen him in anything else. He was always straight-laced and rigid, never a hair out of place. Clare's father was relaxed, wearing shorts and polo. He seemed warm and approachable. Well to everyone else at least.

"So Logan, tell me about yourself, 'cause I've heard and seen plenty," Tom said, his opinion of me clear in voice.

Well, shit. That explained the look. I didn't have a chance with this man from the very start. My father's name and money followed me wherever I go, but it's my lifestyle, the one I chose to live he was questioning. The women, the alcohol, the endless partying. I always wanted to blame my father for everything, but all those choices were my own. No one to blame but myself.

"Well, if you know everything, there's not much to say. Do you want me to deny it? Because I'm not. My choices, my mistakes, my past. But that's exactly what it is, my past. I gave it all up the moment I saw her, because Clare and Maddie, they're my future."

Clare's father didn't say anything for a long time, just

remained quiet, slowly nursing his beer, and thinking. I waited, because I had nothing else to say. I had already laid my cards on the table. All of them. I couldn't change who I was in the past, but I could change who I was now, and would be for Clare and Maddie.

Finally, he turned to me. "Good. Very good, son. Welcome to the family."

He stood and pulled me into his arms, hugging me like a father would a son.

Or at least, how I always imagined it would be.

And just like that, I was family.

~Clare~

I watched as my father and Logan embraced and I felt my knees grow weak. Knowing the importance of this moment for both men brought tears to my eyes that I quickly brushed away. My father had lost a son, and Logan had never had a father. It was a beautiful moment.

"Looks like you have your father's blessing," my mother said.

I nodded, unable to speak, watching the two men.

My father leaned in and whispered something in Logan's ear. Logan's masculine laughter filled the backyard, and he nodded, saying something back to my dad. My father, smiling, gave Logan a swift pat on the back before walking back into the house.

Like gravity, I moved toward him, my hands finding his.

"What was that about?" I asked, wondering what my father and Logan were planning.

"Nothing. Nothing," he said with a wink.

"Jerk," I muttered. I hate surprises.

"Everything went well?" I asked, knowing it had but wanting to hear him say it.

"Everything was perfect. Thank you, Clare."

He didn't elaborate on what, but he didn't have to. I know what that moment must have meant to him, and I just nodded. Arm in arm, we walked over to the swings to find Maddie and Leah. I joined Leah at the swings, while Logan began pushing Maddie, making her giggle and scream.

"So, meeting the parents, huh?" Leah asked as I pushed off, swinging my legs back and forth, gaining momentum. The swing felt about ten sizes too small and made my butt feel gigantic, but I loved the feeling of weightlessly soaring through the air. It made me feel like a kid.

"Yep. He was nervous as hell," I admitted with a slight smirk.

"Ah man, I would have loved to see that," she said sincerely. She loved seeing people squirm. I think it was such a foreign concept to her that it left her completely fascinated. Nothing made Leah squirm.

She was fearless. Well, so far at least.

"Didn't you take care of him before hand?" she asked, confusing me.

I had no idea what she was talking about. Leah was a mystery I had never quite solved.

"Say what?"

"I take that as a no. You sent him in to meet your family, fully loaded? No wonder he's a nervous wreck. The least you could have done was jacked him off before you left so he'd relax a little."

Ladies and Gentlemen, may I present, Leah Morgan, my best friend.

"You're serious?" I said.

"Yep. Men are way calmer after they've cleared the barrel."

"Oh my God. You are ridiculous. And by the way, Maddie is not that far away. She can probably hear you."

"I know I sure can!" Logan interrupted us, speaking loudly

from several swings down.

My pale skin tone had me turning the color of a tomato as Leah started heaving with laughter in her swing. She was laughing so hard she had to stop swinging all together.

"I really, really think you should take Leah's advice on this one, babe. She's a smart girl," Logan advised with a crooked grin, still pushing an oblivious Maddie who was currently singing at the top of her lungs.

I rolled my eyes, still recovering from my massive embarrassment when my Dad opened the door and yelled, "Hey Clare, you've got company."

I turned to see Colin and Ella come through the slider, right on time.

Logan looked at Colin and Ella before looking back at me confused, as I rose from the swing to greet our new guests.

"You invited my friends to your parents' house?" he asked, his eyes taking on a younger, more rounded look than I'd ever seen, making me wonder what he looked like as a boy.

I nodded, and said, "They're your family, Logan. I want our families to know each other."

Taking one quick stride, I was immediately in his arms, completely engulfed in Logan.

"Thank you," he said fiercely.

"Dude, it's just us. No need to flipping cry or anything," Colin joked over my shoulder.

"Flipping?" Logan grinned, turning around to arch his brow in question at his friend's choice of word.

"Ah, yeah. Ella won't let me swear in front of the belly anymore," he confessed, placing emphasis on the word belly as if it were a name or a thing.

"She swears the little monster in there can hear us, and she doesn't want our baby to have a sailor mouth like me. But that hasn't stopped her from screaming like a banshee when we're going at it like – ow!"

I covered my mouth, trying to hold back a laugh as Ella's elbow found its way into Colin's ribs.

"What the hell, I mean heck did you do that for?" he asked as if telling a crowd about his wife's bedroom behavior is totally normal.

"You are impossible," she huffed, folding her arms over her swollen belly. I could see a trace of a smile sneak its way up before she broke out giggling. Colin was a hard guy to stay mad at. He was just so damn cute. The few times Logan and I had gone out with them, I constantly wondered how the hell Ella put up with him. He was high maintenance, had an ego the size of Texas, and the body to back it up. Being a highly successful lawyer didn't help. He never backed down from a fight. They complemented each other and obviously made it work.

My brother chose this moment to arrive and we all stood around and introduced everyone. When the women started cooing over Ella's belly, the men disappeared to go do "guy stuff". My guess was they were going to play around with the grill for a while, nurse some beers and then eventually throw around a football and talk sports.

"So Ella, how much longer do you have?" Leah asked, her nursing instincts kicking in.

"Two months. Two miserable, long months. Next time he tries to knock me up, make sure I do the math first. Being pregnant in the summer sucks." Watching her sit in the hot summer heat, I could commiserate. Ella was tiny, barely topping off at five foot two inches, she looked like a dwarf standing next to Colin's six and a half foot frame. But she was tiny, complaining that she had to shop in the kids department sometimes to find clothing that fit her. Right now, she looked like she was going to topple over. She had a giant belly and two little legs to hold herself upright and we all wondered how she was going to make it to the end without falling over.

"Maddie was born August 11th, so I know exactly how you feel," I said.

Our baby conversation went on from there. We talked about everything from showers to diapers to breast pumps.

Leah, completely out of her element, excused herself and joined Maddie again who had now moved on to hula hoops. She kept swiveling her hips, but the stubborn hoop fell to the ground every time. Leah picked one up, trying to help, and of course mastered it in one try.

Since her night with Declan James, Leah was different. She said it wasn't a big deal, but I think she's still trying to convince herself of that. I tried bringing it up on occasion, but she always managed to change the subject or remind me that it was a one night stand, no big deal. But I think Declan was a much bigger deal than she was willing to admit.

"I wanted to thank you, Clare," Ella said, bringing my attention away from Leah and Maddie and back to her.

"Why?"

"You've gave us back Logan," she said.

Confused, I asked, "What do you mean?"

"I haven't known him as long as Colin. They have a friendship that goes way back, and I know Colin has said that even though they're best friends, there has always been an unreachable part of Logan. But Colin accepted that. He took what Logan was willing to give, and gave back what Logan had always wanted. A family of sorts."

I could see how much this woman loved Logan, and how many years she and Colin had spent worrying over him. After the childhood he had, he needed people who loved him and I was grateful Ella and Colin had stuck by him.

She fiddled with the hem of her skirt, before continuing. "But after the divorce, we lost all of him. He became cold, emotionless. When he called and said he was moving here to be closer to us, we were ecstatic. We thought we'd be able to snap him out of whatever funk he was in and get him back on track. But he just got worse. He'd stop by less and less, and our calls would go unanswered. He check in every once in a while, but we knew he'd given up on everything."

Pausing, she said, "But you," she continued. "You brought him back to us."

Ella's words drifted around in my head hours after as we pulled into my driveway. Maddie had fallen asleep in the backseat on the short ride home and Logan helped lift her out as I noticed a familiar car across the street.

"Leah's here?"

"Yep," Logan said.

"Do you know why she's here?" I inquired.

"Sure do," he answered with a sly grin as we entered the house.

Leah was sitting on the couch, remote in hand, watching some gossip talk shop when we entered. Declan's face flashed across the screen as he entered a Hollywood club with a beautiful blonde. Leah quickly turned off the TV, clearly not wanting to be caught spying on Declan.

"Hey, I'm gonna put princess to bed. You want to fill her in?" he said to Leah.

She nodded, a sly grin replacing the shock I had seen seconds earlier. What the hell is going on? Since when do Leah and Logan make plans behind my back?

I turned and kissed Maddie, who was still asleep in Logan's arms. He gently carried her upstairs to her room.

"Okay, what is going on? Does this have anything to do with what Logan and my Dad were whispering about today?" I asked, still dying to know what my father and Logan were chumming it up about.

"Uh, no. I don't know what the hell you're talking about. Right now my job is to take you upstairs and make you look and I quote, "fucking hot" so your boyfriend can take you dancing," she answered, guiding me up the stairs to my bedroom.

"We're going dancing?" I asked, my voice full of glee. I hadn't been dancing since college.

"Yep, lover boy is fan-fucking-tastic. Let's get you ready!" She walked over to my closet, and pulled out a dress I'd never seen. It was black, and from the looks of it, tight.

"Where did that come from?" I asked, running my hands down the designer fabric.

"I'll give you two guesses."

"He bought me a dress?"

"Yep, and shoes. And they're definitely not from Target," she added, holding up the patent leather pumps with the bright red soles. I jumped up and down, twirling my dress in my arms like a ridiculous little girl, but I didn't care. I felt happy.

We rimmed my eyes with smoky eyeliner, making them look dark and sexy. I decided to leave my hair down, letting the natural curls run down my back untamed. I slipped into my dress and heels and took a peek in the mirror for the first time.

"Hot damn, I look good," I announced, admiring how the dress fit my body like a glove. The black fabric was cinched and ruched down the center giving me cleavage and curves in all the right spots. Tiny straps held it in place, and as I gave myself a twirl in the mirror, I realized just how short it was. Like, don't-bend-down-for-anything short.

"Ready to give him a heart attack?" Leah asked, looking me up and down.

"Do you think he'll like it?"

"Shit, if he doesn't, there's something seriously wrong with him. Even I want to do you right now."

Leave it to Leah to give it to you straight.

"Okay, let's go."

~Logan~

I had already changed into dark jeans, a black button down shirt and my favorite leather jacket. Just as I was congratulating myself on what a good idea this was and how I couldn't wait to see Clare in that dress I bought her, I heard them coming down the stairs. I turned my head just in time to see her take the last step, and I was instantly aroused, miserable and panicked all at the same time.

"Holy fucking Christ," the words flew out of my mouth in a rush as I fought to breathe.

"Um, is he okay?" Clare asked.

Clare's hand was on her hip and it drew my attention to her ass, which looked...*damn*.

"Oh God, this was a bad idea. Such a dumb idea. You've got to go change," I pleaded.

"What? Why?" she asked, looking herself up and down like there was something wrong. There was nothing wrong. That was the God damn problem. She was absolutely flawless.

"I'm gonna kill every man that looks at you tonight," I threatened, feeling my fists tighten and my teeth clench at the mere thought.

A wide grin spread across her face while she slowly walked over to me, gripping the edges of my jacket. Clare paused a moment to admire my clothing choice, her eyes roaming over the jacket I'd worn especially for her. I knew leather would drive her crazy.

"Well, I guess you're just going to have to control yourself...cause I'm not changing," she said, emphasizing the last part slowly, as she ran her finger down her my chest, causing me to groan.

"This is not going to be fun for me," I muttered as she pulled me toward the door.

I prayed that I could make it through the night without

having to kick anyone's ass.

I weaved my way through the thick crowd, drinks in hand, back to our table in the VIP area of the club. It was a small area, and not very well blocked off from the rest of the club, but this wasn't New York. You were basically paying for the table, and surprisingly, they didn't come cheap. But I would pay anything to make Clare happy, and I wanted this night to be perfect. I had seen her dance around the house with Maddie, and I knew how much she loved it. I couldn't wait to be the one she was dancing with.

As our table came into view, I saw Clare politely trying to decline an invitation to dance from a man who had approached the table. My vision blurred, my pace doubled and by the time I reached the table I was seeing red.

Mine.

Clare noticed me bee-lining it to the table, and her look of relief calmed me a bit, knowing she saw me as her savior.

"Hey, buddy," I said to the jackass macking on my woman, "I'd appreciate you backing off my girlfriend a bit. She doesn't want to dance with you," I assured him, setting down the drinks and inserting myself between the guy and Clare.

"Hey Dickwad, I think the lady can speak for herself," the jackass said.

Dickwad? Who said shit like that? This dude must have had the IQ of a turnip.

"Listen asshole, you've got about five seconds to walk away before I kick your ass and you find yourself waking up in a dark alley, permanently walking lopsided if you know what I mean."

Based on his assumed IQ, I was a little afraid he actually wouldn't get what I was talking about, but his eyes grew wide and he nodded his head, walking quickly away.

"That was really freaking hot, Logan," Clare practically

purred in my ear.

"Yeah?"

"Yeah," she confirmed, her eyes roaming over my body again, making me ache and harden all at the same time.

"We need to dance. Now," I demanded.

She agreed and I lead us to the dance floor. The music was loud, the bass low and vibrating against the walls, and there were bodies everywhere. I found an empty spot near the middle, spinning Clare around so her body was flush against mine. She wrapped her arms around my neck, as my hands found her waist, and we began to dance. Her hips slid against my hands as she moved up and down to the music, grinding her body against me. My hands found her ass, pulling her closer, as my mouth descended on hers.

I kissed her deeper, knowing we were going far beyond what should be done on a public dance floor, but I didn't care. At this point the entire club could be watching and I couldn't stop. At least the men would know she was mine and maybe leave her the fuck alone.

Clare broke our kiss, turning around, so her back was to me while keeping my hands snaked around her. She never stopped dancing, swaying her hips, and grinding her ass against my rock hard cock. She brought her arms back up, pulling my head down to her, completely consumed by the music and lust.

We danced like this, in our own world, for what seemed like forever. Panting, glistening with sweat, Clare leaned in to whisper in my ear. "I'm going to go freshen up in the restroom real quick. I'll be right back."

I escorted her back to the table and she fled to the restroom, leaving me alone, horny and sporting a huge erection.

Fuck this.

I had some unfinished business to attend to. And she had just walked into the ladies restroom.

~Clare~

Just as I had finished drying my hands and checking my makeup, there was a knock on the bathroom door. The line was long, but seriously, I had been in here for two minutes tops. Give a girl a break. I needed a breather. If I hadn't fled the dance floor, I was pretty sure Logan would have tackled me to the floor and started ripping off my clothes. I had taken a step back, as hard as it was, to keep us from being arrested for indecent exposure.

As I opened the door and walked out, I was suddenly pushed back in by a familiar set of hands.

"What the -"

Logan kissed me with the force of a windstorm and I could do nothing but willingly take the brunt of his attack. He locked the door, securing our privacy.

He broke away and looked at me. His eyes were heavy with desire.

"You ran away didn't you? Did you think coming in here would save you?" he asked, his voice softly purring in my ear. His skin was still slick with sweat, and I was surrounded by the scent of him. I wanted nothing more than to strip him bare and lick every inch of rock hard body.

"You're wrong, Clare. Nothing will ever keep me from you. I'll never stop chasing you."

His movements were hurried and frantic as he lifted me up, sat me on the sink counter and spread my legs wide. My dress was pushed up to my waist, as his hands found my center, rubbing me through the thin fabric of my panties.

"Always so ready for me," he murmured before gripping my thong and shredding it with his fingers. He took the now destroyed undergarment and placed it in the side pocket of his coat and then began unlatching his belt. The whole scene had me hovering on the edge, so overcome with need that I could feel my legs shaking in anticipation. Unable to wait, I reached out, pushing Logan's hand out the way so I could take over the task of undressing him. I wanted to see him, touch him, and feel him buried deep inside me.

Logan's eyes darkened as he watched my hands undo the button of his jeans, pull down the zipper and let his hard length spring free. As I wrapped my hand around its silky smooth perfection, Logan groaned in response.

Spreading me further, he stepped in between my legs, pressing his body against mine, rubbing the head of his cock against my core, making me moan

"Tell me what you want Clare. I want to hear you say it," he demanded.

"Fuck me," I whispered the words he wanted to hear, and he went wild, burying himself in me with one powerful thrust. Pulling back, he drove in again harder, rattling me against the mirror. It was rough, primitive and God damn perfect. He thrust hard and fast, and I took it all, climbing closer and closer to ecstasy.

"You're mine," he growled, as I felt myself let go, screaming my release in tandem with Logan's.

"I'm yours," I answered, looking into his eyes, making sure he understood.

"I'm yours, Logan."

Chapter Thirteen

~Clare~

"Hello?" I answered, attempting to juggle the phone in one hand and the thermometer in the other.

"Hey you," Logan's melodic voice filled the airwaves between us, making me smile and blush despite the chaos surrounding me. It had been a week since our bathroom escapade. I still can't believe I had sex in a public bathroom! The time we spent at the club wasn't nearly enough to put out the fire we'd created, and we spent the entire night at Logan's making love. I did eventually get the chance to lick every inch of his delectable body, and it was divine.

"Hey, how was your day?" I asked as I inserted the electric thermometer in Maddie's ear and began the ten-second wait that would tell me whether or not I would need to take her to the doctor's office. Maybe I could just take her to Logan's, I thought jokingly.

"Good," he answered. "Went to work. Did the usual hero-type stuff. Saving lives, kicking ass. Whatever." I rolled my eyes in laughter.

"I was about to go for a run, but I wanted to see what time you wanted me to pick you up tonight?" he asked.

He was so happy and I was going to completely ruin his mood.

"I have to cancel. Maddie's sick," I apologized as I shifted Maddie in my arms on the sofa. She curled into my arms, readjusting herself into a ball as I tried to keep the thermometer steady.

"She's sick? Is she okay? What are her symptoms?" he rattled off question after question, humor gone and now in full doctor mode. Realizing the thermometer had already beeped, I pulled it out of her ear, looking at the results. Good. No fever.

"Nothing serious. She's just complaining of an upset stomach and won't eat. She's been lethargic all day. Her temperature is normal so it's not major. But I still better stay home with her. I'm so sorry I'm canceling on you."

"You have nothing to apologize for," Logan assured me. "Maddie takes priority over everything. I wouldn't have it any other way. We'll have hundreds of other evenings to spend together, but tonight Maddie needs you. Take care of my princess," he requested before hanging up.

I snuggled us into the couch with a blanket as Maddie watched Dora the Explorer. I seriously hated that cartoon. I really believed it was created to slowly whittle away the brains of parents everywhere. I did my best to tune it out as I ran my fingers through my daughter's ginger colored curls.

Logan had planned on taking me to the movies tonight. It was something we had yet to do. We had already done so much together including going on hikes and visiting museums. We had been to countless restaurants and even taken Maddie to a movie, but we had never gone by ourselves. I couldn't wait to snuggle up with him in that dark theater as we watched a movie and shared a cherry coke. It sounded cliché and stupid, but it was one of those classic things you did as a couple, and I wanted to share it with him.

But Maddie needed me, and I was a mother first. She was my constant and one of the only reasons I was able to come back after the grief of Ethan's death threatened to swallow me whole. If I had been alone, and her precious life hadn't been there depending on me to get up every day, I probably would have never truly recovered. In a way, I owed that tiny four-year old my life. She had saved me from myself, forcing me to pick up the pieces and be a stronger person than I would have been capable of otherwise.

"I'm sorry you didn't get to go on your play date with Logan, Mommy," Maddie murmured as she watched her cartoon. I found it ridiculously adorable that she called them play dates.

"It's okay, baby. We'll go on another one later," I assured her.

"Mommy?" she asked, her inquisitive brown eyes finding mine.

"Yeah, baby?"

"Do you think Daddy would like Logan?"

Just when I thought I had her completely figured out, she pulled the rug out from under me. How could someone so small have such big thoughts swimming around in her head? And how did I answer that? Did I think Ethan would like the man I had fallen in love with? Would he approve? Most days I thought he would, when I felt like maybe he was the one who sent Logan to me in the first place. But there were still moments, in all honesty, when I felt guilty. When I would look down at the picture of the two of us I still had sitting on my nightstand, and wonder if he was looking down on me screaming because I was with another man.

"What do you think, baby?" I asked, taking the coward's way out by not answering.

"I think Daddy would be happy Logan's here. He makes everything better."

I was stunned. Leave it to a child to take something that seemed so complicated and involved and reduce it to two sentences.

Plain and simple.

Logan *did* make everything better. Of course Ethan would be happy me, for that very reason alone. My daughter was a genius.

As I continued to play with her hair, contemplating my newest epiphany, our doorbell rang. Sliding myself out from under Maddie's sprawled out body, I ran to the door wondering what type of cookie or popcorn tin I was going to be talked into now.

"Logan?" I cried, completely shocked as I opened the door.

His arms were full of grocery bags, boxes of pizza and two bouquets of flowers.

"I missed my girls," he said with a shrug.

Seeing him there, I couldn't help myself. I launched myself toward his arms, completely overcome by emotions. Forgetting that he was carrying about fifty pounds of groceries and take-out, I was stopped short by the many obstacles separating us. Laughing as he noticed my frustration, he dropped the bags he was carrying and grabbed me around the waist, pulling me tight.

"Thank you," I said.

"Like I said, I missed you, and I had to see Maddie. The thought of her not feeling well was killing me," he admitted.

"I would think you'd be used to that by now Dr. Matthews," I teased.

Leaning his forehead against mine, he said, "I know, but Maddie's different. I can't be clinical with her."

Of course he couldn't. He loved her. He loved us both. The words hadn't been said, but I felt them. I could see the love he had for Maddie every time he picked her up, cradling her like she was the most precious thing in the world. I knew he loved me every time he looked at me, and every time we made love, branding me as his own. But the word "love" wasn't something he said before, and I knew for a man who believed he was essentially broken, it would take time.

"Come on, let's go inside so I can check on my patient," he suggested before placing a kiss on my cheek.

I helped him with the bags that are strewn on the front

stoop, giving myself a little peek to see what goodies he had brought. I saw boxes of Kleenex, Tylenol, movies, and popcorn.

"Hey, is there any chocolate in here?" I asked as we made our way inside.

"Of course. Do you think I'd show up without chocolate?" The man was well trained.

Maddie saw us round the corner into the family room, on our way to the kitchen, and yelled "Logan!" mustering up as much excitement as she could from the couch.

"Hey princess, how ya feeling?" he asked, dropping his bags on the counter and moving toward Maddie.

"My tummy hurts," she complained. She really did sound pitiful.

"Well we can't have that, can we?" Logan said.

I pulled down some plates and absently watched him with Maddie as he looked at her throat and felt her tummy, causing her to softly giggle. He finished up his mini exam, covering her with a blanket and returning to the kitchen.

"Well, I don't think I discovered anything more than you did. It's probably a stomach bug. We just need to get her to drink water and maybe chew on some crackers," he said, sounding very doctor-ish. It was kind of hot. He just needed a pair of scrubs.

I helped him unpack the groceries, touched by his thoughtfulness, when I notice the Band-Aid at the crook of his arm.

"What's this?" I asked, grabbing his arm so I could have a closer inspection.

"Oh, nothing. Had to get blood work," he said dismissively.

The blood drained from my face, and I felt weak. He said it was nothing, right? So I should have calmed down, but I couldn't. Visions of blood tests and chemo flashed through my memory and I struggled to stay upright.

"Whoa there...Babe, you okay?" his voice filled with concern.

I nodded absently, but he didn't believe me for a second, grabbing my hand to sit me down at the kitchen table. Kneeling down on the tiled floor, he took my hand in his, gently rubbing with his thumb.

"Hey, look at me," he urged gently as my eyes slowly locked with his.

"I had a physical. Just standard blood tests. I'm not going anywhere, Clare. Okay?"

I nodded again, letting a tear escape down my cheek. I was being ridiculous. But the thought of losing him, going through that again. I didn't think I could do it.

He pulled me into a tight hug, wrapping his arms around my back, enveloping me in warmth.

"Even doctors have to visit the doctor's office every once in a while," he said, trying to lighten the mood. It seemed to work, because I fired back with, "Oh yeah, you can't give yourself a physical? I'm pretty sure you could do that 'turn and cough' thing pretty well solo."

He laughed against my ear as we stood and headed back to the kitchen. He was fine and everything was going to be okay, I assured myself.

We got our pizza, which wasn't nearly as good as the pizza Logan had made, and joined Maddie in the family room. Thankfully, I was able to talk her out of more Dora, and we watched a Disney movie instead. Cuddled up on the couch together, with Maddie resting between us, I could see it.

The three of us, like this, forever.

But it was a conversation we had never had. He said I was his and he would always be here, but was he ready to be a father? I knew he loved Maddie, but becoming a father to her was different. Could I ask that of him? I knew what I wanted, and it was him. I could only hope he wanted us, and everything that came with us.

Maddie fell asleep and Logan helped carry her upstairs to her room. We both tucked her in, giving her kisses goodnight. Logan began to head back for the stairs, and I grabbed his hand, stopping him.

"Stay. Please, Logan."

"Always," he vowed, before following me to the bedroom.

I shut the door, locking it, making sure I heard the click before I turned. Giving myself a few moments to stand there, I admired the man before me. Sometimes I couldn't help but stare. He was like a magnet pulling me in, and I was helpless to stop. He was the perfect combination of pure sin and superhero, and I wanted all of him.

Right now.

"Clare, you've got to stop looking at me like that," he groaned.

"Why?" I asked, letting my hips sway as I sauntered toward him. Finally reaching my object of desire, I reached out, running my hands up and down the blue t-shirt that covered his perfectly formed chest.

"Because Maddie's down the hall and I can only handle so much before I throw you on the bed and take you anyway."

What was this? Take me anyway? I don't know about him, but sex was definitely in my plans for the evening. Oh. I understood.

"You're scared to have sex with Maddie in the house, aren't you?" I couldn't help but grin. Seeing him squirm was pretty damn funny.

"Well, that would definitely be a first for me," he agreed.

Who knew a full grown man would be so freaked out about having sex in the same house as a child. It's not like she was *in* the room with us.

"Logan?" I whispered.

"Yeah?"

"Do you plan on living with me? Ever?" I asked, hoping and praying I didn't just step over a line trying to make a point.

"Dear God, I hope so," he said like a prayer.

I gave myself a second, or five to let that sink in, making sure I remembered those words forever.

"And exactly how did you foresee this future of ours? Are we just going to practice abstinence whenever Maddie's in the house? For the next fourteen years?"

His eyes widened, causing me to laugh.

"What if she wakes up? I mean, we're not exactly quiet," he argued, clearly warming to the idea.

My hands moved to the edge of my tank top, lifting it over my head, and exposing my purple satin bra. His eyes flared with heat, and I knew he wasn't thinking about anything else but me now.

"Then we'll just have to learn to be silent, won't we?" I said before I pushed him onto the bed to teach him the art of quiet lovemaking.

~Logan~

I woke in the middle of the night to Maddie calling out for me. My eyes tried to focus in the darkened room as she poked at my head. Again. Sleep still tugged at my every thought making my movements jerky and lethargic. Suddenly remembering the hours of lovemaking Clare and I had spent before going to sleep, I ran my hands down my body, exhaling in relief that I had the forethought to throw on a pair of boxers and shirt before collapsing into bed.

"Maddie? You okay princess?" I asked as I pulled her toward me, noticing right away the immense heat radiating off her body.

"I don't feel very good," she said, wrapping her arms around my neck.

I gathered her into my lap, exhaling as I let this moment sink in, because it was a big one. She had come to me. She needed someone and she chose me. I don't know what it was like to be a father, to watch your child grow in your wife's belly, be born, and hold her in your arms for the first time. It wasn't a life I had ever pictured for myself. But I did know what it was like to hold Maddie in my arms, to feel her head rest on my shoulder when she was sleepy, to see the joy in her face when we danced. She may not be mine by birth, but I would give up everything I had to be her father. To belong to her, to them both.

"Come on princess, let's go downstairs so we won't wake your Mommy," I said, before picking her up and heading downstairs for the kitchen. Clare had earned the sleep, and I would gladly stay up the rest of the night if needed. But that wasn't why I was doing this. Seeing Maddie in the darkness tonight, as she reached for me, her body sick and frail. I wasn't ready to give her up yet. She came to me, and I wanted to be her healer and protector. I would let Clare take over in the morning when I had to leave for work, but for now, I needed a night taking care of the little girl who had stolen a piece of my heart.

I took Maddie's temp which was high, as expected. She sleepily took the medicine I gave, and drank some of the water I put in her Dora Sippy cup, but she was having a difficult time settling. I put on a movie, and we burrowed ourselves under a blanket while I began running my fingers through her hair. It was something I'd seen Clare do on numerous occasions, and it always seemed to soothe her. About fifteen minutes later, her eyes fluttered, and eventually closed, and she fell asleep in my arms.

I purposely remained awake a while longer, watching the breath move in and out of her body through her rose colored lips. It's amazing how life can change on you in an instant. A few months ago, I was afraid of my own emotions, and I protected myself with a thick layer of ice. I pushed away the few people in my life who actually loved me, scared that the love I felt for them was a long standing lie as well. I had convinced myself that someone who grows up without knowing love was incapable of giving it. It was the reason why I couldn't love Melanie, the reason I had ruined our marriage. And so I gave up. If I didn't know how to love, why bother? Why bother with any of it?

And then I walked into an exam room and met two redheads that took my bitter, pathetic excuse for a life and turned it upside down. I was so afraid that I'd never be able to love anyone, and here I was, holding a child I desperately wanted to call my own and upstairs was a woman I would give my life for.

Turns out I was always capable of love, I just hadn't found it yet.

"Hey," Clare's sleepy voice wafted in as she entered the

family room and sat next to me on the couch.

"Hey." I answered back, "She woke me. Said she didn't feel good, so I took her down here. I hope you don't mind."

She smiled, looking at Maddie in my arms, as she placed her own hand over mine and we begin to stroke Maddie's hair together. "It's perfect. Seeing you there with her, it's perfect," she whispered.

"I love you." I told her without hesitation, saying the words I've been holding inside of me for far too long, "I've loved you Clare, every minute of every day, since the very first day."

A single tear escaped down Clare's cheek before I heard the single greatest words of my life.

"I love you, too. Oh God, I love you too, Logan," she said, her voice raw and heavy with emotion.

I pulled her toward me, kissing her gently, making sure not to wake Maddie who was still asleep in my arms. We kissed, hugged and cried for hours as we held Maddie throughout the night. Exactly like a family would do, because that's what we were now, a family. After years of being ignored in my own family, I had found one of my own. I no longer needed anyone else, as long as I had Clare and Maddie in my life.

Chapter Fourteen

~Clare~

"This is where we're supposed to be?" Logan asked as the cab pulled up to the curb. I looked at the hotel, admiring its beautiful exterior, complete with historic brickwork and elegant overhang.

"What's wrong with it? It's stunning," I said as I helped Maddie out of the bright yellow cab.

"Yes, it is. It's also subdued and understated," he said with a frown. "Are you sure we're at the right place?" He checked the address again and shrugged. He handed the cab driver several twenties causing the man to leap from his seat to help with our luggage.

The three of us waited on the New York street corner while the cabbie and valet unloaded our luggage. I looked down the busy street as cars zoomed by and peopled hurried along. New York was a different world. Seeing it now, I wondered how Logan survived the slow paced life of Virginia after living here. Looking over at him now, he was still busy staring at the hotel like it was a Rubix Cube he couldn't solve.

"You okay?" I asked.

"Yeah, I guess. This just isn't the place I would have envisioned. My mom is a certain type of woman," he chose his words carefully.

"We'll call her extravagant. She marries for money, and when the man she married stops giving her money, she moves on. Her last wedding was in Paris. Everyone was flown in for the week long affair, and it ended up costing her husband over a million dollars. They were married about a year."

My jaw dropped to the floor. Who spent that kind of money on a wedding? I had that much sitting in the bank from Ethan's life insurance and I was hoping to make it last a lifetime, but Logan's mom had spent that and more for a wedding ceremony that rivaled Kim Kardashian's.

"I guess we'll never find out if we don't go in, huh?" I picked up Maddie, who had been bouncing up and down gabbing about her first plane trip and entered the lobby. She had quieted down a bit, taking in the sights of New York as we drove here from the airport. It was adorable to see her tiny nose glued to the window of the cab as she tried to see the tops of the skyscrapers.

The lobby of the hotel was breathtaking, and everything you would expect from a historic New York hotel. Majestic marble floors led to a grand mahogany staircase. There were plush sofas and chairs grouped together making intimate seating arrangements. People wandered about reading and drinking coffee, speaking in just about every language known to man.

Logan went to the desk and checked us into our suite.

Once the valet escorted us to the elevator, I asked, "Is it weird to be back?"

"No," he answered.

"No? Why?" I asked.

He shrugged, saying, "I have you and Maddie with me. I'm here, making new memories with you and that erases all the bad."

I grasped his hand in mine, feeling the warmth seep into my skin. Sometimes I had to touch him just to make sure he was real and wasn't a figment of my imagination. Why the universe had decided I was lucky enough to get this second chance, I would never know, but I wasn't letting it go.

Exiting the elevator, the valet opened our suite and Maddie

raced inside to one of the two bedrooms, immediately jumping up and down on the pristinely made bed.

"I guess that one is hers," I laughed.

"I think they're both fairly equal, so it doesn't really matter. Besides, all I need is a bed...and you." His voice suddenly became sexier and lower, taking on a rougher quality. I called it his "sex voice" and it was my favorite of all the different variations of his voice.

Logan had gotten over his fear of being intimate in the same house as Maddie very quickly. After Maddie's bout with the stomach flu, he had spent every night with us and it had been pure bliss. Seeing him walk through the door after finishing his shift at the hospital, and waking up next to him made me never want to see him go. Maddie loved having him around. I secretly asked myself if we were moving too fast, having only dated for a few months, but it felt right. He fit in our world perfectly and we fit in his.

Ethan still filled my thoughts, as he always would. One night while Logan was working a late shift, I found myself sitting on my bed holding the letter he left behind. I smoothed my hands over its frayed edges, like I had done so many times before, staring at the words he'd written.

I had done the impossible. I had fallen in love. I'd been given a second chance at happiness, and I was diving in, headfirst. I placed my trembling hand on the seal, ready to break it and finally read what my late husband had written so many years earlier. I had so many sleepless nights wondering what he had written on those pages, and I was finally going to take the leap. At the very last second, as my breath was coming in short staccato beats in and out of my lungs, I threw the letter back into my night stand.

I was happy for the first time in years. What if there was something in this letter that changed that? I always thought "When You're Ready" had something to do with moving on, but what if it didn't? What if something in that letter changed the way I felt about Logan?

Looking back on that night, I felt angry. I had second guessed myself and made stupid excuses for my cowardice. I knew Ethan and I knew in the very depth of my soul that there was nothing in that letter but love. I'd made stupid excuses up for my inability to open that letter. I wasn't ready. Still. When would I be ready? I had fallen in love with another man for God's sake! I even had the strength to remove my wedding ring, tucking it away in my jewelry box to give to Maddie one day. But I couldn't open that letter. Even now, feeling the heat of Logan's body as he pulled me into his arms, I still didn't know if I would ever have the courage to open it.

A knock at the door interrupted my thoughts. Logan kissed me on the forehead before walking over to greet our mystery visitor. We weren't expected until the rehearsal dinner in a few more hours, so I had no idea who this could be.

"Mother?" I heard a surprised Logan say as he pulled the door open, revealing a beautiful middle-aged woman wearing a pretty summer dress and matching sweater. She looked nothing like what I would have pictured, and based on Logan's reaction, I gathered it was a new look.

"Hi, Logan. I'm so glad you're here," she said sincerely before pulling him into her arms.

A stunned and very stiff Logan returned the hug briefly, taking a step back toward me to grab my hand, as if he needed the contact to keep him grounded.

I had never met the woman, but I think this new look and the way she was acting had completely shifted Logan's entire view of his mother. He looked lost and confused, and for once, I didn't know how to help him because I was just as confused as he was.

"Are you going to introduce me?" she asked, looking down at our joined hands.

"Of course, how rude of me. Mother, this is Clare Murray. Clare, this is my mother, Cecile Carrington," he said formally.

I stepped forward offering my hand, but she pulled me into her arms as well.

"Just call me Cece. The last name is going to change tomorrow anyway," she insisted, letting me go so I could return to Logan.

"Who's that, Mommy?" I heard Maddie say as she came to stand between Logan and me, her favorite spot nowadays.

"This is Logan's Mom, Cece," I said.

"Hi Cece. I like your name," Maddie said, taking a step toward the woman. There wasn't a shy bone in that kid.

Cece bent down so she was at the same level as Maddie, her eyes full of excitement as she looked at my daughter.

"Well I like yours too, pumpkin. I love your shirt, do you dance?" she asked, admiring Maddie's pink shirt with ballerina frog on it that Logan had bought her.

"Yep. Mommy takes me to lessons. She says I'm a natural," Maddie answered proudly, puffing out her chest to show off her shirt.

"Well, I was just in the gift shop downstairs, and saw the cutest ballerina necklace. If your Mommy says it's okay, do you want me to show you?"

"Can I Mommy, please?" Maddie begged, bouncing up and down. Logan gave me a look that said the decision was all mine.

"Of course, baby. But, best manners okay? Cece's in charge," I instructed.

"Okay Mommy!"

"I'll bring her right back. Just thought you two might enjoy a few minutes alone," Cece said before scooping Maddie up in her arms and heading out the door. I could hear them chatting down the hallway and I found myself thinking Cece would make a wonderful Grandmother, which was odd considering the type of mother I knew she was.

"You okay?" I asked Logan as he stared out the picture window down at the busy street below, his body tight and rigid. He was so deep in thought, I could practically see them coming off of him in waves.

"That was not my Mother," his voice was distant, as if he was still processing the last few minutes.

Closing the distance between us, I wrapped my arms around him, resting my head against his broad back, breathing in his unique scent.

"Talk to me Logan. I need to understand."

"That woman you just met was warm and inviting. She was everything I wanted in a mother as a child, but never had. The mother I know is obsessed with material possessions and making sure she has someone around to buy them for her. She would have never allowed anyone to call her Cece. She was always Cecile. She gave up parental rights to my father when they divorced and I barely saw her after that. My sister and mother were just people I visited once a year when my father had nowhere else to send me," he snarled.

"Something's obviously changed. She's different. Maybe she's trying to make amends," I offered as an explanation.

"I don't know, but I have a hard time trusting this new version of her. So many years of neglect, how do I forgive that?" he said quietly, all the energy draining out of him.

"Just take it one breath at a time, Logan. That's all you can do."

The rehearsal dinner was lovely, and after being introduced, I was quickly becoming a fan of Cece's fiancé, Robert. He was a banker, but although he was very well to do by most standards, he was by no means wealthy. He was, however, very handsome. He had dark features and piercing green eyes; he was the perfect example of what age did to good-looking men. It made them even finer, like a well-aged wine. It gave me a little thrill, thinking of Logan, and what he would look like in ten, twenty or even thirty years. Robert seemed very down to earth. He carried himself well, giving the impression that he was well educated, but he was very easy to talk to and made everyone in the room feel at ease.

The wedding was scheduled for tomorrow afternoon in the hotel's ballroom. The guest list was small, only family and a few friends would be in attendance. The venue was beautiful, something I would have chosen actually, but it was peanuts in comparison to Cece's previous nuptials.

After the food was cleared, the few guest mingled about, everyone stopping to congratulate the happy couple. And they did look truly happy. As I sat at the table solo, while Logan took Maddie on a walk around the lobby, his mother sat next to me.

"Hello, dear. Are you having a good time?" she asked, trying to making small talk.

"Oh yes, thank you. Everything is lovely," I answered politely.

"I wanted to thank you for getting him here. I know he wouldn't have come otherwise."

I didn't know what to say. Luckily I didn't get the chance to, because she continued.

"I've been a terrible mother. Actually I've been a terrible human being. I don't know if he'll ever forgive me for all the sins I've committed against him, and I likely don't deserve it. But I'm going to spend the rest of the life I have left trying to make up for it," she confessed.

God, I hope this woman was being truthful. I wanted so badly to believe her.

"If you don't mind me asking, what changed?" I asked, hoping she wasn't offended by my boldness.

"You can ask me anything Clare. I may not know my son

well, but I can see the love he has for you and your daughter. I want to be part of your lives, and I'm hoping you can help with that. As for the reason for my drastic life change? Well, it's the reason we do many things in life. Love," she answered simply.

"Robert?" I asked.

"Yes," she said with a smile, "I met Robert after my divorce to Mr. Carrington had just been finalized. I was at a charity event doing my normal thing, showing off my latest designer gown, and flashing the many layers of jewelry I had on display for the evening. All those things I had to have, it was like a disease," she shook her head in obvious disgust.

"While at the bar refilling my drink, I met a man. Robert. He was ridiculously handsome, and I thought I'd have him eating out of the palm of my hand by the end of the evening. But he didn't fall for any of my usual tricks. Instead, he handed me a business card and said if I wanted to go on a date with him, I'd have to agree to get dirty. And then he walked away. Our first date was a hike. I was miserable the entire way, but I'd never done anything like it. When we returned the car, I was covered in bruises and dried dirt, but I felt amazing. I accomplished something and it didn't require anything but me."

"He changed you," I said, when she paused.

"Well, I'd like to say I changed myself. He just helped. He taught me there was more to life, more to marriage than a bank account and a walk-in closet. When we moved in together, I sold almost everything I owned, and then donated the money to charity. It was the most selfless thing I'd ever done."

She really had changed.

"Wow, Cece...that's amazing."

"Don't give me too much credit," she laughed, "I still buy designer jeans and I'm not planning on going to Africa to live in a hut, but I'm learning to live with less and look beyond myself. And for the first time since Logan's father, I'm marrying for love."

"Love has a way of completely altering your life, doesn't it?" I said, watching as Logan held Maddie on his shoulders and they walked back into the dining room.

"Yes it does, my dear. Yes, it does."

~Logan~

I had to admit, she looked beautiful tonight. I had never been to any of my mother's other weddings, always finding excuses for why I couldn't be there. She'd never been there for me, so why should I put forth the effort? But seeing her tonight on the dance floor with her new husband I felt the last of my icy layers beginning to melt.

When the three of us had returned to our suite last night, I asked Clare what she and my mother had been talking about for so long. She smiled wistfully and simply said, "Love." She then proceeded to tell me about a woman I didn't know, a completely different mother, and I found myself listening to every word. Could a person really change that much? I looked at Clare, remembering the man I was mere months earlier, and thought *yes*.

Love could do anything.

"They look happy, don't they?" Clare said, sliding down in the seat next to me, a second slice of cake in hand.

"You know, I think they have a one slice per guest max on the cake," I teased.

"Well then you should have given me yours," she fired back. Realizing she left with Maddie, and came back alone, I asked "Where's princess?"

"She met Robert's mother at the dessert table and the woman fell victim to Maddie's charm. They're over there," she pointed to the corner of the dance floor where Maddie was twirling around in her pink sparkly dress while Mrs. Erikson clapped from the sidelines. It was an adorable sight, and reaffirmed my belief that Maddie's joy was the most infectious thing in the world.

As I was admiring Maddie's performance, I saw Robert, my new father-in-law, approach our table.

"Logan, would you mind if I stole your lady for a dance?" he asked, holding out his hand to Clare. She looked over at me, batting her eyelashes with a sly grin, waiting for my answer.

Chuckling, I said, "I don't know, Robert. Can I trust you?"

"I'll be the epitome of a gentleman, I assure you," he promised before taking Clare's hand and escorting her to the dance floor. She graciously followed, her coral gown swishing behind her as she took his lead, looking beautiful and elegant.

"She's lovely, Logan," my mother said, taking the empty seat Clare had just vacated.

"I know," I answered curtly, cursing myself for my rudeness. I knew she was trying, but a lifetime of hurt was a difficult thing to get over. Growing up with my father was hell, and I spent numerous nights staring out the window as a child wondering what I did wrong to make her leave, and how I could fix it.

"I'm sorry, I know you're trying," I said as an apology.

"You have nothing to apologize for, Logan. I have no right to ask you to forgive me. It doesn't mean I'm not going to try. I want to be in your life, in their lives," she said, motioning to Clare and Maddie.

I nodded, unsure of what to say.

"You really love her, don't you?" she asked, looking at me as I watched Clare dance with Robert.

"With everything I am," I answered with conviction.

She smiled, fiddling with the new ring on her left hand, twisting and twirling it around her finger.

"When are you going to ask her?"

"As soon as we get home. I've had the ring for weeks,

carrying it around in my pocket, waiting for the right moment," I confessed.

I hadn't told anyone about the ring, not even Colin.

Clare and I had been out shopping one afternoon and stopped at an upscale antique store. We roamed around, looking at furniture, picture frames and artwork. I loved watching Clare in her element. She loved touching and connecting with anything historic and always ended up chatting with the store keeper about half a dozen pieces. While Clare looked at a nineteenth century armoire, I wandered over to the jewelry case below the register and that's when I saw it. A flawless three carat oval cut diamond, surrounded by at least another dozen smaller glittery white stones, set in platinum. It was vintage, probably nearing a hundred years old and had recently been purchased from an estate sale. I knew it was Clare's the moment I saw it. The second I dropped her off that night, I rushed back to the store, buying it on the spot.

"You're nothing like your father," my mother said gently, placing her hand on mine. I didn't know if she was trying to convince me or herself.

"Is that why you left me with him?" I needed to know. I needed to know how a mother could give up her only son and never look back. It had haunted me my entire life, and I needed closure from this woman.

"Yes," she said quietly, letting out a long breath, as if the confession has just released twenty-seven years of tension and guilt from her body.

"I loved your father. He was harsh and cold to the rest of the world, but never with me. I never knew why. I don't know, maybe he saw me as some sort of exotic flower," she laughed harshly. "I came from new money and he came from old. My parents were eccentric, and his were refined. I always thought our differences would keep our love new and alive, but in the end, it destroyed us."

"You embarrassed his precious image," I said plainly. I knew that much. Although I didn't know why.

"Ah ,yes," she said, "Something you've learned firsthand. I thought he'd stand by me, but no. He sent me away, like a discarded piece of trash." The hurt was still evident on her face, even after nearly three decades.

"What happened?"

Taking a deep breath, she told me the story of her fall from grace.

"We were members of a country club. Very upscale, very affluent. Your father's still a member if I've heard correctly." I nodded. I knew the club she was talking about. It was a club for old money, a term used for people who came from wealth. My father had made his own money, but he had a head start from his own father, the grandson of an oil tycoon. Our family's money went back generations.

"I was there for a charity meeting with all the other wives. I hated those meetings. In fact, I hated everything about that club. I was judged the minute I walked in just because I didn't have the right last name. I excused myself to head to the ladies room, and was approached by one of the valets. He was around my age, working the club on his summer break from law school. He was very handsome, but I was not interested. Unlike many of the other women in the club, I was not helping myself to the staff," she said defensively.

From what I had observed at the club, they still did. Apparently it could be a very lucrative career for the right person. I still remember Declan telling stories of the waiters being able to fund an entire year of tuition in one summer.

"He cornered me, saying I was a tease and a flirt. He pushed me up against a wall, pinning my hands so I couldn't get free. Around that time, the women from my table walked by. They of course assumed the worse of me, and the rumors started. I tried to explain, but it was too late."

If I hadn't already hated the man, I would now.

"So why did you leave me with him?" I asked.

"You were only five, but you were the exact replica of him. I could see you becoming him. You worshiped him, did everything he asked, always trying to make him proud. If I had been a better woman, I would have pulled you out of that home and never looked back. But I was weak, heartbroken and stupid. I saw a small version of the man who'd just broken me, and I ran," she confessed.

I looked out onto the dance floor, Clare and Robert's dance long since over. I think she was staying away on purpose, giving me some time with my mother. Time I needed to process everything I had just been told.

"But you took Eva. You left me and took Eva," I emphasized, trying to understand why I was left to be raised by a heartless monster. That was something I never understood. I was the one she left behind. My sister was the chosen one, and I was the one forgotten.

Tears trailing down her cheeks, she said, "I know. She was so young, only two. And I figured if I could save one of you, maybe I'd be redeemed for leaving the other behind. Unfortunately, I was probably the worst type of person to raise a child. Eva is the exact replica of me, before Robert."

It had been years since I had seen my sister. The last time was her college graduation. She'd barely made the grades for the diploma and blew every dime my father gave her less than a week after it hit her account. I doubted much had changed.

"I owe both of you so many apologies. But it warms my heart to see you happy finally. Don't wait too long, Logan. You never know what life is going to throw at you. Ask that woman to marry you and start your life."

I nodded, agreeing with her for maybe the first time in my life. I was not going to wait any longer. The second the plane touched down and we had a second alone, I was going to ask

Clare to marry me. We had an entire life to plan, and I didn't want to spend another second without her as my wife.

The evening wore on and Maddie's energy level bombed, so we said our goodbyes and congratulations to my mother and Robert, knowing we wouldn't see them again. They were leaving first thing in the morning for their honeymoon in Hawaii. I smiled thinking of our vacation plans coming up in August. We were taking Maddie to St. Thomas for her birthday. She didn't know and we weren't going to tell her until the morning we left. I couldn't wait to see her face. I also couldn't wait to spend an entire week with Clare on a secluded beach, seeing her beautiful body in a bikini...or not.

"Do you want me to take her?" I asked Clare as we headed for the elevator in the hotel lobby. Maddie was draped over her, arms wrapped tightly around her neck and completely asleep.

"No, it's okay. I've got her. She was the life of the party, wasn't she?" Clare said, laughing.

"Yeah, she was," I chuckled, completely happy and contented.

Just then, I saw a familiar looking blonde headed our way, coming from one of the other larger ballrooms.

Fuck.

Maybe she wouldn't see us.

"Logan!"

"Rachel," I said calmly, turning to greet her, "So nice to see you." I leaned into Clare, placing my hand on the small of her back, hoping Rachel got the hint to go the fuck away. She apparently didn't, because she continued.

"You too. It's been ages! I've missed you. Have you moved back?" she asked as her eyes inquisitively lingered over Clare and Maddie before returning back to me. She looked exactly the same as she did the last time I saw her. Same fake blonde hair, same fake smile.

"Uh no. Just visiting. My mother was married today, and we were just here for the wedding. This is my girlfriend Clare, and her daughter Maddie," I said.

Dear God, can we please leave now?

"Clare, this is Rachel. She and I used to work together." Clare gave a cursory nod and Rachel did the same, before saying with a wink, "Wow, didn't take you for the monogamous type Logan."

This woman was relentless. What had I seen in her? Oh right, nothing.

"Yes, well I am. Very. We need to get Maddie upstairs. It was nice seeing you."

What I wanted to say was "Go the fuck away," but I opted the high road, hoping for a quick exit.

"You too, Logan. The hospital's not the same without you. If you ever want to come back, just let me know. You'll always have a job ready and waiting for you," she purred. I'd never heard a job offer dripping with so much sex before, and if it hadn't been obvious that we'd slept together, it was now.

Tension and anger rolled off of Clare in waves as we entered the elevator.

"Clare, I..." I stuttered, trying to find the words to explain.

"Don't. Just don't. I'm not ready yet."

The elevator stopped at our floor. We walked in silence to our suite. I unlocked the door and Clare disappeared, taking Maddie to her room, while I collapsed on the sofa, wondering how much my past was going to fuck this up.

Minutes, hours, days went by before she came out of the bedroom door. She was still dressed in the coral strapless gown she had worn to the wedding. She looked like a goddess come to life. Cautiously, she sat down next to me, tucking her feet underneath her as she smoothed out her skirt.

"I'm sorry," she whispered.

"Wait, what? Why are you apologizing to me?" I asked,

stunned. It hadn't been her past walking around eye-fucking her in the hotel lobby. And if it had, the asshat would have left with a broken nose.

"When I fell in love with you," she started, "I accepted all of you, including your past. I refuse to let my jealousy over some hussy doctor or anyone else get in the way of our happiness."

"You were jealous?" I asked, astonished.

She snorted, saying, "Jesus, Logan. She was practically purring, like she was reliving the entire event right there in the lobby. Damn right I was jealous. I wanted to scratch her eyeballs out."

I couldn't help it. I laughed, feeling so relieved she's wasn't storming out the door.

"You're vicious, you know that right?"

"Don't laugh at me," she pouted, "Besides, if the tables had been reversed and that had been my casual fuck we'd run into, how would you have reacted?"

I instantly saw red. My fists tightened, and my breath grew rapid. Just the thought of seeing another man, knowing he had touched Clare, seen Clare....

"Exactly," she said. "See? I was quite reserved."

"I don't want to talk about this anymore," I stated. I was done with talking about our pasts, the many mistakes I made, and a lifetime of regrets. I wanted Clare and Maddie, and nothing else.

"Really?" she grinned," 'cause I think I would really like to continue this conversation. It's titilating"

"Nope, sorry. We're done talking for the evening." I announced right before I stood, pulling her from the couch and swinging her up in my arms with my intention set on the bedroom.

"Put me down! Why do you insist on carrying me everywhere?" she laughed, throwing her arms around my neck.

"I thought it would have been obvious by now," I answered, "I'm not whole without you in my arms."

Without warning, she pulled my head down, kissing me hard, as I stumbled in the doorway to our room. Struggling to stay upright as we devoured each other, I entered the dimly lit room, setting her down near the middle. We continued our frantic kiss as her body slowly slid down mine.

"You know, I never had a chance to dance with you tonight," I said, pulling back to whisper in her ear.

"We don't exactly have the best track record when it comes to dancing in a public place," she laughed softly.

"Ah, but we're not in public now, are we?"

"No, we're not. But we don't have any music," she pointed out as I wrapped my arms around her and began to move us back and forth.

"Who needs music?"

Our bodies swayed as I led us in an intimate waltz.

Ever so slowly, my hand found the zipper of her strapless dress, pulling it down inch by inch until the fabric pooled to the floor in a billowing heap. Clare was left wearing nothing but coral panties and a matching strapless bra. She looked radiant, and I didn't think I would ever grow tired of seeing her body, touching her skin, or feeling her writhe below me. Tucking my fingers under the waistband of her panties, I slowly slid them down until the joined her dress on the floor. I made quick work of her bra, unsnapping it with a flick of my hand and it too fell to the ground, leaving nothing but Clare.

She took her time undressing me, running her hands over my naked skin, making me groan. We danced to a symphony of beating hearts, slow lingering kisses, and our combined breath. It was the most beautiful song ever created.

When we finally made it to the bed and our bodies came together, I found my home again. My solace. My shelter from every terrible memory of my life. This woman with the beautiful red curls and bewitching green eyes who captured my heart had given me everything.

"I love you, Logan," she murmured as our tangled bodies moved together in tandem

"I'll love you forever, Clare," I vowed before we both fell over the edge, lost in our mutual release.

She was my salvation and if she would have me, I would spend my entire life worshiping at her feet.

Chapter Fifteen

~Clare~

"There's something wrong with him, Leah," I said to her on the phone, while continuing to slice vegetables for a salad.

"What do you mean?" she asked.

"His mood, it's all over the place. He's been distant, making excuses and staying at his place for several nights in a row. And then he'll show up out of the blue and practically attack me on the doorstep, like he's afraid I'll disappear," I explained, throwing the remainder of the carrots into the bowl.

At first I thought it might be work, maybe he was just stressed. I was dating a doctor. They had stressful jobs, right? But this was something else entirely. The longer he acted this way, the more worried I became.

"When did it start?" Leah questioned. I could hear her at a checkout stand, the familiar sound of items being rung up, and her speaking to a clerk as she paid. Clearly she was buying her contribution to today's cookout.

"Right after we got back from New York. He got a call when we landed at the airport and he's been distracted and moody ever since. He usually shares his entire schedule with me, but now I don't know where he is most of the time, except when he's at work, and he doesn't answer many of my calls. You don't think he's changed his mind, do you?" I asked, biting my lip in worry.

"About what? You? No. That man is head over heels in love with you. You can just flip a switch like that," she assured me.

I nodded, even though she couldn't see me. I set down the knife and dumped the rest of the vegetables into the bowl. Today, Logan and I were hosting our first cookout together. I had brought up the idea when we got home from the wedding. He'd nodded absently, looking at something on his phone and said he thought it was a good idea, but hadn't mentioned it since. It was a good idea, right? I wasn't moving too fast, was I?

No, no...I was being ridiculous. He told me he loved me, and wanted to be with me forever. He wouldn't change his mind all the sudden.

"I'm sure he's just planning on proposing or something like that. Men get all sorts of weird when they decide to pop the question. Don't you remember what Ethan was like the weeks before he asked you?"

Yes, I do. He was a nervous wreck. Fumbling and tripping over himself. If I had known that was what he was planning, and the reason he was such a nervous ball of energy, I would have just done it for him.

"You're right. I'm sure it's nothing," I said, trying to convince myself.

"Exactly. Besides, men are known for having PMS symptoms occasionally. It's like a scientific fact. So, it could just be his time of the month," she teased, causing me to roll my eyes and laugh. But I silently thank her. I needed that. Even though I told her I agreed and it must be nothing, there was still a nagging feeling in the pit of my stomach that told me something was wrong. That soon, my world was going to come crashing down, again. And I didn't know if I was strong enough to pick up the pieces again.

~Logan~

It was ironic how a single phone call can change your life. Some for the better, others for the worse. Clare, Maddie and I had stepped off that plane several weeks ago and I was elated. I had a plan. The ring was in my pocket, like a beacon and symbol for the rest of my life, and then my damn phone rang, and everything changed.

It took one moment for me to walk into that exam room that held Clare and Maddie and have my entire world changed. It took a single phone call for it to come crashing down like a pile of rubble.

"I bet you know how that feels, huh?" I asked the four foot granite slab my body was slumped against. It didn't answer back. I took another swig from the half emptied body of amber colored whiskey I'd been working on since arriving here some time ago, feeling the liquid burn all the way down to my belly. I didn't know what brought me to that specific spot, but after leaving the hospital, I didn't know where else to go.

"I'm in love with your wife. Just thought you should know," my words slurred and eyes were blurry as I tried focusing on the words in front of me.

Ethan Oliver Murray. Loving Husband, Father, Son. His grave laid before me, a living testament to the love he and Clare shared. The love she lost and grieved every fucking day.

I pulled out the ring I had been carrying with me for weeks and held it to the light, watching it sparkle and flash, imagining how it would look on Clare's finger. Knowing now, I would never know.

Logan, is there anyone we can call?

No, there's no one.

Bringing the bottle to my lips again, I let out a harsh laugh, hating the irony of it all. How could fate hate us so much? What was the point of it all if it was supposed to end like this? Why show me how to love if I had to give it up?

"How did you do it, Ethan? How did you let her go?" I asked, hating the thought.

I don't know what I expected to hear in return. All I got

was silence. Nothing but fucking silence.

I hadn't come here for answers. I knew what I had to do. It would kill me, but I couldn't put her through this. She deserved better.

She may hate me, but at least she'd never have to lose me like this, I thought, giving one final glance at Ethan's final resting place.

~Clare~

It was really late when the knock on the door startled me awake. I rushed from the couch, throwing the blanket off my lap to open the door.

"Logan!" I cried, so happy to see his face.

He was dripping wet, rain pouring down his lean body, drenching his hair and clothes. I leaped into his arms, not caring about his water soaked state, needing to feel him, solid and safe in my arms.

"I've been so worried. I tried calling half a dozen times. Where have you been?" I rattled off a million questions, holding him tight.

The cookout had been over for hours and he had been a complete no show. Our first couple hosted event and I had to make excuses for him all night. When the evening wore on and he still wasn't answering his phone, I became worried, and then worried turned into frantic. I called hospitals, and police departments and then finally fell asleep on the couch in tears, convinced he had left me for good.

His arms wrapped around me tightly, for one brief second, before pushing me away completely.

"I'm sorry, I had some things I needed to think about," he answered coldly.

"Um, okay," I stammered, "Why don't we get you inside? Here, let me take your jacket."

He handed over his leather jacket, completely drenched with rain water. I laid it out to dry before sitting next to him on the couch. His eyes were vacant, hard, and completely unrecognizable.

"Have you been drinking?" I asked, the putrid smell of whiskey coming off of him in waves.

"Listen," he said, ignoring my question completely. "I've been doing a lot of thinking since New York."

The feeling I had been having, that terror in the pit of my stomach flared to life, warning me that my life was forever about to change. And not for the better.

"I miss the city. I don't think I'm cut out to live here," he confessed stoically.

"Logan, what are you saying? Do you want us to move to New York?" I asked, hopeful.

I didn't want to move, but I will. If it meant he wouldn't leave us, I would go anywhere.

"There are other things, too. I miss my job, my life there."

"I thought we were your life," I whispered.

He continued, spilling out the words, like he was unable to get them out of his body quickly enough. They sounded practiced and rehearsed, like he had written a speech before coming here. A "how to break up with Clare" speech and he couldn't wait to get it all out.

"I thought I was ready for this. Ready to be with one person for the rest of my life, and ready to be a father. But I don't think I am. I'm sorry. I know that sounds selfish, but it's where I'm at," he said, like he wasn't ready to place his order yet, or he couldn't decide between two shades of paint. No big deal.

"Why are you doing this?" I asked softly, seeing something flash in his eyes that he was desperately trying to keep blank for my benefit. He was hiding something.

"I just thought it'd be better this way. At least I figured it out before it was too late, right?" he shrugged.

Unable to sit next to him anymore, I jumped up from the couch, hurt and angry and so damn confused.

"Too late? There's a little girl upstairs who adores you. What am I going to tell her, Logan?"

He turned from me, shielding his face from my view so I couldn't see his expression.

"You goddamn lying bastard," I seethed.

"I'm sorry, Clare."

"Don't apologize to me, Logan! Tell me what's really going on here. This isn't about some stupid job. What happened to make you run like this? Just tell me and we can work through it."

He stood, running his hands through his hair for a few seconds as if trying to decide what to do. He finally looked up at me. I saw the hurt and pain in his eyes and I felt myself relax, knowing if he was opening up, we could get through this. But he turned his emotions back off and resumed the icy cold demeanor he had arrived with.

"There's no other reason. Clare. I'm just not ready for this."

"Please don't do this Logan, please...you can't leave," I begged, the panic taking over every molecule in my body.

"I'm sorry, Clare. You have no idea how much I wish things were different," he said, and it was the first thing he said all night that I actually believed. Everything else was a lie. One big goddamn lie he's concocted. Like a big get out jail free card.

"You're a fucking coward!" I roared, slapping him hard across the face. He just took it, as his head snapped back against the impact. No emotion, no angry words. Nothing. The Logan I knew was gone, buried underneath newly formed sheets of ice. This was the old Logan, the one that existed before me.

"Get out!" I yelled. "Get out, please," my yell turning into a whisper, as the energy in my voice drained. I could barely stand, my knees fought to keep me upright. Seeing my struggle, he hesitated, taking a step toward me, but just nodded, walking out the door and never looking back.

I collapsed onto the floor, tears flowing down my cheeks as my entire body shook and that nagging terror I had felt earlier took over my every thought.

~Logan~

Sitting at my familiar barstool in the same bar I had gone to the night I'd met Clare, I felt like shit. It was really a dumb move on my part, but I didn't want to go home. Too many memories to haunt me, reminding me of everything I had lost. Everything I'd given up.

You're a fucking coward!

I was a coward. I had set myself on this course thinking I was doing something noble, saving her another life of pain and suffering, but who was I really trying to protect? I never asked what she wanted to do, never told her what that call was about so many days before. What I had found out today. I'd kept to myself, saying I was protecting her. But I was protecting myself from the possibility of seeing her walk away. What if she didn't want me anymore? What if she looked at me differently? I didn't know if I could handle the possibility that one day I could stop being Logan, and instead be a constant reminder of Ethan and everything she'd lost.

Walking into that house, telling her I wasn't ready and acting like what we had wasn't the most goddamn important thing in my life was the biggest shame of my life.

She looked slain, like I'd ripped out her heart and thrown it to the wolves. And I just stood there, cold and emotionless while she'd fallen apart. I wanted nothing more than to close the distance between us, and tell her I was sorry, that I didn't mean any of it, and everything would be okay. I would have pulled out the ring in my jeans pocket, the ring I would carry with me until the day I died, dropped to my knees and asked her to marry me. I would have begged forgiveness, carrying her upstairs and making love to her all night rather than sitting here in this bar alone, like I would be for the rest of my life.

"Hey, Doc," Cindy said, as she made the rounds to refill drinks. "You haven't been around in months."

"Been busy," I answered coldly, not bothering to look up from my glass.

"Yeah? Well I sure hope she was worth it because you look like hell," she commented before walking away.

I felt like hell. I felt like I left my soul on that doorstep as I walked out of that house, leaving Clare and Maddie forever.

All that was left was numbness, that constant void of nothingness.

"Hey, stranger, long time no see," a familiar woman's voice greeted me from behind. I awkwardly swiveled around in my bar stool, seeing double. As my vision cleared, I couldn't help but grin, stunned by who stood before me.

"Well, aren't you a sight for sore eyes, gorgeous."

Chapter Sixteen

~Clare~

Sitting alone, on the floor in the middle of the family room, reliving the horrid events of the last night, I felt like there wasn't enough air left in the room. I took another gasping breath, trying to fill my lungs between the echoing sobs, but it wasn't enough.

Why did he leave me? I didn't understand.

Would it always feel like this? I made it through Ethan, but I didn't know how much more my heart could take. As my sobs filled the room, I silently thanked God Maddie's wasn't here. Leah had arrived early this morning, after I finally broke down to make the call and told her what had happened. After fifteen minutes of convincing her not to go to Logan's place to rearrange his anatomy, I asked her to come here and pick up Maddie for the day.

"Don't tell her. She can't know yet. It will destroy her," I whispered in her ear as they walked out the door, slapping on a fake smile as I gave Maddie a hug and waved goodbye. It was a miracle she didn't notice anything, overjoyed to be spending breakfast with Leah.

And now it was just me.

And the silence. The deafening silence.

I've loved you, Clare, you every minute of every day, since the very first day.

Had it been a joke, a sick way to pass the time?

No.

I had felt it and seen it in his eyes when he looked at me,

when he brushed his fingers across my skin and trembled as he came deep inside me. Whatever this was, whatever reason he had for leaving me last night had nothing to do with loving me.

Looking around the room, my eyes narrowed in on something spread across the corner chair next to the door, Logan's jacket. He had left it here in his mad rush out the door. Out of my life. Knowing it would only cause more hurt, but unable to stop myself, I rushed over to the chair like someone in the desert desperate for water. I grabbed the now dry leather in my hands, bringing it to my nose, inhaling the rich spicy smell of Logan. Fresh tears blurred my vision, knowing this was the only thing I had left of the man I thought I would spend the rest of my life with.

Knowing I looked ridiculous, but figuring the silence wouldn't care, I slid the jacket on, letting the scent engulf me. I tried to imagine it was him wrapped around me, holding me tight. Slipping my hands inside the pockets, I wrapped my hands around my body, picturing his hands replacing mine.

My fingers rubbed against a piece of paper that was folded in his pocket, and I pulled it out and read it.

"What is this?" I asked out loud.

I saw lab results, something about a biopsy, and the worst part was Logan's name at the top.

I'm sorry, Clare. You have no idea how much I wish things were different.

I gasped as everything fell into place. The mysterious phone call at the airport, his distant behavior over the last few weeks ending in his abrupt departure last night.

"Oh my God, no,"

Before the next thought was even formed in my head, I was rushing out the door, needing answers only one person could provide. I don't remember the drive to Logan's house, just the overwhelming desire to see him pushing me forward. When I arrived, I jumped out of the car, racing for the front door, ringing the doorbell in desperation. A few seconds passed and then I heard the growing sound of female laughter moving toward the door.

My heart plummeted and I felt sick. He wouldn't. Would he?

Oh, God. I can't see this.

Before I could turn and run, the door opened, and I was face to face with a gorgeous brunette. Judging from the long Harvard t-shirt and coffee cup she was carrying, it's was no secret she'd been there all night. The image of her with Logan in his bed made me want rip out her throat, and wipe that charming grin right off her face. He told me I was the only one he'd ever taken into his bed, and now he was bringing bar trash home.

"I'm sorry, I must have the wrong house. Sorry to bother you," I blabbered, slowly backing away from the door. It was the best thing I could come up with. Lame yes, but I hoped it would get me out of there faster so I can go back to my hole and die. If I stayed any longer, Logan might see me. Seeing the two of them together would only confirm the awful picture I had swimming in my head.

"Are you Clare?" she asked.

Why would the bar trash know my name?

"Um, yes. And you are?" I asked, rudely.

"Oh God! What you must be thinking! I'm so sorry! I'm Melanie," she said brightly.

"Logan's ex-wife Melanie?" I was not impressed. Her introduction was so *not* helping.

"Yes. Oh! And I'm here with my husband. With whom I'm expecting a child....and love very much!" she exclaimed, resting her hand on her belly. Now that I looked beyond her face, and was not willing her to die, I noticed the swell of her stomach.

"Sorry. Should have included that part in the beginning," she added.

"Come on, why don't you join me for some coffee? It's decaf, but if you close your eyes and pretend, you can almost taste the caffeine," she winked before leading the way inside.

"Is he here?" I asked quietly, following her to the kitchen.

"No, Colin came by about an hour ago and picked him up. Something about sobering him up and then kicking his ass," she answered as she moved about the kitchen, grabbing another mug of hot coffee and handing it to me.

"Logan didn't tell me you were coming to visit," I said, making myself comfortable at the counter, unsure how to continue this awkward conversation.

"Oh, he didn't know. Colin called us. He said something was wrong with Logan and he didn't know what to do. He thought Logan was about to do something stupid. So we can down to intervene."

Uh, okay.

"No offense, but when was the last time you even spoke to Logan," I asked, knowing I was being kind of rude.

"No offense taken. And it's been awhile. But he needed help, and I will always be here for him. Whether he wants it or not."

Like Colin said, sometimes Logan needed a kick in the ass.

"He and I were completely wrong for each other. I was in love a man who didn't love me, and Logan was in love with the idea of love. It was doomed from the start. But the man I saw last night, he was a wreck. And the only thing that can cause that type of agony is love."

"Then why did he do it? Why did he leave me?" I asked bitterly, the hours spent in tears weighing heavily on my mind.

"That's something only he can tell you."

"Did you really love him?" I asked, unsure why I was asking, but this woman had once loved Logan and I guess I felt we had some weird kinship. God knows I wasn't going talk about how great Logan was in the sack.

"Yes, as much as I could. How much can you love someone who doesn't love you?" she replied.

"You knew?"

"Yes," she admitted.

Shocked, I asked "Then why...?"

"Did I marry him?"

I nodded, waiting for her to continue.

"I was young and he was my first love. In my mind, I thought I could make him love me. That, eventually, over time, the love would grow. But it doesn't work that way. Love can't be forced."

"And then came Gabe," I guessed.

"Yes." she said with a wistful smile. "I had a crush on him in school, but he'd always been seeing someone else. When he moved to New York and asked me to help with his practice, I gladly said yes. It was innocent at first, but eventually we gave in, letting our passion take over."

She shook her head, her face lined with regret. "It was so wrong, what we did to Logan," she said quietly.

"He doesn't blame you, Melanie," I said reassuringly.

"It still doesn't make it right. I took a vow. I made a promise."

"And now you can ask for forgiveness," I told her, joining our hands, as a tear trickled down her cheek.

"I don't deserve it," she whispered, as her tears fell.

"You have it," Logan's voice said softly, causing my heart to flutter as he stood at the entrance of the kitchen. Another man, Gabe I guessed, trailed behind. Logan's hair was a disheveled mess, and he had dark bags under his eyes. But he was most beautiful sight I had ever seen.

His eyes briefly connected with mine before walking to Melanie to pull her into a tight hug.

"You have nothing to apologize for, we both made mistakes," he assured her, as she sobbed in his arms. They stayed like that for some time, and I let them have their moment. They both needed to heal and move on.

Eventually Melanie pulled away to wipe the tears from her eyes and looked up at Logan.

"You're a good man, Logan. You deserve happiness," she said.

Kissing him on the cheek, she turned to me, gave me a quick hug and then walked out with her husband, giving us privacy.

With his back still turned, he said, "She told you." It wasn't a question.

"No, she didn't. She didn't have to. You did," I said.

He turned, confusion scattered all over his worn face as I held up the test results to him.

Understanding quickly set in, and he nodded, saying, "My jacket."

I set the test results down on the counter and said, "Although, I don't understand half of the stuff on this paper. Are you sick?"

Time seemed to go by slowly as I waited for his answer.

"I have cancer," he finally said.

"No....no," I wailed in disbelief.

Deja vu hit me hard, and I was suddenly in two different places at once, reliving the moment when Ethan told me the same exact thing. It couldn't possibly happen twice.

It can't be true.

Violently shaking my head in disbelief, I said, "But you're so healthy. Maybe there's some sort of mistake. We should call the hospital. Make them run the tests again."

I ran to the phone, intent on doing just that, but Logan caught me before I was able to lift it off the cradle.

"The test results are correct, Clare. I have a form of lymphoma, Hodgkin's disease. Very easy to miss, since the symptoms are so slight. Sometimes non-existent for many patients."

No, dear God no.

"Ethan has a rare form of brain cancer", the doctor said "It's why it was missed on the CT. We're so sorry, Clare."

The floor rushed up, and the room spun as I felt Logan's sold arms wrap around my waist.

"It's okay, Clare. Breathe," he said, brushing the hair out of my face as he tried to calm me.

"No, it's not okay Logan. It's not okay."

It would never be okay. How could fate be so cruel?

"This is why I didn't want to tell you,"

"So, you broke up with me instead?" I snapped, anger replacing fear, flooding my system.

"I wanted to save you the pain of having to go through this again. I couldn't ask you to do that for me."

"How dare you make that decision for me? What gives you the right?" I seethed.

"Do you really want to go back to that hospital? Sit in the waiting room while I go through chemo treatments, give blood samples, and wait for test results? Can you honestly tell me that your heart can take that again, Clare?" he asked, his words full of emotion.

His words brought back every memory of Ethan's sickness crashing back, watching my strong husband turn into nothing short of a weak child. It was a horrid experience no person should ever have to endure.

"It's not your decision to make," I whispered.

"No? I've been agonizing over this for weeks while I waited for those results. How would I tell you? Would you stay? I've seen the pain in your eyes, the grief you still endure over Ethan's death. How could I ask you to stand by my side, knowing it could all have the same result?"

"You don't think I'm strong enough?" I asked.

"I think you're strong enough for anything. But how can I

ask you to willingly suffer?" he admitted, his voice filled with regret and longing.

"But I love you," I said softly.

"But for how long? Did you love Ethan until the very end, with all your heart?"

My heart skipped a beat, its pacing quickening, as my breath became irregular.

"What did you just say? Of course I did! How dare you!" I snarled.

"Did you really? You'd spent all that time caring for him, raising Maddie practically by yourself, and after everything, he was still dying."

"It wasn't his fault." I whispered.

"But it didn't change anything. He was still leaving you. How did that make you feel, Clare?" he demanded. I felt anger welling up in my veins, and the words erupted from my mouth before I could stop them.

"I HATED HIM!" I screamed, "Is that what you wanted to hear? I hated him for leaving me! I hated him for abandoning me and Maddie."

Raw, angry tears splashed down my cheeks as he pulled me into his arms, and the sobs continued to rake through my body. With every sob, I felt like I was purging the soul-sucking secret from my body, like a dark weight had been lifted off my chest.

I had just uttered my darkest shame, my most unforgivable sin and I felt like I could breathe for the first time in three years. In my darkest moments, as I watched my husband, frail and sick, dying before me, I hated him. It was sick and wrong, and I could never forgive myself for it. He was the most selfless person in the world, and I sat there angry at him for something he couldn't control.

"Shhh, Clare. Baby, it's okay," Logan soothed, running his hands through my hair and we held each other on the floor of his kitchen.

"No, it's horrible." I sobbed, "What kind of person am I?"

"You were losing the man you loved, Clare," he said.

"It's no excuse."

"There's no 'how-to' guide for death, Clare. You were faced with unimaginable circumstances and you faced them with so much strength and courage. Don't carry around this burden," he told me.

I let him hold me, feeling the security his arms gave, afraid I'd never know this feeling again.

"So where do we go from here?" I asked hesitantly.

He pulled back slightly so that I could see his face, still rough and unshaven from the night before.

"I still can't ask you do this Clare, but it's your decision. I understand that now," he acknowledged.

"But," he continued, "I want you to think about it, long and hard. It can't be rash decision. I want you to take time, remember Ethan and everything the two of you went through, and decide if you can do it again."

"Logan, I don't..."

"Yes, you do. Please Clare. For me, give it some time. If you say yes, I want to know it's for me, and not out of guilt, honor or a split-second decision. Those emotions you just felt. I need you to remember all of them. Every heart crushing moment. And then I need you to decide if you can go through it again, if that is where this road may lead us."

Nodding, I started to pull away, knowing there was nothing else to say, but I needed one thing before I went.

"Logan, can you do me one favor?"

"Anything," he vowed.

"Kiss me."

"Always," he answered, before pulling me back into a fierce kiss, full of desperation, passion and fire. It was the type of kiss that left you breathless, permanently altered, and stayed with you for the rest of your life. Slowly I pulled away, taking one last look into his beautiful blue eyes before I left, the fate of my future before me.

~Logan~

"So, you just let her go?" Gabe asked hesitantly as he entered the living room.

I didn't bother looking up, continuing to strum my fingers on the strings of the guitar. The melody changed haphazardly from one song to the next, mimicking my thoughts.

A complete clusterfuck of chaos.

"Yup," I said.

"You're not going to run after her? Fight for her?" he inquired, settling himself on the sofa opposite from me.

"Nope. This is something she's got to figure out."

"And you really broke up with her, hoping she wouldn't find out?"

It had been a dumbass move, I'll admit to that.

"I was trying to protect her," I explained as I plucked out the notes to "I Gave You All" by Mumford and Sons, before switching to something by Oasis, which was a little less depressing. Apparently, I was in a British mood tonight.

"Man, a little heads up, woman *hate* when you make decisions for them."

"The ball's in her court now," I muttered.

"Oh, that's good. Right? I mean, she'll come back?"

God, I hoped so. I'd resigned myself to a life without her. My booze and I would live a very miserable life together, in hell, and that would be that. But when I walked in my door today, and saw her in the kitchen, all I wanted to do was fall at her feet, and beg forgiveness. When she became so angry at me for making such a crucial decision without her, I let myself hope that she would follow me, no matter where life may lead us. But I couldn't chance it. It had to be real. I couldn't be a constant reminder of Ethan's death. To win her back now, and lose her all over again when she decided it was too hard? It would end me.

So, I let her go. Gave her time. And now I waited.

It fucking blew.

"So, we're cool, Logan?" Gabe asked, leaning back into the couch. Realizing this conversation wasn't going to end soon, I set my guitar down, grabbed the glass of bourbon I'd poured myself and settled into the sofa opposite him.

"Yeah, man. We're cool. No hard feelings. You and Melanie look really happy," I answered honestly.

"We are. She's my world."

"I'm happy for both of you, really," I affirmed. "So, parenting huh?" It was a vain attempt to lighten the mood and change the subject. I couldn't handle any more heavy shit today.

"Yeah," Gabe said, getting a goofy grin all over his face.

"I'm scared shitless. Every day, her belly grows, and we get one day closer. I mean, I'm excited, but I am a complete mess," he confessed.

"You'll be great, Gabe. You'll hold that child in your arms and you'll instantly fall in love, needing to protect her and your family above all else," I said, thinking of Maddie and how much I already missed her.

"You sound like a father," he smiled.

"I guess I do."

"I hope everything works out for you Logan," he said sincerely.

"Me too, Gabe. Me too."

Chapter Seventeen

~Clare~

It had been an entire week. I could only come up with so many more excuses for Logan's absence before Maddie clued in that something was wrong. I told her he had to go on a trip, he had to work late, and that he had a cold. I was running out of options. She'd caught me crying at least three times, and I'd brushed it off, blaming anything from allergies to my contact lenses. She was a smart girl and she was bound to figure it out sooner or later. I needed to make my decision or tell her. My stomach churned in response.

When I'd left Logan's house last week, I was so angry with him. I didn't need time! I knew what I wanted, and it was him. I didn't care what he had or how bad the cancer was. We were in love and we would get through it, right? That was until I walked into the front door of my house. I saw the couch where I had cared for Ethan after his numerous chemo treatments. I walked past the guest room which eventually became his when he had to move into a hospital bed. As I took a shower, I remembered having to bathe him when he was too weak to do so himself. I collapsed into a worthless pile on the shower floor, letting yet another round of tears take over.

I didn't understand. Did fate hate me? Why give me love only to have it end like this? Logan was my second chance. I had gone through the horror of losing my husband, and had come to terms with living a life alone. Fate showed up and gave me Logan, and I fell in love. It was so easy, knowing I had an entire lifetime to love someone again. But, that was all ripped away last week when Logan told me he had cancer. Now I had to decide how strong I was, how much I was willing to give up again for love.

With Ethan, I had no choice. He was my husband, the father of my child. I stood by his side and I wouldn't have changed a thing. Could I be so choosy with Logan? Could I actually walk away?

No, I couldn't. But I was afraid to take the first step.

I paced the floors back and forth for days, wondering what he was doing, how he was feeling, but was never able to take the leap and walk out the door.

The house was quiet now. It had been quiet a lot lately. Me and my good buddy Silence had been hanging out quite a bit.

Leah, my constant rock, had been the great distractor this week, taking Maddie all over the city. They had visited the zoo and gone to a baseball game. Maddie was in heaven and I couldn't thank Leah enough. I needed the time alone, as selfish as it was.

It was the middle of the afternoon and I was lying in bed. Again. At least I was dressed and showered. I guess that counted for something.

I pulled the sheet closer, tucking my knees to my chin, and wrapped my arms around them like a child.

Logan probably thought I had abandoned him by now. He told me to take time, but how much time did he think I would need. A normal person, a good person, would have just turned the car around and came back to declare their undying love. But, here I was, a week later, curled up in the fetal position, waiting for what?

Shouldn't I be ready by now?

Ready...

Clare, you're such an idiot.

Heart racing, I reached for the night stand and grabbed the letter that had been its sole occupant for the past three years.

Racing downstairs, I grabbed my car keys and headed out the door to the one place I knew I had to be. The only place I could be when I read this letter. With Ethan.

I pulled up to the old cemetery and walked the path I'd traveled so many times before, listening to the soft rustle and moan of the trees as they moved. Eventually, I made it to my destination, looking at the place we had laid Ethan to rest three years earlier when I thought my life was ruined and could never be whole again. And here I was again, feeling like my walls were crashing down around me. I needed him, so I knelt down and began to speak.

"Hey baby, it's me. I brought your letter," I said, holding it up and waving it like he was there to see it. "I don't know what to do, Ethan. I don't know how to take that leap of faith I so desperately need to take right now. Please help me," I pleaded right before turning the worn envelope over and breaking the seal. With shaky fingers, I unfolded the letter I had waited three years for, and read.

Clare,

I've started this letter half a dozen times, and they've all ended up in the trash, and now I don't have much time. You've taken Maddie out for her first ice cream cone, and I stayed behind, saying I'd catch the next one. We haven't discussed it yet, but as I feel my body growing weaker, I know there isn't going to be a next one for me. This is it, and I'm so sorry Clare. I'm sorry I've failed you. I'm so sorry I won't be there for you and Maddie.

I have so many things I want to say to you, so many words that I could write. But how do you fit a lifetime into a letter? How do you tell your wife everything you feel when there aren't enough words to describe them? I've loved you since the moment I saw you standing in that disgusting bar, trying to fend off that drunken ogre. You've always been my number one, and my reason for living.

I thought we'd have a lifetime together. I thought I'd have decades to tell you and teach you all the ways in which I love you. I thought we would grow old together, watching our children conquer the world. But I don't have years, or months, and I hate the thought of leaving you alone.

I know you will survive without me because you're a fighter. You're strong and brave and willing to give up everything for the ones you love. I've seen it firsthand. You will be the best parent to Maddie a child could ever possible have. Don't doubt yourself. And please, make sure she knows about her old man. At least the good stuff.

You are my soul mate Clare, and the love of my life. Thank you so much for giving me your heart and your soul. It was the greatest gift a man could receive. But, now I have to give it back. My life is ending, but yours carries on. You can't go through life without love, and you have too much of it to give. If love finds you again, don't fight it. Don't let grief hold you back. Love is a risk, there are no guarantees. But, in the end, it is always, always worth it.

The love of your life is still waiting Clare, go find him.

Yours always for eternity,

Ethan

The tears slid down my face as I read it, knowing Ethan had poured his soul into this letter. It was exactly what I needed to hear. Even now, he was still taking care of me.

I slowly rose, taking one last look at the marker where our shells still rested at the top. I counted them, making sure they were all still there and got to…eleven? I counted again and reached the same number.

Taking a step forward, I picked up the foreign shell, flipping back and forth in my hand, until it dawned on me where I had seen it before. Logan's house. On his mantel.

Placing the shell back on the headstone, I said, "Thank you, Ethan," and quietly turned, walking to the parking lot. As soon as I got into car, I began punching in numbers on my cell phone, waiting for an answer.

"Hello?" a gruff voice answered.

"Colin, I need to find Logan. Now," I said as I sped out of the cemetery.

~Logan~

You would think I would be used to these types of rooms, stark white walls, and the pungent smell of cleaner. But being on the receiving end, the side that wasn't in control? It made my skin crawl. Give me the lab coat and scrubs any day.

Unable to sit on that paper-covered exam bed, I paced the exam room like a lion, waiting for the oncologist to come in. He was someone I knew, which would either make it better, or really awkward.

So, Dr. Matthews, heard you have cancer? That's a total bummer.

Yeah, I was going for awkward.

The nurse who had brought me in here and took my vitals had given me the "I'm sorry you might die look". She must be new. I thought they would have trained that right out of them in a place like this, and instead replaced it with something more nurturing like "We're here if you need us."

Fuck, I didn't want to be here. But a doctor refusing treatment probably wouldn't look good. And, as much as I hated these walls, and the creepy nurse, I really preferred to be alive and kicking. Even if I was alone.

It had been a week.

She'd listened and stayed away for an entire week. I don't know if that was a good sign or bad. I missed her more than I could put into words. After Melanie and Gabe left, it was just me in that great big house. Colin and Ella would stop by occasionally, making sure I was fed and watered, but it wasn't the same without her. I saw her and Maddie everywhere I went. At the ice cream shop around the corner, at work when I'd examine a small child, and when I'd lie in bed wishing Clare was beside me.

But I told her I would give her time, and I would. As much as she needed, or as much as I had to give. I just hoped she didn't wait too long.

A knock sounded at the door and I gave the okay for the doctor to enter.

Looking up, I saw a familiar set of green eyes and burgundy red hair enter the room.

"Clare?"

She rushed into my arms and brought her lips to mine.

It had been too long and my control snapped. I deepened the kiss instantly as my hands wrapped around her body.

Breaking our kiss, she looked at me, her eyes full of purpose.

"I'm so sorry. I'm so sorry it took me so long. I was just so confused. I couldn't get myself to take the leap," she said.

"What changed your mind?" I asked.

She was here. In my arms. I was never ever letting her go.

"Not what. Who," she said.

"Who?" I inquired, confused.

Reaching into her purse, she pulled out a piece of paper, a letter, and as I quickly scanned it, I realized it was a letter from Ethan.

"Read it."

"Are you sure, Clare? Where did you get this?"

"I've had it for years. I just wasn't ready. Please Logan, read it," she begged, her eyes bright and full of excitement.

I took a seat in the corner, reading the letter that Clare entrusted me with. It was a beautiful letter and I would have normally felt jealousy reading someone else declaring their undying love for Clare on paper, but I felt nothing but gratitude. When I finished, I looked up at her, tears blurring my eyes, humbled by Ethan's selfless words.

"I've found him. You're the love of my life," she whispered.

A single phone call had made me feel like my life had ended, but two sentences had brought it springing back from the depths of hell.

"But, what if..." I started to ask.

"No. No 'what if's'," she said, "We're meant to be, we can handle anything."

Hearing her words, seeing her stand before me baring her soul, made me feel invincible. She was right. Cancer or no, we could handle anything life threw at us, as long as we were together.

"Marry me," I said, pulling the ring I had carried in my pocket for weeks, finally placing it on her finger where it belonged. It was about the most unromantic place for a marriage proposal ever, but considering everything we'd been through, and everything we would go through, it was perfect.

"Oh my God! Where did you get that?" she cried, looking down at mammoth ring now residing on her finger. It looked perfect, just as I knew it would.

"I've had it for weeks. Your Dad thought he was pulling a fast one on me that day at the cookout, when he told me I better make an honest woman of you soon. I think I surprised him when I laughed and said it was already in the works," I said, a wide grin spreading across my face.

"So, that was what I saw!"

"Guilty. And, Clare?"

"Yes?" she said, tearing her eyes away from her hand.

"You haven't answered me yet."

"Oh! Yes!" she squealed, looking down at her ring again before I pulled her into my arms and swung her around the exam room.

The doctor chose this moment to knock and enter the room,

looking startled at the sight of us spinning around the room.

"Um, sorry Logan. I'll give you two a minute. Just let me know when you're ready," he said, obviously feeling awkward.

Clare and I looked at each other and grinned, before she said.

"We don't need any time. We're ready for anything."

Epilogue

Two years later...

~Clare~

"Oh, God...why does this have to be happening now?" I said to myself as the double doors to the ER whooshed open, and I rushed to the counter.

"Do you need to see a doctor?" the attendant asked. Hmm, she looked vaguely familiar.

A feeling of deja vu swept over me. Her nametag read "Tammy" and I remembered the last time I'd seen her in this waiting room. The night I'd met Logan.

"Yes, I need to see a doctor. One doctor in particular," I requested, but before I could continue she cut me off.

"Ma'am, you'll just have to sign in and they will assign you a doctor when you get back there. You can't request a doctor in the ER. We aren't a doctor's office," she said, her voice filled with annoyance.

Don't kill the nurse, Clare.

Breathe in, breathe out. Isn't that what they teach you to do?

"I don't think you understand. My name is Clare Matthews. My husband is Logan Matthews."

Her face quickly changed from annoyed to pleasant as she said, "Oh, I'm sorry Mrs. Matthews. I can page him. Is there anything you'd like me to tell him?"

"Yes, please," I said, feeling another wave of pain take

over. "Can you let him know I'm in labor?"

~Logan~

I ran my hands through my hair, trying not to let the exhaustion take over. It seemed like a lifetime ago, but I remembered what it felt like to run my hands over my head and feel nothing. Clare said I looked sexy, and I had to admit, it wasn't a bad look if you took away the black bags under my eyes and the yellowish skin. I don't know how the women who went through chemo handled it. Men weren't nearly as attached to their hair. But I did love having it back, feeling Clare run her hands through it, tugging on it as we made love.

They always said going through something life-altering like cancer made you appreciate the little things in life, and that was true. But it also made you appreciate the larger ones as well, like family, friends and being able to wake up in the morning. There were mornings I would wake up and just lay there staring at her, so grateful she stayed. There were rough days. Hell, there were rough months, but we pulled together as a family. I eventually shed my last layer of ice, and allowed my mother to become part of our family. Not that I had much of a choice. After meeting "Grandma Cece" in New York, Maddie insisted that she visit, and that was that. As always, Maddie knew what was best for our family.

When Clare said yes to my exam room marriage proposal, we didn't waste any time. Our St. Thomas summer vacation turned into an impromptu wedding. We flew our family and friends out, renting out a small resort for the occasion. It was intimate and beautiful, and Maddie thought we threw the entire event in honor of her birthday. After the wedding, we decided two houses was one more than we needed, and sold her house. I told her we didn't need to, that I would gladly sell mine. But she was adamant, saying we needed a fresh start with new memories. Watching her pack up the house she'd shared with Ethan was difficult. I felt like I was taking him out of her life, but she insisted it was just a house, and he would always live on. We still went to the cemetery each year, placing shells on his grave, and we made sure to keep photos of him scattered throughout the house so Maddie never forgot the man who gave her life.

The day they told me there were no signs of cancer left, and I was in remission, I thought my life was complete. I had everything I needed. I had my health back, the love of my life at my side, and a daughter who thought I was a super hero. Clare went back to work at one of the local high schools, and we started our life as a normal family. Finally.

About a month later, I came home to a silent house. I called out for Maddie. No answer. I called out for Clare, no answer. I finally found her in the master bathroom, curled up on the floor crying. I rushed to her fearing the worse. But she just handed me a positive pregnancy test, smiling, with tears of joy running down her face. They had told us it may not be possible after the chemotherapy. But it happened for us. Turned out my life was far from complete. It was just beginning.

"Paging Dr. Matthews, Paging Dr. Matthews," filled the airwaves. I picked up the nearest phone and dialed the extension listed with the page.

"Hi, this is Dr. Matthews. I was paged."

"Hi, Dr. Matthews. This is Tammy from the front desk. Your wife is here, and we're currently checking her in through L&D. She wanted to let you know she's in labor."

"Fuck!" I shouted, before taking off in a sprint for the waiting room.

~Clare~

"He's beautiful," Leah cooed as I watched my husband

hold our new son for the first time. He'd been a father since the moment he laid eyes on Maddie, but there was always something special about seeing a new father, no matter how many times around.

I chuckled to myself, remembering the sight of Logan in his scrubs, barreling down the hall, and throwing the double doors open to the ER. You would think a doctor, especially one trained in trauma would be calmer. But I guess every new father was entitled to his moment of crazy, even a doctor.

He had check me over from head to foot even though I assured him I was perfectly fine.

They escorted us to Labor and Delivery, and five seconds later, an attractive blonde nurse walked in. Apparently Leah wasn't going to let anyone else near her godson, or goddaughter. We decided to leave the sex of the baby a mystery, driving everyone crazy. With everything that we had gone through over the last two years, having a little mystery that wasn't a dire circumstance was nice.

Once I was hooked up to the monitors and given some medication for the pain, Logan was able to relax and play the role of expectant father, for the most part. He still watched the monitors like a hawk and checked my vitals more than necessary. When our son was delivered, all notions of being a doctor were dropped and Logan became a father to our child instantly. Seeing him cut the cord and running his hand down the baby's tiny cheek made me proud to call him my husband.

There was a knock at the door, and Maddie entered, proudly displaying the "Big Sister" shirt Grandma Cece had bought her. My parents hung back in the hallway, giving Maddie a few minutes with us before entering. I knew the wait must be killing them. Seeing the blue bundle in Logan's arms, she stopped short and frowned.

"It's a boy?"

I winced, knowing she had really been hoping for a girl.

Well, there's always next time I guess.

"Yes, you have a brother. Is that okay?" I asked

She was silent for second, before she said "Yeah, I guess so. Boys can dance, right Daddy?"

As soon as we told Maddie we were getting married, her first question was whether she could call Logan "Daddy." He'd broken down in tears, pulling her into his arms. It brought a smile to his face to this day to hear her say it.

"Uh. Sure, princess. But he might want to do something else. Like play guitar like me. Or football like Uncle Colin," Logan suggested.

"Hmmm, well I don't know about football, but he could play the guitar! He can play music, and I can dance!" she exclaimed with excitement.

Problem solved. No problem was ever too great for a child.

"Hey, does my baby brother have a name?" she asked.

Logan and I smiled, looking at each other. It was a name we both decided on a long time ago.

"We thought we'd name him Ethan. Ethan Oliver Matthews."

"I like that name. Daddy would like that name."

"We think so, too."

Ethan knew me better than I knew myself. He gave me the push I needed when I was scared to take a risk. But with love, the risk is always worth it.

Some love stories begin with a chance encounter in an

emergency room.

Others start in a crowded bar, with a heated gaze and a one-

night stand.

Never Been Ready

The Second Novel in The Ready Series.

Coming February 1st 2014

Acknowledgements

A while back, I had this crazy idea to write a book. Many months later, after pouring my heart and soul into this novel, there are so many to thank. It may have been my crazy idea to start with, but without the support of my family, friends and special people I met along the way, it would have never been ready.

First of all, I have to thank my husband, Chris. He's always there for me, whether it's taking care of the kids so I can write, or being my sounding board for new ideas. You are my rock, babe. I also have to thank my children and official cheerleaders. They are so proud of Mommy, even though they have no idea what it is that I wrote. All they know is "Mommy wrote a book!" If they only knew.

Words cannot express how grateful I am for the family I have. I am so incredibly thankful for my parents, big brother and sister in-law, and huge extended family. A very special thank you goes to my BFF Leslie. I don't need to say why, she knows. Thank you to Megan Peterman for taking the time to offer wisdom and support.

One huge thank you to my editor, Ami Deason, who has saved my ass more than once. A big thanks to my cover designer, Sarah Hansen from Okay Creations for making an absolutely stunning cover. Thanks to all of my beta readers who gave such wonderful feedback. Lisa Filipe - you are amazing and go above and beyond always. I have been so lucky to be surrounded by such amazing bloggers, especially Jenny and Gitte from TotallyBooked - thank you for your awesome support.

And lastly, thanks to the readers, who have supported me from the very beginning.

J.L. Berg

About the Author

J.L. Berg is a California native living in the South. She's married to her high school sweetheart and they have two beautiful girls that drive them batty on a daily basis. When she's not writing, you can find her with her nose stuck in a romance book, in a yoga studio or devouring anything chocolate.

Photo Credit: Studio FBJ

55939033R00163

Made in the USA
Charleston, SC
11 May 2016